Daddy's Girl

Marian O'Neill

POCKET BOOKS

TOWNHOUSE

First published in Great Britain and Ireland by Pocket/TownHouse, 2001

An imprint of Simon & Schuster UK Ltd and TownHouse and
CountryHouse Ltd, Dublin

Simon & Schuster UK is a Viacom company

1 3 5 7 9 10 8 6 4 2

Simon & Schuster UK Ltd
Africa House
64–78 Kingsway
London WC2B 6AH

Simon & Schuster Australia
Sydney

TownHouse and CountryHouse ltd
Trinity House
Charleston Road
Ranelagh
Dublin 6
Ireland

A CIP catalogue record for this book is available from the British Library

ISBN 1 903650 19 4

Typeset by SX Composing DTP, Rayleigh, Essex
Printed and bound in Great Britain by
Omnia Books Ltd, Glasgow

For Stephen

CHAPTER 1

For as long as Lisa could remember it was her and her mum. Always her and her mum, and her mum always looked out for her. Her dad couldn't – her dad wasn't there, never had been – but her mum looked after that too. Her mum told Lisa all the stories she had to tell about Lisa's dad and Lisa never got tired of hearing them.

She loved the stories about how handsome her dad was, how his hair licked down low over his face, almost as low as his chin, and how his trousers clung tight and his shirts gleamed white. How all the girls flocked and twirled around him as he stood sideways to the mike clicking his fingers with a swing to the beat. He sang all the songs, Lisa's dad did, he crooned them deep and dangerous and all the oul' ones called him a show.

But the girls knew better. They preened themselves and pushed each other out of the running and sweated their mascara loose in an effort to earn recognition, but Lisa's mum didn't have to do anything like that. She just had to sit and smile and Lisa's dad came running.

'The first time I met him! Ah Lisa, love, you can't want that story again.'

'But I do, Mum, please, please, Mum, and I'll go asleep straight away then, I promise.'

'All right then, love, but it's your choice and it's your promise to keep.'

And the Lisa of four and five and six and onward
would curl up tight under her blankets and listen to her
mother's voice come out of the twilight of the darkened
bedroom. When other girls were falling asleep, lulled by
the promised romance of fairy stories, Lisa was
comforted to sleep by the familiarity of her mother's one
romantic adventure.

'I met him first in November and it was a very cold
November that year and I had just started working in
Mitchell's. I was on the factory floor then, and do you
know, but it was much more fun than the office. Oh, it
was hard all right, when you weren't used to it. The cold
and the standing would kill you, eventually, but the girls
had a sight more life in them. They were wild, those girls,
but they were good, even though there were a lot of
people with a lot to say about them and none of it nice.

'But anyway, when I turned eighteen, the girls insisted
that I go with them to the pub. Nothing would satisfy
them except to see me drink my first legal drink.

'So we went, me and about five others, and they
forced me fit to bust with dirty great glasses of beer.
They had me feeling sick in an hour and I was all for
leaving when your dad came on.

'He did a turn in the pub every Wednesday and
Saturday night. There was a little stage in the corner
beside the bar and him and his pal would do their turn
there. His pal played the piano. They were both of them
hoping for a talent-scout to see them and break them
into the big time. And do you know, but I think that that
is exactly what would have happened, they were that
good. Especially your dad, sure can't any old monkey
learn the piano, but no one can learn how to sing.
Singing is real talent.

'Well, your dad got up on stage and all the girls went wild. He was the reason they went out of a Wednesday. And didn't they all leave me to run up to him and gaze at him close up, and to tell you the truth that was exactly what *I* wanted to do. I don't think I had ever seen such a long streak of gorgeousness in the flesh before. Oh, I wanted to run forward with the others, but I was afraid to, on account of being filled with beer and feeling so sick. So I just sat quiet and hoped for the best.

'Your dad says that that's when he fell in love with me, the very first minute he saw me. He said I was beautiful and that I looked a bit lonely and he said I seemed smarter than the screaming girls, but I still looked like I had a bit of life in me. He always said that, he said that I had a funny bone the size of my knee joint hid deep inside me.

'And do you know when I fell in love with your dad?'

'When he sang *Moon River*.'

'When he sang *Moon River*, the last song in his set, and all the girls screamed for more and I felt a right charlie because I started to cry. It was the music. It was so beautiful. I looked up with my eyes filled with tears and your dad looked down and then he walked off the stage and straight over to me and I took his hand and without as much as a "hello" we both of us walked out of that pub. And do you know what?' Lisa's mum spoke softly now, because she was only questioning Lisa's heavy breath and Lisa, deep asleep, never answered. 'From that day on your dad never sang *Moon River* to anyone other than me.'

That was only the first story, the first of hundreds. Lisa's mum said that she and Lisa's dad were together for seven months and every day for seven months they saw each other, and every hour of every day had its story. When Lisa turned eighteen herself she still hadn't heard all the stories, but she knew the most important ones by heart, the story of the beginning and the story of the end.

The end story was only told on special days. It was told when Lisa's mum had drunk too much. It was told at Christmas time and on Lisa's birthday. And, every year, on the twenty-first of May, it was told over a special but solemn dinner. Lisa never asked for this story. She knew that it would never come on demand. She had to wait for her mum to volunteer it, and even though it made her cry, she loved it.

'Did I ever tell you, Lisa, love, how it came to be that your dad doesn't live with us?'

And the Lisa of four and five and six and onward would shake her head, even though she knew what was coming.

This was no bedtime story. This was a daytime-together type of story, so Lisa's mum would take Lisa on to her knee, or she would pat the seat beside her on the sofa, and she would wait until Lisa was cosy and snuggled before she began.

'Your dad was a good man, Lisa, love, but he lived at a bad time in a bad place. He could sing fit to turn you inside out, and he was strong, and smart. He read all kinds of books, but it was a bad time and so he had to work as a hand down the docks on a daily wage and with no better prospect. But he didn't mind much because he knew that his voice would some day carry him away from it all and me with him.

'Your dad had a friend, Lisa, love, and your dad set

great store by friendship. We'll call this friend Tommy. I forget his real name. Now Tommy wasn't as good a man as your dad, but maybe that's mean of me to say. Maybe he wasn't so good because he had to work down the docks too, but he had no voice and so he had no hope and it got to him that working for a daily wage with no prospects just wasn't a good enough life and so he did something about it. He got involved in all sorts that shouldn't concern a good man from a good family.

'I never knew exactly what it was that Tommy did, but whatever he did, he did it wrong and he got himself all messed up with some very bad types and then he did them wrong and then they came looking for him. They found him easy enough, lining up for work one morning down by the docks.'

At this stage Lisa's eyes would grow wide with horror and the proximity of tears, because she knew what was coming.

'They – the bad men – they took Tommy aside and there was an argument. There were three men and as they all got angrier they crowded tighter and tighter around Tommy and Tommy got scared and backed away from them and backed away from them, until he backed himself off the pier and into the deep water. The men just turned and walked away without a backward glance and your dad raced past them and still in his shoes and still in his jacket he dived after Tommy.

'He came up twice, your dad did, and dived down twice, but he never found Tommy and he never came up a third time. That was the morning of the twenty-first of May, but I didn't hear until that night when I was waiting for him outside the Royal.

'One of the men that were there saw me and recognized me and told me and I fainted and, after a week, when I was still fainting, I went to the doctor and he told me about you, love. So you see Lisa it wasn't all a sad story, you're my happy ending.'

So, before Lisa was aware that her mother had done a bad thing she knew that her father had done a great thing. And that was a necessary weapon to have when the taunts started coming.

Lisa and her mum lived in a short street with a high wall at the end. Lisa always knew it as the cuddle sack and she rightly associated it with the security and comfort of her bed.

There were four houses on one side of the street and four houses on the other. Lisa and her mother lived in the house on the left, closest to the high wall. On the other side of the high wall was a busy road and Lisa wasn't allowed even to try to climb the wall. Not even if she promised to climb high enough just to peek over the top.

'No!' Lisa's mum would say. 'No, a peek might cost you your nose and a fall might cost you your life, love.'

Lisa loved her house, even though it was the smallest on the street, even though it rattled when the trucks went past on the busy road, and even though its windows were always blackened by the filth of the cars.

And she loved her yard even if it was just big enough for a clothesline, a seat and a few dirty geraniums. Lisa's mum said that that was the right way to look at things.

'We have to remember that it's big enough for what we need and not always be reminding ourselves that it's too small for what we want.'

Lisa loved her road. She loved the way it slanted a little so that it was easier to pedal down and harder to pedal up. She pedalled down the left-hand side, stopped, stood up and pushed her trike carefully across the road and on to the opposite path. Then, she pedalled up the right-hand side, stopped, stood up and pushed her trike carefully across the road, along by the high wall, and she pedalled down the left-hand side again.

Sometimes Lisa tied one end of a rope around Mr Philips's cherry tree, the trunk of which had burst through his rotten wooden fence and was now deemed public property, and spun the other end herself and imagined a playmate with pigtails flying, skipping high singing, 'A, my name is Annabel, my husband's name is Alan, we live in America and we sell almonds. B, my name is Brenda . . .'

Sometimes Lisa bounced a ball against the high wall and caught it and bounced it and caught it and pretended that she was two little girls. Sometimes she drew hopscotch squares on the path in coloured chalk and practised and practised all day long. She rathered hopping on her right foot. She could hop on her left one, but she always had to stick her tongue out a bit when she was doing it. Lisa knew why she stuck her tongue out. Her mum had told her. It was because she was concentrated like MiWadi. Lisa supposed that when she was taller her tongue would stay in.

The only thing that Lisa didn't love was that there was no other little girl, not even a little boy, in her cuddle sack. The second only thing that Lisa didn't love was that she had no bigger, or even littler, sister to play with and the third only thing that Lisa didn't love was that when her mum went to work all day, fat Mrs Tyler came to sit in Lisa's house and make sure that Lisa didn't climb the high wall.

Fat Mrs Tyler sometimes said funny things and sometimes cooked lovely dinners but she never played games with Lisa like Lisa's mum did, and she never told stories like Lisa's mum did.

And Lisa loved her mum. She loved to sit by her mum and watch the funnies on television. She loved to laugh when her mum laughed, even though sometimes she didn't know what was funny and her mum would pull her ears and say, 'You little goose, if you're laughing why I'm laughing you must have the brain of an old woman in there.'

And Lisa loved having her tea with her mum and how she would drink her milk from a glass that was big enough to swallow her whole face. And Lisa loved going to bed with her mum and how they both slept in the same room and how they both had the same bedspreads, both spread with tight red rosebuds. And Lisa loved how her mum read late into the night and how her bedside lamp had a red shade with gold tassels. And Lisa loved how her mum would say, 'I spy with my little eye something beginning with G.' And the answer was always Guardian Angel. And Lisa loved how she was supposed to say, 'I spy with my little eye something beginning with S.' And her mum always knew the answer and the answer was always the Sandman.

And it wasn't until Lisa was older that she questioned the depth of her love. And it wasn't until Lisa was old that she appreciated it.

CHAPTER 2

When Lisa went to school, things changed. Every morning she left the house with her mum, and hand in hand they swung each other over the pavement, heads down, careful of the cracks that could spread wide at any moment and swallow an elephant in a second.

'An elephant in a second,' said Lisa.

'An elephant in a zoo in a second,' said Lisa's mum.

'An elephant in a jumper in a zoo in a second,' said Lisa.

'An elephant in a trunk in a jumper in a zoo in a second,' said Lisa's mum.

And every afternoon Lisa was collected by fat Mrs Tyler and every hour in between was spent with the fleshy materialization of all Lisa's imaginary friends.

She sat with girls who poked her ribs with their elbows and whispered cherished secrets in her ear. She stood for prayers beside all shapes and types of girls and clamped her hand tight over her mouth to stop the giggles from spilling out. At break time she hurried on to the yard deep in a flurry of girls, all eager and all ready to play.

She played skipping with girls with braided hair and she watched their plaits fly high. She brought her ball to school and bounced it to the other girls and they bounced it back and she brought her chalk to school and beat all the older girls at hopscotch. When fat Mrs Tyler came to collect her, Lisa always waved a sad goodbye. The afternoons were longer now, after these newly tasted joys.

As Lisa got a little older she settled on a small group of girls and called them her best friends and, secure in mutual regard, this group of girls picked another group of girls to be their worst enemies and suddenly life was too intensely social to be limited to a morning. Soon Lisa organized her afternoons around the homes of other little girls and in doing so did fat Mrs Tyler out of a job and exposed herself to a world that demanded explanations.

Jill and Katie and Anne and Jane all had back gardens that stretched and stretched. They all had mummies who sat home all day and talked to other mummies and they all had daddies who worked all day and arrived home for tea in shiny cars. They all had kitchens with deep-set lights and rows of presses and they all had bedrooms of their own with frilled curtains. Jill had a big brother and Katie and Anne had big and little sisters and Jane's mummy was very fat from just sitting down all day making a baby.

Lisa watched and stayed silent and kept her secret of her mum and their bedroom and their yard to herself. She sensed that her differences would not be appreciated.

Lisa didn't mind much about the daddies and the shiny cars or the mummies who talked all day. She knew why these things were different in her life. They were different because her dad had done a good thing for his friend.

And she didn't mind about the gardens that stretched and stretched because she and her mum knew that they had all they needed and never reminded themselves about what they wanted.

And she didn't mind about the bedrooms with the frilled curtains because they would be lonely places at night without the glow from a red lamp with gold tassels.

And though she did mind about the brothers and sisters, she understood why she couldn't have any. It had to be always just her and her mum because brothers and sisters had to come with a daddy and her dad was deep under the sea.

But she did mind that all the mummies who talked all day looked at her funny and treated her funny and stopped talking when she came into their neat and shiny kitchens. She couldn't understand why, so she asked her mum for reasons.

'Why does Anne's mummy call me poor?'

'Does she, love?'

'Yes. She says Anne and Jill and Katie and Jane and poor Lisa.'

'Well, I suppose we don't have as much money as they do.'

'Why does Jane's mummy give me prayers to learn instead of letting me watch telly with the others?'

'Well, I suppose she must have taught the others the prayers already and maybe she really loves God.'

'Why does Jill's mummy think that I'm a bad imfluent?'

'She said what?'

'She said I was a bad imfluent and then Jane's mummy said that it wasn't my fault that I was a bastard.'

Immediately after that conversation, fat Mrs Tyler resumed her place in the after-school queue of waiting mothers, and for a long time after that conversation Lisa spent her afternoons back in the loneliness of her cuddle sack. Whenever Lisa questioned her position her mother slanted her replies into stories or bounced the questions back to her daughter unanswered.

'But why can't I go to Jane's?'

'Why's the question, because is the answer.'

'Why have I to come home? Why can't I go with Jane?'

'Go with Jane! Goodness me that reminds me. Did I ever tell you about the first fight I had with your dad?'

Lisa shook her head and listened.

'After me and your dad started going about together I started to listen to what people said about him. They said that he was no good and that he drank and was wild but I didn't care, I could see that they were all just jealous even the oul' ones and they were worse 'cause they were jealous of me as well as of him. I was pretty in those days though you wouldn't think so now.'

Lisa laughed because her mum was still very pretty and she knew it too, and so she laughed as well.

'I didn't listen to most of what they said but there was one thing that worried me and that was that everyone kept telling me all about this girl called Jane and how her and your dad were really friendly and how he had been with her for months and how she was talking to all her friends about getting married.

'Well, I was worried about Jane, but I was too scared to ask your dad in case it was all true and then I'd have no option but to leave him and you know, Lisa, love, I couldn't bring myself to do that, so I never asked and I kidded myself that I had no worries, and do you know but that's a dangerous thing to do, because worries have a way of growing beyond you and bursting out.

'One evening there I was walking home from work deciding in my head what to wear that night to meet your dad in and didn't I see him talking to that girl Jane. Well my head just about exploded. I had only been with your dad about a week and I'm sure I had no ties on him, but I marched right up to them and I screamed a filthy word at him before I ran home as quick as I could.

'I didn't expect it and I'm sure I didn't deserve it, but your dad came running after me. He caught up just by the railway lines at the end of my street and grabbed a hold of me. He held me and told me all the sweet things I wanted to hear. He told me that he had to meet her to tell her about me and would I have it any other way? Would I want to be with a man who wouldn't act decent by a woman? I just shouted at him and hit him off me and cried at him, because . . . do you know why, Lisa, love?'

Lisa shook her silent head.

'Because deep down I thought that I was no match for a man like your dad. I couldn't believe he wanted me like he said, like I wanted him, and he couldn't make me understand that he did no matter how many words he used. So, finally he walked away and said, "If you don't believe words maybe you'll believe this."

'And do you know what he did, Lisa, love? He walked out on to the railway tracks, right out in front of the six o'clock commuter. You know I'll never forget that sight. It was dark and cold and we were standing just out of the lights of the station. The only light facing us was the big and growing light of the train. And the noise! It wailed and screeched and howled and your dad acted like he couldn't hear me above it though I screamed myself hoarse.

'Oh, I screamed that I needed him and I wanted him and I loved him and I was sorry and I ran to him, screaming and screaming, and then just when I was going to close my eyes to block out his death he casually walked towards me and over the roar of the train he asked all calm like, "Did you say something, love?"

'And I laughed and cried and hit him and hugged him because he had been nothing but teasing and he had heard every word I said. Well, after that I could never pretend that I wasn't mad for him and we never mentioned Jane again. But do you know what, Lisa, love? To this day I can't trust a Jane, so let's not talk any more about your Jane.'

And they didn't.

Lisa settled for a less demanding circle of friends and she learnt to fill her afternoons with books and elaborate games of hopscotch. She and the Famous Five hopped forward, clear over every crack and landed safely on the island. Then she and William Brown hopped home, dirty from the woods but happy without Violet Elizabeth.

Then she got a little bit older and all the girls in her class got a little bit older and life became more complicated.

The girls in Lisa's class discovered the illicit joys of adulthood. They learnt that if you stayed very still and quiet in a room your mummy might forget you were there and she might let slip something unsuitable, or if you stayed very still and tried to look very dim your mummy's friend might forget what age you were and she might let slip something unsuitable. And even if you had to leave the room, you could nearly always manage to leave the door a little open and if you stayed very still beside an open door it was almost as good as being in the room.

Lisa didn't really understand this new obsession that blotted out skipping and catch and hopscotch and added an unknown dimension to games of pretend. No one in Lisa's house ever spoke behind closed doors. Lisa's mum never spelt out words instead of saying them and the adult world where Lisa's mum lived seemed just the same as Lisa's, except Lisa's mum had to go to work instead of to school. But Lisa tried. She spent break time sitting with the other girls in closed huddles whispering about the latest piece of information, trying to twist it to fit into their haphazard perception of adult reality.

'Mrs O'Brien has been killed with her hip!'

'Nah, says who? I saw Mrs O'Brien last Sunday.'

'My mummy, she said, "Mrs O'Brien is killed with her hip."'

'But that's stupid. Everyone is killed with all their bits in.'

'Yeah, unless doctors have to take your hip out if you're dying.'

'That must be it. That must be where you get hip replacements from. My granny got a hip replacement 'cause her old one was bad. Doctors must keep people's hips.'

'Mr Byrne has fallen off of a wagon.'

'Is he hurt?'

'No, he seems to be really happy about it. He keeps singing and telling everyone jokes and forgetting what the end of them is and just laughing anyway.'

'Maybe he landed on his head when he fell.'

Lisa would always carry these conversations home to

her mum and her mum would always laugh and shake her head and say, 'I must write all this down.'

And then her mum would unravel the half-truths and weave the broken phrases back into the context of their reality. Lisa was often disappointed by the mundanity of her mum's explanations and she seldom shared her knowledge with her friends, they seemed so happy with their whispered half-truths.

But the more they listened, the more they learned and the more they learned, the more dangerous the whispers got.

'Did you know that Mary's daddy isn't living in a big house at all, he's in prison?'

'Did you know that Ruth Brown's daddy drinks?'

'Did you know that Mr Forster goes to bed with Hilda Benson and Mrs Forster is the last to know?'

Lisa carried these conversations home as well, but with increasing trepidation because they would always make her mum sigh and shake her head crossly and say, 'Some women should have their tongues tied in knots at birth.'

Then her mum would sit Lisa down and tell her stories, and give her examples, and try and impress on her the philosophy of liberal morality. Lisa listened and tried to understand, but she never shared her knowledge with her friends. They seemed so happy with their comfortable condemnations.

But then it was Lisa's turn.

'Did you know that Lisa's mummy and Lisa's daddy were never married?'

'Did you know that Lisa's mummy won't even give her old mother the time of day, even though she has a watch?'

'Did you know that Lisa's mum doesn't even know who Lisa's daddy is?'

'Does too know who my dad is.'

And Lisa went crying home and wouldn't talk to fat Mrs Tyler and Lisa's mum had to come home early from the factory to see what was wrong.

She listened carefully to everything that Lisa told her and she didn't laugh the confusion away or she didn't talk about the ideas of great men and the differences between everyone. She didn't even shake her head crossly. Instead she sat very still with her head bent low and Lisa saw a tear stain the wool of her skirt a darker blue. It was only one tear and when Lisa's mum lifted up her head she was smiling again, a kind, nice smile.

She patted the empty seat beside her on the sofa and Lisa sat down and snuggled close. She was expecting the story of her dad's death. It felt like a sad time, like a time for that story, but it was time for a different story.

'Lisa, love, it's true that me and your dad never got married but that's all that's true out of all those lies. If someone spends their whole life lying they're bound to get lucky some time and hit on the truth. Isn't that right?'

Lisa nodded, though she did think that if people were imaginative enough with their lies, they could probably get away with avoiding the truth for ever.

'When I was going about with your dad, people started out by saying bad things about your dad to me and then they stopped 'cause they decided that I was just as bad as him in my short skirts and high boots. In the end they made up their minds that I was even worse than your dad and they started telling him bad things about me. But your dad never believed them and he never minded them. He used to say to me, "What you tell me is what I believe and what you show me is what I see because you are my truth and you are my eyes."

'It was his prayer to me and his prayer to us. So I started doing what he did, I stopped minding what people said, and soon everyone stopped talking. I think that once they realized we weren't bothered they thought that maybe we knew more about our business than they did.

'And though it's hard, I think that that's what you have to do. You know better than them don't you, Lisa, love? You know why me and your dad didn't get married and you know that you're my happy ending.'

Lisa nodded, because she did.

'But, Mum, do you have a mum and do you not tell her the time when she needs to know it?'

'Yes I have a mum all right, but she has a big, shiny kitchen clock of her own and anyway that's a whole new story.'

CHAPTER 3

Lisa's mum was right as usual. Lisa shrugged her shoulders against the gossip and the gossip filtered away, diluted by the romanticism of Lisa's position, a romanticism she exploited.

'My dad died so young, God must have missed him very much,' was one of her claims. Another was, 'My dad was a musician, but Mum says he was a great artist as well. Who knows what he could have become.' Another was, 'My dad died a hero. Mum says that he would have thought that that was better than living a coward, but she says a dead hero is no good to anyone.'

At one stage it got to be all the rage to deny one's father and boast the imaginary affairs of one's mother. Although there were always the few who laughed at Lisa's stories and intimated at their own truths, they never knew enough to thoroughly undermine Lisa. Their bottom line was always, 'My mum says that's nonsense.'

And all the little girls rathered Lisa's imagination and Lisa's stories to such basic realism.

Of course, one of the main reasons for this was that Lisa's features had settled into the line and form of prettiness. A similar line and form that had worked its way deep into her mother's face, leaving its mark of matured beauty. Lisa's eyes were far-set and rounded, her nose was small and sharp and her mouth pouted full-lipped in repose and, when animated, spread itself wide over delicate, brilliant teeth. Her hair crowned the whole with black, fat, bouncing curls. No one could associate such looks with loose morals, not even Lisa's classmates.

Lisa grew older and it was still her and her mum, and her mum always looked out for her. They still walked to school in the mornings, though now they walked further, to the big girls' school, and they walked slower, untroubled by the threat of elephant-swallowing chasms. In the afternoons Lisa walked home alone and set the fire and started the dinner before her mother's return. Fat Mrs Tyler, by now old, fat Mrs Tyler, visited on occasion, but was no longer a part of Lisa's world.

Lisa's afternoons still seemed lonely. They stretched long and silent in the winter months and listless and sultry through the summer. Lisa knew that they could be filled with friends but she wasn't willing to risk exposure.

As she grew, an awareness of her position grew with her. She knew that three-roomed cottages with leaking bathrooms were not the norm amongst her peers. She knew that the fashions that dictated casual wear were as strictly adhered to as the rules that dictated the restrictions of the school uniform, and she knew she couldn't compete.

If she had been sent to the school around the corner she would have been all right. She would have been thrown in with the hurly-burly of her neighbourhood street life. But Lisa's mum worked hard so Lisa could attend the convent school on Chester Road, and Lisa's mum did overtime to ensure that Lisa always looked crisp in her well-tailored uniform, and Lisa's mum couldn't work any harder, so Lisa's afternoons remained quiet and lonely.

*

It was during one of these afternoons that Lisa's grandmother appeared for the first time.

'There's things need sorting,' was her reason for
calling.

Lisa had laid the fire, had washed the vegetables and
was filling the coal scuttle from the bin in the yard when
the doorbell rang.

The cottage was too small for a doorbell. Its loud peal
echoed around the small, tight rooms, shaking whoever
was inside and alarming whoever was outside. No caller
ever expected to create such a disturbance.

Lisa went to answer it when she was ready. She wasn't
expecting a guest, and so she was prepared to face a
slightly apologetic petitioner of some sort. Her grandmother was neither a guest nor a petitioner; she was
neither alarmed nor apologetic.

'You must be Lisa,' she stated and she advanced into
the cupboard-sized hallway. 'The passing of the years
always surprises me. I had expected to see you grown,
but you seem to have outgrown yourself and any idea I
had of you, though I am pleased to see that you have the
look of the Fitzgibbons. My father's family were all dark
and it suited them. Of course it suited the men more than
the women but dark looks always do.'

Her flow of speech was articulate and definite – it did
not stem from nerves – and it always had the effect of
undermining her listeners. Lisa wiped her blackened
hands nervously on the seat of her skirt and followed
what she gathered was a relation into the sitting room.
She sat opposite the already seated visitor, on the other
side of the fireplace, and waited for an explanation.

'There's things need sorting,' was all she got.

It was a strange moment for Lisa. Up until then she

had never met a relative, aside from her mother, and had never felt the loss, but now she understood their function. A reason for being and a blind sense of belonging were suddenly presented to her. Here was an elderly woman with Lisa's nose and Lisa's mum's habit of turning her head to the side when finishing a sentence. The performance was as fascinating to watch as the woman was enthralling to listen to.

'. . . without as much as a card. I'm not a proud woman but I'm no one's fool, and I tried as often as I was turned away. The girl did wrong, though she wouldn't be told, but I'd have done my bit if I was let and I would have liked a sign of a sorry. Not that that's your fault, but there's many that say that the sins of the mother and there's no need to finish that old saying is there? You don't have any brothers or sisters do you? There's not any more of you I should know about?'

Lisa shook her head.

'Well that's something to give thanks for. Maybe the girl learned, albeit the hard way. Well here I am. As I have said, I am not a proud woman and there's things need sorting so where's your mother?'

They didn't have to wait long for Lisa's mother to return from work, but they waited long enough to form a solid opinion of each other.

Lisa, still uninhibited by adult decorum, stared. She stared at the strange lady's hat, wide brimmed and overly trimmed, and at her coat, which was still wrapped close about her against the cold of the unlit fire. It was black wool with broad, showy, unfashionable, astrakhan trimmings. The visitor allowed herself to relax into her surroundings only so far as to remove her gloves. They were black with three buttons apiece and they were now neatly laid across her lap. Three rings, of obvious worth, were embedded into the soft flesh of three of her fingers, and her mannerisms reflected her pride in them. Her fingers kept twirling over each other turning the rings and smoothing the stones, and her hands kept flying to her face with the decorated fingers outstretched. Her face was lost in folds of flesh, not because she was a heavy woman but because her features were so small. Lisa saw more of herself the more she looked. She recognized the colour of her eyes and her own nose was definitely there, but there was no trace of her mouth. This lady was speaking through bloodless thin lips that sporadically curled in what appeared to be scorn, but what Lisa rightly interpreted as a show of humour. Lisa prepared herself to be very fond of this elderly lady. She was, after all, family.

As for Maud Gaskell, née Fitzgibbon, she was later quoted as professing herself 'pleasantly surprised by the beauty I found in that hovel'.

But she wasn't one to be won by beauty alone. She thought it necessary, but only as a means to an end, and so she probed her granddaughter, looking for that something extra.

'You go to school, I presume?'

'Yes. Saint Brigid's.'

'A good school and a steady voice. I wonder which came first. Are you a scholarship girl?'

'No.'

'Are you a dim girl? Did you not qualify?'

'Mum didn't let me try.'

Maud Gaskell sniffed with approval.

'Your mother has the Fitzgibbons' approach to poverty. Never admit to it and it will not defeat you.'

Lisa laughed, although her grandmother spoke without inflection and punctuated her comments with a sneer. Lisa's mum walked into that laughter and shattered it.

In later years, Lisa marvelled at her mother's reaction. After her initial shock, she immediately reverted to her role of disgraceful daughter. Her language changed and her tone changed. She was torn between the urge to disagree and the desire to please; she was a child again and she was a bold one.

'Mother! How did you get here?'

'Bus, what would you expect? But I can see that you don't expect a lot. Goodness, child, when did you clean those windows last?'

'It's the traffic. No amount of cleaning keeps them. You would have to pick on the windows, when the rest of the house is spotless.'

'Believe me, it is hard to ignore those windows, but there's a lot worse than them I could pick on if I had a mind.'

And both women turned to look at Lisa as if she had been mentioned by name.

'Well, if you're just going to start that again. Please don't, Mother. How are you? And May? It is good to see you. Is there anything wrong? Why did you come?'

'I came because there's things need sorting. Things perhaps that the child shouldn't hear.'

'The child, as you call her, is thirteen. Thirteen long years old. She's old enough to listen to anything that needs saying.'

But Lisa could hear that her mum's heart was not in her words and, fighting valiantly against her natural curiosity, she saved her the embarrassment of a retraction.

'I'll go and check on the dinner. Will . . . you stay?'

Lisa hesitated before her use of 'you'. This woman obviously deserved a more formal title.

'I will not and you can call me Granny.'

Lisa almost laughed out loud. That stiff and opinionated old lady was the furthest thing from a 'Granny' that Lisa had ever encountered.

It was the first time that Lisa had been excluded from a conversation in her house and she tried the trick she had learnt from her classmates, but her mum made sure that the door was firmly closed and, a moment later, appeared to do the same to the kitchen door. Shut into the kitchen, Lisa heard nothing except the rise and fall of rumbling voices. An hour later she heard the front door close and she and her mum sat down to a slightly cold, slightly charred meal.

Lisa still loved mealtimes with her mum. They were usually filled with stories and anecdotes from school and the factory, but tonight there was a new tension.

'That was your granny,' said Lisa's mum, and then lapsed into silence and a forced enthusiasm for her food, but Lisa demanded more.

'Where does she live?'

'Down by the park, the river side of the park.'

'But that's not so far away. Why haven't we seen her? Why did she come today?'

'She came to tell me that a friend of mine was dead and to remind me that I have a sister.'

'Who's dead? And a sister! I have an aunt!'

Lisa had the feeling that perhaps she should be angry, but she was too interested to waste her time on a false emotion and she could see that her mum had been through enough already.

'A friend that I had a big falling-out with, but she was a good friend and it hurts that she died thinking the worst of me. And yes, you have an aunt and a fun one too if she hasn't changed too much. I'm sorry, love. All this must be a bit of a shock, but families are strange things. Me and my mother never got on too well and your Aunt May, well, she went away but she's back now and your gran has asked us all to dinner on Sunday. I'm sure it'll be worth it. Your gran always did know her Sunday dinners.'

Lisa winced. 'Gran' sounded even more incongruous than 'granny'.

'Do you want to go?'

Lisa nodded. She couldn't bring herself to finalize the agreement with words. There was something new and frantic in her mum's expression, and Lisa didn't know which answer she had to give to ease it. So she just nodded, because she desperately wanted to go.

CHAPTER 4

Sunday came as Sundays always do, and Lisa woke early into a still-dark world. She stretched under her rosebud bedspread and turned to the bed opposite. Her mum was sitting up, a book limp in her hands, and her lamp, with its red shade and gold tassels, still on. She had not slept at all. Lisa registered this before she sank back into the warmth of her dreams and the luxury of a late sleep.

At breakfast, three hours later, everything was overly normal. There was no mention of the planned visit. There hadn't been since the day of the invitation. Lisa longed to start the questions but her mother's composure almost belied the forthcoming event.

They sat together in the sitting room eating sausages and watching the treat of Sunday morning television. Lisa's mum said that the wholesomeness of Sunday morning programming was as beneficial as any organized religion and so they neither of them felt bad about wasting their morning watching reruns in their nightwear. It seemed to be more of a duty than a failing.

Finally, Lisa's mum broached the subject. 'We should probably walk through the park. We'll need some exercise to be ready to eat the lunch I'm expecting.'

Lisa took her cue. 'When will it be? When are we expected? Is it a big house? What should I wear?'

Lisa's mum laughed and answered every question as best she could. But before Lisa left to get dressed, her mum called her back and patted the empty seat beside her on the sofa. Lisa sat down, and although she felt herself to be almost too big, she snuggled close and her mum folded an arm around her shoulder.

'You're going to need a lot more answers over the next while, but the problem is, you don't know any of the questions yet, so if you listen a bit I'll fill you in on enough to get you by.

'My mother, your gran, was a strict woman. I'm not putting her down. It was the way it had to be. She was a widow with two young girls and she just didn't have time for the frills of mothering. Your Aunt May was three years older than me – she still is if she hasn't put a spurt on – and we were the best of friends, unless we were the worst of enemies, but that's just how sisters are. And life went on and then I met your dad.

'Up until then there were three of us that were as tight as eggs in a nest. Me, your Aunt May and Fran from down the road. We did all there was to do together until I met your dad and then I just wanted to do everything with him. Oh, your dad knew better. He would try and push me out with the girls. He said that he would never be able to take their place, but I didn't want him to, he was making new places just for him and me.

'And maybe you can guess the rest of the story or maybe you're still a bit young, but what happened was straightforward enough. My mother hated your dad. She hated him for being wild and cocky and for being the punchline of so many stories, and Fran and May, well, they were maybe jealous of him or jealous of the time I spent with him, but whatever their reasons, there was no one stood up with me when you came along.

'Now you're not to get me wrong. They're the best

people in the world and Fran is dead now and that's a terrible sad thing and the falling-out was my fault. Fran believed that I had done a terrible thing to her and instead of hanging my head with shame, even instead of explaining, I left the house. I thought they'd all come running after me and they did, but not enough for me, and so I've sat on my pride like a fool for all these years.

'I'm telling you this, Lisa, love, so that you'll know what all the nods and winks are for 'cause, mark my words, there'll be some nodding and winking going on. And another reason I'm telling you is so that you don't ask the wrong people questions. Grown-ups never like to talk about past fights and your dad was nothing except a big fight.

'So here's the deal, Lisa, love. You don't mention your dad and I won't make you sing.'

Lisa laughed and disentangled herself sufficiently to shake her mum's hand. It was their joke. It wasn't that Lisa couldn't sing or that she was shy, it was because as a child she had been terrified of microphones.

Then she left to put on her plain brown dress and her mum put on her shiny red dress with the white polka dots.

'We look a treat,' said Lisa's mum.

'We look a chocolate treat,' said Lisa.

'We look a strawberry-filled, chocolate treat,' said Lisa's mum.

'We look a minty, strawberry-filled chocolate treat,' said Lisa, and they stepped into the early afternoon and swung their hall door closed behind them.

'Did I ever tell you about your dad's and my special bench?' asked Lisa's mum as they neared the park.

Lisa nodded her head and listened. It was comforting just to listen. It eased Lisa's nerves and she knew that her mum found comfort in talking – the telling of her story eased her own nerves. And it was a lovely story, one of Lisa's favourites.

One night, Lisa's dad had lifted Lisa's mum over the railings and into the park. Then he had vaulted over to join her. They had walked by the lake and by the frozen rose garden and then they had found their seat, a stone one, under the delicate branches of a willow. Lisa's mum had never shown Lisa the seat and Lisa had never asked to see it. She knew it would look smaller in real life. Lisa's dad put Lisa's mum sitting down and then he presented her with a single twig instead of a flower, because it was wintertime, before asking her to dance. Lisa's mum put the twig in her hair and Lisa's dad hummed a sad, slow song and danced her around the trunk of the tree, beneath its drooping branches.

The following Sunday they arranged to meet by the same bench and Lisa's dad did the same thing. It was a bright Sunday and the park was filled with strollers, but Lisa's dad didn't mind. He hummed his sad, slow tune and he danced Lisa's mum around the trunk of the tree, and he was so handsome and she was so pretty and so shy that the strollers stopped and watched, and when the dance was over they clapped and when they strolled on they did so hand in hand.

It was the end of the story. Lisa's mum stopped talking and she turned out of the park and plunged into a maze of terraced streets. Lisa followed slowly, busy staring about her. She felt as if she were entering a strange new life, one that had always been waiting for her. A life populated by people with her nose.

Lisa's granny lived in a house like all the others, in a terrace like all the others, in a street like all the others.

Lisa was sure that she would never be able to find the house on her own. It was a two-storey red-brick and it opened straight on to the street. It was small – much smaller than the visitor's grandeur had led Lisa to expect – but it was as proper as its owner. The brasses gleamed gold against the polished warmth of the mahogany hall door and its three windows were washed transparent and were dressed in white lace. Lisa slipped her hand into her mum's and her mum let the brass knocker fall.

The door was opened promptly and Lisa and her mum stood staring at Lisa's Auntie May and Auntie May stood staring at them. It was a long moment. Lisa's mum squeezed Lisa's hand hard and then dropped it. It may have come a moment too late, but May's cry of greeting was inarticulate in its sincerity. She fell against her sister and when they finally broke apart, they were both smiling helplessly with the emotion of it all. Lisa watched and noted that May's smile spread wide over delicate, brilliant teeth, even if her nose was disappointingly large.

'Is that them or is that just a draught at the door? Either way please shut in the heat. Can you not respect an old lady's need for warmth?' Lisa's grandmother's words might have been harsh, but her tone was friendly.

'It's them.'

May took Lisa's hand and led her into what could only be described as a parlour. It wasn't a lounge or a front room or a sitting room, it pre-dated them all. It was a small room burdened with oversized, over-polished blocks of furniture. Its carpet and its curtains were faded and worn, but had obviously been the best in their day. It was a perfect room for Lisa's new grandmother.

'It's them all right.'

May seemed to be having difficulty believing it all. She

stood between the parlour and the hall, between Lisa and her mum, smiling at the two of them. Eventually she put Lisa sitting in an over-stuffed chair and briefly kissed her and thoughtfully ruffled her hair. 'She has the look of you, Elsie.'

Lisa's mum smiled her encouragement at Lisa before she drew her sister away. 'She has your smile, though, and that's what a girl needs most in this life – a smile she can count on.'

They left Lisa alone then and gathered in the kitchen behind her. She could hear them as they busily avoided the topics of past rows. It was eerie to listen to the disembodied voices and to hear the need behind the mundane exchanges.

'You're looking well.'

'I'm looking older.'

'The two of you are looking your age,' said Lisa's grandmother. 'Did you expect anything else? Or would you want it?'

'Are you home for good?' Lisa's mum asked.

'Yes.'

'And Bill?'

'He'll follow. I came early for the . . . you know.'

'Can you not say "funeral"? And will one of you girls help with the carrots. Where's the child? Alone with my china and her with huge hands and at the awkward age.'

Lisa started when she heard herself mentioned and carefully glanced around before she trusted herself to relax. Her grandmother's china was displayed behind her, in a wide, glass-fronted cabinet. It was all carefully shelved and locked away, safe from breakages, and Lisa relaxed.

'And is Bill well?'

'You peel the carrots and you, instead of standing chattering with your arms swinging, would you not think to busy them with a cloth. You two! Children still, will you never grow?'

There was the sound of laughter and the clatter of work.

'And Fran did she . . . how did she . . . ?' asked Lisa's mum hesitantly.

'It was a bus. She didn't live long enough to know which number.'

'Mother!'

'There's no loss of love, now, between me and Fran. You two left to remember her in her prime, but I had to stay to see her grow bitter. I think she thought that the sins of the child should be visited on the mother. Or maybe she was just one of those women who would have turned out bitter anyway, she took to it so well, mother's milk it was to her.'

'I'm sorry, Mother.'

'For what? What have you done to the carrots? This room isn't big enough for three, especially with a visitor inside being ignored. Go in there, May, and get to know your niece.'

Lisa could hear her grandmother's orders being carried out. There was a shuffle of movement and a creek of a door. She sat up and smoothed herself down, making herself ready to be made known to. The last she heard from the kitchen, as she watched the knob on the door turn, was her grandmother saying, 'Now that she's gone you can answer a few questions and you can do that facing me.'

*

'Well, Lisa, I would have known you in a crowd.'

May spoke loudly. She obviously knew that her role was to block out the kitchen conversation. 'You have my smile on my sister's face. As long as you don't have my brains and her cheek you'll stay in employment and out of trouble.'

Lisa smiled. She didn't know how to respond, and her mum had taught her to look affable when in doubt.

'Well, it's good to know you and I'm sorry we've missed each other for so long. We've got thirteen years to catch up on, so between us we must have some gossip. I'll go first. When I was seventeen, I got fired from Hall's Central Stores for falling asleep in the ladies' shoe department.'

Lisa laughed and found herself smoothed into comfort and conversation. She forgot to concentrate on the continuous rumble coming from the kitchen and lost herself in her Auntie May's memories – her mum's old world, but a brand new one for Lisa.

'. . . and school . . . don't get me going, but if you do, don't tell your mum what I've been saying. The things Elsie would get up to and drag me into. I bet she never told you about the time herself and Fran organized a birthday tribute to the headmistress, although it wasn't her birthday and no one had rehearsed anything?'

Lisa shook her head.

'Oh, it worked all right. Everyone sat in the assembly hall singing "Happy Birthday" for all they were worth and Elsie and Fran reciting poetry and calling on us all to do a turn. The head was delighted, although she was a bit confused, and Elsie and Fran got away without doing their maths exam. That had been the whole reason behind the affair. Do you know, I think we even got off early that day. And of course there was the strike against the introduction of volleyball . . .'

'And that's one story Lisa will never hear about.'

Lisa's mum had crept in on them and was smiling down on them. Lisa's smile dazzled back up at her. She was smiling at her mum, but she was smiling at May too, and for the first time. It was no longer just Lisa and her mum. It was bigger and better. It was Lisa and her family.

CHAPTER 5

The four women finally sat down to lunch in the cramped formality of the parlour. They sat one on each side of the square table, which had been cleared of plants and pulled free of the shallow bay window. Lisa sat between her mum and her Auntie May, facing her grandmother, and listened to the slow thaw of the conversation.

'I saw Veronica died a few years back. I'm sorry.'

'Not sorry enough to care to see her off.'

'I went to the church. I was at the back.'

'And you wouldn't step forward for your own aunt. You'd let me bury my sister alone.'

'You weren't alone. I'd have gone to you if you were alone, but you were surrounded. I couldn't face everyone at once.'

'No, you let me do that.'

'It was my fault too, Mother,' May said. 'I wasn't there either.'

'And you had reason not to be. You were an ocean away. An ocean is an excuse.'

'Well, I had an excuse as well,' Lisa's mum said defensively.

And everyone looked at Lisa as if she had been mentioned by name.

There was a roast-pork-filled silence, and then Lisa's mum tried again. 'The street's not changed.'

'Did you expect it to? Did you think you were that important?'

'I've missed it. I didn't know how much until today. I'm so pleased to see it the same.'

'Bricks don't change, but people do and that's always a good thing. You're still at Mitchell's then?'

'Yes.'

'I know. I've checked with personnel every now and then. Thought it only right that I should know something about my daughter.'

'Did you?'

Lisa helped her Auntie May clear the dishes. When they returned from the dark kitchen with the bowl of bright trifle there was a softness in the room and a dampness about Lisa's grandmother's eyes.

May held the bowl high. 'We made trifle, Elsie.'

'With black jelly and juicy sponge?' The silly words cut through the break in Lisa's mum's voice.

'Isn't my sponge always juicy and of course we made it with black jelly. Sure wouldn't you spit it out if it was any other colour?'

'Lisa, love,' said Lisa's mum, 'you've not lived until you've tasted this. It's made with God's own recipe.'

Everyone laughed and Lisa, once remembered, was questioned for the rest of the meal by her grandmother. She was asked about her school work, her ambitions, her friends, her wardrobe, her tastes and her fears and almost every answer was attributed to a relative.

'A fear of the dark. Now, that would be from my mother and, come to think of it, she could never hold a number in her head either. But the flair with languages, you'd get that from the Gaskells, along with your teeth. They always had good teeth.'

Lisa listened, enthralled by the history of her component parts. Out of the corner of her ear she could hear her mum and May fumble through their years apart and fasten on their past together. They were lost in the joy of each other and all that they had once been. Gripping each other's arms and wiping away tears of laughter, they spoke in shorthand with snorts of enthusiasm and overlapping squeals.

'Tommy Delaney!'

'The bus shelter!'

'Remember, remember Shirley?'

'Not curly Shirley?'

'And I was sixteen and madly in love with Paul.'

Lisa picked at her second helping of trifle and relaxed into the comfort of home, but behind all this new warmth a strange coldness was growing inside her. Her mother had denied her all this. She had denied her communal Christmases and birthday treats and trips to the park and people to make presents for and birthdays to remember and all the knowledge of all these people, both alive and dead, with her nose and her smile and her fondness for radishes and her skill at swimming.

Lisa had already accepted that there were things about the adult world that she didn't understand, but she was just now beginning to feel that maybe there were some things about it that she couldn't forgive.

The clatter of the meal died suddenly. The reunion was not strong enough to extend far into casual silence and everyone was too tired to work hard on conversation. The heavy meal was dragging on them all. Lisa rose with her mum to help clear the table, but her grandmother stopped them both firmly.

'You've not come far enough to be anything other

than a guest, Elsie. Put those dishes down and behave like one. Anyway, I need something to keep me busy for the afternoon.'

And so Elsie and Lisa settled back into the silence for a moment – Lisa's grandmother was not a woman to argue with – and then Elsie rose to go.

'It was lovely, but we'd better be going now. It gets dark early these nights and if we leave now we can still cut across the park.'

'As you wish.'

May quickly covered her mother's abruptness: 'I'll walk with you, Elsie. You can show me your house.'

'No.' Elsie and her mother spoke together.

'I'll need some help with these dishes.'

'I want to have the house nice for your first visit.'

May didn't protest. The initial meeting had been long enough for everyone.

In the small hall, May squeezed Lisa's shoulders and promised her a meal in town, and Lisa's grandmother kissed her on her forehead, pressing her old, dry lips down with hard urgency. When she straightened herself, she barely paused before hugging her daughter, Lisa's mum.

'This is always your home, Elsie. As long as I am alive it always will be. You should never have forgotten that. Now that Fran is dead, there is no one around here to bother you. May won't be here for ever and when she's gone there'll be two empty bedrooms upstairs. I'll say no more, except that you should think of the child.'

'I always think of her. I always have.'

Lisa had never heard her mum speak like that, in a cold controlled voice. It was almost how the visit ended, with a cold finality and a brief handshake between May and Elsie. But Lisa and her mum were barely down the road before May was with them again.

'Elsie!' she called, waving at them to stop, taking quick, running steps away from her own mother. 'Elsie, you never gave me your number.'

Lisa and her mum stopped and Lisa's mum fumbled for a pen.

Behind them, Lisa's grandmother called out: 'I have it May. Weren't you with me when I rang them? May, come in, the heat's getting out.'

May waved to her mother that she knew, that she heard, that she was hurrying, as she whispered close to Elsie's ear, over Lisa's head, 'He never came.'

'Who?'

'Burrows, to the funeral. He never came. No one has heard from him at all. I knew you'd want to know. I couldn't mention him in front of mother.'

And she was gone.

Lisa's mum looked a little shaky, but she soon recovered herself. She visibly forced herself to recover sufficiently to talk all the way home. She talked noisily over all Lisa's unasked questions.

'This is Station Road if ever you need to ask, but if you're around this area and you need to ask, chances are you'll be lost for good. There's few will be able to direct you to Station Road when there's a Station Terrace, a Station Lane and a Station Square and they're only the ones I know. The joke is, of course, that there's no station. They closed the one at the back there when they started the 36 bus route. Your dad used to tell me that one day our train would stop at the old station and we two would get off and walk straight into a world that would welcome us as a couple and would offer your dad a job with a collar and tie. When your dad was gone, I rode the train almost every day for a month. I had myself convinced that it would stop at the old station and your dad would be waiting for me there.

'But that was then and this is now, and now we know what has changed since then. And do you know, Lisa, love, but not a lot has. Of course that video shop wasn't there and I'm sure that that newsagent used to be a butcher, but I might be wrong. Streets like these don't take to change.

'And here's the park already. I haven't been around this end of it for an age, for a lifetime of yours. It reminds me so much of your dad. We used to always meet by that gate. Your dad called it the gateway into our world. Did I ever tell you about the midnight picnic we had?'

'And for the first time Lisa said, 'Yes, a few times.'

She wanted to shout, 'You've told me too often, but you never told me that I had my Auntie May's smile and that my grandmother was born a Fitzgibbon.' But she didn't. She just bowed her head to the familiar story and, despite herself, was carried away with it.

'We went to a dance that night, your dad and me, and I had dressed up in all my finery. I remember I was wearing a blue frock that was cut tight at the waist but seemed to have a skirt made out of fairy wings. I was dead proud of myself in it and I was delighted showing it off, so you can imagine that I wasn't too keen on your dad when he insisted that we leave early. I was so cross with him that I walked home in a sulk and I stormed off in a right fit when he said he was going to whoosh me over the railings into the park for a short cut. Well, he caught up with me and we nearly had a blazing row and then of course I did as I was told. I always did what your dad said, not 'cause I was naturally obedient – it was just because he always seemed to have the best ideas. So, I allowed him to whoosh me over and we walked through the park until we came to our gateway and there, under a clump of bushes, your dad had hidden a basket of food, a bottle of wine, a tablecloth and even a silver candlestick. He made me close my eyes and I wasn't allowed to open them until he had set out the meal. He even had glasses for the wine and no one drank wine back then. I think that was my first glass.

'Oh, I couldn't believe it when I opened my eyes, and everything smelled and tasted of grass and the night air.'

Lisa and her mum walked on hand in hand, both lost in the beauty of a beautiful night and a beautiful man, but when Lisa disentangled herself and before she could start her questioning, her mum snapped back to the present and swamped the child with mundane queries.

'Do you have socks clean for tomorrow? Are you sure that you finished your homework? Remember the coal is due tomorrow around four – the money's behind the clock.'

It wasn't until later, in bed, under the comfort of her mum's red lampshade, that Lisa got a chance to talk.

'Why did you never tell me, Mum?'

'I've been waiting for that question, love, for as long as I've had you and I still haven't thought of the answer. There maybe is no answer to emotions. I was sad after your dad, I was scared of my mother, I was disappointed in Fran and May – all bad emotions and all mixed up. You can't blame me for the odd bad decision. And it wasn't all my decision. May left with her Bill and your grandmother took your coming very hard – people did back then and your grandmother was always of an older generation. Like I said to you before, I flounced off and no one came following hard enough. And maybe I never wanted them to know you, maybe I thought that all they could teach you was their stories about my hurt and shame. I'm so happy I was wrong. What do you think of May? Isn't she pretty? Oh, I've missed May so much.'

'And Fran?'

'Oh yes, I've missed Fran too, but we were never as close and we fell out.'

'Why?'

'I think she was jealous of me, though that sounds big-headed. Go asleep now, I want to read for a bit.'

'Who was my dad?'

'Ah, don't push me for a story now, Lisa, I'm tired.'

'No, who was he?'

'Haven't I told you often enough? He was Jimmy to me, but he called himself Jim Bowles. He said it rumbled off the tongue like a singer's name should.'

'Yes, but who was Jim Bowles?'

'Jim Bowles was your dad.'

And Lisa was too young to get any further. She still didn't know which questions to ask and something new inside her sensed that her mum wasn't going to answer her. For the first time, Lisa understood what her old playmates had been talking about. For the first time she understood the thrill of half-heard conversations and overheard scandals.

CHAPTER 6

The following Wednesday, Lisa's Auntie May called before Elsie arrived home from work, and she stayed until long after Lisa went to bed.

For Lisa, that Wednesday afternoon had started off as a lonely, ordinary, grey, rainy one and then the doorbell rang and she opened it to a startled May.

'Goodness, but I thought that I had let off an alarm. What an important doorbell you have.'

She stayed politely on the step until Lisa invited her in, and she stayed politely in the cramped hall until Lisa directed her into the sitting room and the still-cool fire. Then, having established her niece as hostess, she took control of the conversation.

'What a lovely house and what awful directions your mum gave me! It's a wonder I'm here at all, but now that I am I'm not going anywhere for a while. Don't worry. I've provided for myself. I've brought some chops for dinner so here's the plan: you make me a cup of tea now and after I'm thawed I'll make the dinner for us three. Is it a deal?'

And Lisa laughed and agreed and headed for the kitchen. She took her time laying a special tray, complete with chocolate biscuits and white napkins, and all the time she was accompanied by the flow of May's conversation. Her words came from all corners of the cottage. She was shameless in her curiosity.

'Well isn't this toilet so compact, and I see you have a power shower – aren't they gorgeous things? And the bedroom! Lisa your bedspreads! They're just like what we used to have, me and Elsie. It's such a cosy room, you must love it.' And then her head popped around the kitchen door. 'Am I being rude? Can I help?'

'No, no, it's just ready.'

Lisa lifted the tray and followed her aunt into the sitting room and the warmth of the fire. Once they were seated, facing each other, the conversation started for real. May went first.

'I am very glad to know you, Lisa, and I'm very sorry that it took this long. I was away, you know. If I had stayed, things would have been different. Your mum and your grandmother are as stubborn as each other. It's what they are – you can't blame them for that.'

Lisa blushed. She had never supposed that her resentment was visible. 'Are you going to stay here now? Are you going away again?'

'No, we're home for good. Your Uncle Bill has got a job back here. It's what we always wanted. It's the job he wanted, and I'm looking for the house we've dreamed of for the money we have.' She laughed. 'He'll be home soon. He's just finishing up over there. I came home early for the. . . well, you know why I came. But there's something else. Don't let on that I've told you first, promise to look surprised when I tell your mum later on.'

'I promise.'

'Well . . .'

The two of them, both smiling the same smile, leaned forward towards each other and, although they were alone, May spoke in that important whisper that some women save for the more delicious scraps of scandal. 'I'm three months gone.'

Lisa, being only thirteen, looked confused. May laughed, settled back and continued in her normal voice from the depths of her armchair. 'I'm pregnant. In six months' time you'll have a cousin, and now that we've met, I hope that I'll have a baby-sitter.'

'A baby! Oh, brilliant!' Lisa's smile split wide open, encompassing everyone in this new world of hers, her family, her auntie, her uncle, her grandmother and now her cousin. She hoped the baby wouldn't look like her Uncle Bill. She wanted a child with her nose and her smile and her hair. She wanted people to mistake her cousin for her sibling.

May watched and laughed and seemed to follow Lisa's thoughts exactly. 'They say that black hair and brown eyes are dominant, so, with any luck, the child should look like us.'

Lisa blushed again. She felt that her need was obviously as transparent as her resentment. She still didn't know that genetics ran to thought patterns.

May didn't look to see the blush. Still talking, she stood up out of the depths of her armchair. 'The child could do without its dad's looks. Bill's a good man, not a handsome one. Not that I'm complaining. That was my choice. I don't think the two ever come in the same package. Now, show me where your pots are and tell me if your pans are kept separate and I'll get cooking. You do whatever school stuff needs doing and then you'll be free all evening to listen to me and your mum talk nonsense. Is it a deal?'

'It's a deal.'

But Lisa found it hard to leave her aunt. She showed

her the ins and outs of the tiny kitchen and then she hung about behind her, cluttering the already poky space.

'A deal is a deal,' said May, 'and this room ain't big enough for both of us and pork chops. Either one of us leaves or that there dead pig.'

Lisa laughed and shuffled towards the door, but she didn't go through it. Her unasked question was keeping her there and her uncertainty was keeping her quiet.

'Well?' May stopped her bustle and turned. Her tone seemed to demand a query from her niece. Relieved, Lisa felt that she had no choice now – she had to ask.

'Why did my mum not see my grandmother? What did Fran do?'

'Fran did nothing.'

'Why did my grandmother say that Fran would have bothered my mum?'

'Did she?'

May bent about her bustle again, dividing her attention, giving herself an excuse for vague answers.

'Why did my mum never go home? Was it because Fran was there?'

'Maybe a bit. Do you like prawns? I brought some for a starter.'

'Why did Fran not like Mum and my grandmother?'

'Ah, Lisa, that Frances Burrows, she let herself get bitter. She ended up not liking anyone.'

'Frances? Was that her name?'

'Yes, sad old Frances Burrows. That's how she died, even though she was still young, but I'd like to remember her as Fran O'Leary, the girl with the best legs in the school.'

Lisa left then, and she left quickly. She was scared of

her new transparency. She didn't want her aunt to see her thinking, *so it wasn't Bowles, then*.

But May misinterpreted the abruptness of her niece's departure and followed her into the sitting room.

'I've not upset you, have I?'

'No, I'm not upset.'

'What did your mum tell you about your dad?'

'Everything, I think.'

'Did she tell you who he was?'

'Jim Bowles.'

'Who's Jim Bowles?'

'My dad.'

'Oh.'

There was no time for anything more. Lisa's mum's key turned in the lock and both May and Lisa went to greet her, smiling their smile.

'I came calling,' said May.

'She came calling and brought dinner,' said Lisa.

'She came calling and brought dinner and will have to stay and eat it,' said Lisa's mum, and everyone laughed.

It was a very happy night. They ate the food that May had cooked in her new, foreign way, swamped in a sauce, and they ate it off their knees, sitting in a semi-circle around the fire. It was only after the dinner that conversation started in earnest, but not before May had made her announcement.

'Ahem,' she said and stood and winked at Lisa. 'Ahem, ahem, and can I have a little bit of order here please. Speech time.'

Lisa and her mum sat back, smiling.

'It has come to my attention that now, after almost

fourteen years of marriage, my trousers are growing a little tight.'

Lisa giggled, but her mum looked confused. 'Diet if you must, but don't start tonight,' she said and Lisa and May laughed.

'It's not a dieting matter.'

The two sisters stared at each other and a light dawned slowly in Elsie's eyes. But instead of the expected squeal and hug she just sat up and shook her head.

'But I thought . . .'

'Well, all that was sorted out.' May paused. 'It's one of the main reasons I came home.' Her voice wavered with uncertainty. She obviously felt foolish now, standing alone, waiting to be hugged. Lisa looked to her mum, but Elsie didn't need telling. She leapt forward with all the enthusiasm that was expected of her. It was that enthusiasm that dictated the tone of the rest of the evening.

Without their mother there to check them, the two sisters bounced loudly and wildly from topic to topic, person to person, year to year and Lisa listened to everything, soaking it all up, relishing every anecdote, recognizing them all as part of her pre-birth history.

All the stories were new stories. They were all stories about three little girls, or three teenage girls – Fran, May and Elsie – and that was all. The stories never went any further. They never mentioned Jim Bowles. But Lisa didn't mind. She had heard all his stories before.

The night sped on.

It was long past eleven when May rose to go.

'Good lord, the time,' she squealed, and sprang up. 'Mother will be frantic. But if I run I'll still catch the bus.'

'Steady, steady there, May,' said Elsie, the older sister.

And, because old habits are quick to resurface, May stopped flapping to listen to what she had to do.

'You ring Mother and tell her we're busy talking and you'll be along later in a taxi. Have you a key? Well and good. Tell her not to wait up. And you, missy cheeky! Lisa's Mum said pointing at Lisa. 'You go straight to bed, shut your eyes tight and close your ears and try and be asleep an hour ago. And I will make more tea and fish out the Christmas brandy.'

Lisa hated going to bed alone. Usually her mum came with her and sat up reading. It was hard to sleep without the secure sound of rustling pages. It was harder still knowing that the fire was still burning and one's pre-birth histories were still being unfolded. Lisa did try. She counted sheep and lessons and tables and rhymes. She imagined the most perfect frock and her first proper kiss with a still-faceless boy, but nothing worked and she soon stopped trying. She just lay still, facing the ceiling, listening to the adult rumblings coming from the room opposite.

She must have slept, because suddenly her mouth felt muzzy and the voices rose high.

'Jim Bowles? Where did you get Jim Bowles?'

'A name is just a name.'

'It's not just a name she wants, it's a father. She'll know sooner or later. She's been asking me questions already. The first conversation I've had with her and she's asking.'

'And I suppose you were quick to tell her.'

'I was, but you came home. And I wasn't just telling her for the reason you think. I assumed the child would know. I thought you'd have seen to that by now. It's been thirteen years, Elsie, the man is just a name now anyway. All I'm saying is, the child deserves the right name.'

Lisa had to strain to listen now. She sat up in her bed, clenching her fists tight, waiting for her mum's answer.

'Jim Bowles is the right name. She loves Jim Bowles. I've given her that much.'

The sisters settled to disagree and their voices dropped back down to their companionable volume. Lisa didn't hear anything else until the alarm went off and her bleary-eyed mum drew the covers off her, forcing her to react to it.

They were both tired at breakfast, but it was more than that and whatever it was, it was in Lisa. She had never known a tense meal before. A week ago she would have confidently demanded the truth. Now she didn't even know if her questions were worth asking. She ate slowly, washed and packed her bag slowly, and finally, just as they were leaving, broached the subject. 'I heard Auntie May last night.'

These new, family names were still novel enough for Lisa to make sure to use them at every opportunity. 'What did she mean about the right name and Jim Bowles?'

'You were sleeping, love. You must have heard us muddled.'

Lisa was standing in the cramped hall and her mum was standing in the kitchen, checking her bag for the day. The door between them was wide open and Lisa could see her bent over her bag. She knew that her mum's mind was filled with lists – keys, purse, lipstick, lunch vouchers, bus pass. It was the same every morning. Most mornings she chanted her list out loud.

Lisa's mum had never learnt the art of smooth morning management.

'I was awake and I heard it all.'

'What did you hear?' Lisa's mum snapped her bag shut and joined Lisa in the cramped hall, reaching over her head to get her coat.

'Auntie May said that I should have the right name.'

'Your Auntie May would have me married, you with a stepdad and us all living in a cottage in the country surrounded with beauty and dead with the boredom of it all.'

But Lisa didn't laugh. She just turned slowly out of the house.

'Lisa, love, there's nothing to bother yourself with. Your dad answered to Jim Bowles and I always called him Jimmy and you know him almost as well as I did, and May has been too long from home to have the right to poke her nose in. And now we're off and quickly.'

The door was slammed shut and Lisa's mum was away down the road at a pace that didn't allow for conversation. But Lisa tried. She ran behind her panting her questions.

'But who was he? Who was Jim Bowles? Did he have a mum or sisters? Do I have more uncles or aunts? Did he live around here? Would his family still be here?'

Eventually Elsie stopped. 'Lisa, love, I loved Jim Bowles. I loved my Jimmy, and that's all I knew or wanted to know. He could have had a family of monkeys or he could have had a family of kings, but he was still my Jimmy. When he was gone, everything was gone except my happy ending. Do you understand, love?'

Lisa nodded. She couldn't help being impressed by such a show of honest emotion. She stopped asking her questions.

CHAPTER 7

For a while Lisa's life was very different and then that difference faded into a new norm. Every Sunday she and her mum would cross the park to Station Road for their lunch. Every Wednesday May would come for the evening and, at least once a week, more often twice, Lisa would go to Station Road alone, after school, to visit her grandmother. On those nights, both she and her mum arrived home at the same time to a dark, cold house and a makeshift dinner.

The first few times this happened Lisa came bursting home filled with all she had done with her grandmother, the new stories she had heard and the old photographs she had seen, but her mum never joined in with her enthusiasms, and soon Lisa learnt to keep them to herself. She loved her stiff, kind grandmother. She loved her new sense of belonging. She loved her afternoons frozen in the warm dust of age, and she hated to expose these loves of hers to her mum's indifference or deliberate coldness. She was too new to the family dynamic to understand the subtleties of jealousies or the deep strength of battling wills.

All Lisa knew was that her mum didn't much like her grandmother and so Lisa stopped gabbling her mish-mash of sentences starting with, 'My grandmother says' or 'My grandmother told me' or 'My grandmother showed me'. Meals in the little house became quieter, and suddenly the little house seemed too small. Lisa felt her mum's presence for the first time. Before she had always seen herself and her mum as a unit.

But May was different. Whenever May was around, everyone laughed and the cramped house became cosy and the cold was great because the fire was warm and the telly on the blink meant that they could chat all the better and candles were prettier than lights and meals were tastier when they were eaten away from the table and rainy days washed the city cleaner than any Corporation man. Lisa's mum said that that was May's gift, that she was one of those people who knew how to store sunshine.

May's disposition may have helped everyone around her, but it helped herself as well. She always got what she wanted. Lisa's mum said this as well, but she said it in a happy way because anyone who ever met May would have to know that she deserved the best of everything, so it was only right that she got all she wished for.

May didn't stay in Station Road for long. She soon managed to rent the house she and Bill wanted, for the money that they had. She said that some day she hoped to buy it and everyone believed that she would.

And she soon managed to get a job that could be done amongst people she liked for as long as she liked, and at home after the baby came. She was to be a saleslady and, although some people saw telesales as a poor job, everyone knew that May would make it work because a phone call from May would cheer anyone up and happy people were more inclined to buy things. Now, all May was wishing for was that Bill would hurry home.

'It's not just Bill, though bless him I do miss his round,

bald head, his round, bald face, his round, bald tummy – well, just the roundness and the baldness of the lot of him.'

They were sitting in their semicircle around Lisa's fire drinking hot chocolate and Lisa and her mum laughed at the thought of a round, bald man.

'No it's not just Bill. It's my three-piece suite and my king-size bed and all my lovely crockery. It's no joke living in that great bare house, literally waiting for my ship to come in. If he doesn't hurry himself up I'll be too fat to help unpack as much as a spoon.'

She patted her tummy and Lisa and her mum laughed at the thought of a fat May.

As usual May got what she wished for and Bill arrived home within three days of that conversation. He turned up in Station Road early on Saturday morning to get directions to his new house from his mother-in-law who did what every good mother-in-law would do. She fed him, and while she was cooking for him, she rang May and May rang Lisa's mum and Lisa answered the phone.

'He is!' she squealed. 'Oh yes, of course we will.'

And she dropped the phone and ran to wake her mum. 'Uncle Bill's back. He's in Station Road and I said we'd go and say hello. Hurry up. Auntie May said that they wouldn't be there for long.'

Lisa's mum sat up straight away and smiled a cross kind of smile. 'I suppose there's nothing for it. Now's as good a time as then for welcoming the man home.'

She told Lisa to wear her brown frock and she wore her smart navy one and the pair of them ran across the park to Station Road. Lisa's new Uncle Bill was still in the kitchen mopping up his egg mess with a fistful of white sliced bread when they arrived.

It was Lisa's first real family occasion, and to her eyes it held all the rich glory of Christmas films and greetings cards. Her grandmother's kitchen was dark, but it had all the trappings a kitchen should have, a scrubbed, bare table, a Sheila Maid, pots hanging from hooks, vegetables in a round wicker bin, a Belfast sink and a flagstone floor. It was a perfect setting for an informal, warm reunion and her Uncle Bill looked the perfect focal point for cosy affection. He was round and he was bald and he did look pleasant.

'This is your niece, Lisa,' May said proudly, and Bill got to his feet and held out his hand.

'Hello there,' he said. His voice was nice; soft but rumbly.

'Hello,' said Lisa.

'You're the picture of your mum.'

Lisa smiled. She liked it when people said that because her mum was so pretty.

'Hello, Bill,' said her mum.

'Hello, Elsie,' said Bill. 'It's been too long.' He sounded as if he meant it.

For a moment everyone was standing close together, looking pleased with each other, looking close enough to hug, and then the picture postcard shattered. Lisa's grandmother stepped away, through the door, into the hall, and on into the formal parlour, calling after her for everyone to follow.

'We deserve more comfortable chairs than kitchen ones. Shut the door after you, May, keep the smell of frying in. Would you see thirteen years on Elsie's face Bill?'

She was sitting on her throne now, the large armchair,

the one right beside the fire and far away from the draughts.

'No, I wouldn't see a day.' He laughed.

'But you'd see the years in Lisa all right. Without her I'd hardly credit the time passing.'

'Oh, you would, yes.'

'You'd see the years on Bill, though, wouldn't you, Elsie?' May asked and without waiting for Lisa's mum she answered herself. She ruffled Bill's head and prodded his side. 'The years have rounded him and polished him up a treat.'

Everyone laughed because when May said such things they were funny, even if they were true, even if they would have hurt coming from anyone else. Bill laughed the loudest and he laughed a little too much. Lisa thought that it was just because he was so pleased to see May, but she was to learn that he always did that. Later, when Lisa's mum offered to make some tea and he laughed. And when Lisa's grandmother told a story about the local shop he laughed, even though she had been complaining about the prices. And then when May told him about their new house and asked about their furniture, he laughed and told a silly joke.

'That reminds me,' he said. 'What's the difference between a woodworm and a bent lawyer who deals in wills?'

Everyone shook their heads.

'One eats chairs and the other cheats heirs.'

Everyone laughed, even Lisa, although she was blushing inside at the silliness of the joke. By the time Bill left, Lisa was upset to find herself relieved.

'We'll be off, then,' said May. She had refused tea and had withdrawn from the conversation some time earlier, leaving it tense and brittle. It was always like that between Lisa's mum and Lisa's grandmother. Their words were always teetering on the verge of an argument. May stood up and Bill followed.

'We will, then, eh, ha ha ha.'

'You have to see the house and get yourself unpacked and we have to arrange for the furniture coming on Monday.'

'Yes, we do indeed, yes, ha ha ha.'

'I'll see you Wednesday.' May said this directly to Lisa. 'Bill will have to cook for himself then.'

Lisa smiled. She felt mean, but she knew that her Uncle Bill wouldn't fit well into their Wednesday nights.

Lisa and her mum waved May and Bill down the road. They looked funny, like two young, old people going on holidays. They each had a large suitcase and Bill had two bulging plastic bags. Just before they turned out of Station Road, Bill stuffed all his bags around one arm and put the other around May. She put her head on his shoulder and they disappeared. Lisa turned to her mum to smile because it had looked so lovely but her mum was gone. She was in the parlour.

'And I suppose you'll be off now?' Lisa's grandmother was asking.

'Well, we have things to do.'

'Anything more important than helping your sister? You could have left with them, held on to something for them.'

'It was time they were left alone.'

'They'll have time enough for that. It was time they were given a hand.'

Lisa closed the front door and walked into the parlour and both women stopped to smile at her.

'What did you think of your Uncle Bill then?' asked her grandmother.

'He was nice. He had a nice voice.'

'He's better than nice, Lisa. He's a good man. It's important for a young girl to know a good man, helps her recognize the bad ones.'

'Lisa knows her good from her bad.'

'Then she knows more than her mother.'

Lisa and her mum left then. They walked slowly through the park and Lisa's mum told Lisa the story about her dad and the magic daisies.

'The park is beautiful isn't it, Lisa, love?'

It was late November and the trees were almost all bare except for a few yellowing leaves. The black branches were spread stark against a cold, blue sky, so Lisa agreed. There could be no question about it, the park was lovely.

'Poets talk all the time about how lovely nature is and how romantic and all, but me and your dad never did have much of nature. We had this park and the embankment down by the railway and the scrap of woods along by the river, but we had all the romance we needed.

'One Saturday, just before the end, your dad and me were down the embankment and I was making a daisy-chain and your dad stopped me. He said I was killing the flowers for themselves and everyone else. He said there was something about the way daisies opened and closed that made him think that they counted the days in an intelligent way and I was doing them out of their tomorrows. So of course I stopped and I was a bit upset with him because I knew he was right and that always hurts. So, to cheer me up, he said that he would find a way to have the daisies thank me and I laughed and forgot about my sulk, because he was down on his knees low to the ground pretending to be whispering to them. I had to go then, but he went on with his foolishness and told me to meet him early the next morning at exactly the same place and he would have the daisies coached.

'Of course I thought he was teasing and of course I met him the next morning. I met him at about six. I was that foolish with love. He was waiting for me, sitting among all the daisies that were only half-open. And we talked for a bit and the day warmed up a bit and the daisies opened up fully and eventually I noticed. Do you know what he had done, Lisa, love?'

Lisa shook her head even though she knew the answer.

'The night before, after I had left him, he had written messages on the petals of the daisies. A letter in black on each white leaf. It took me an age, but I pieced all the letters together and the daisies said "Thank you" and "Good morning" and "Jimmy loves Elsie".'

They walked on a bit in silence. That's what they did after every story. It was to give themselves time to digest the beauty of the memory.

Then Lisa asked, 'Was Uncle Bill always so round and bald?'

'Not quite.'

'And did Auntie May have any other boyfriends?'

'No.'

CHAPTER 8

Soon it was Christmas. Christmas for Lisa and her mum had always been a lovely time. They always had turkey, and stockings filled with sweets at the end of their beds, and a tree, and Santa presents wrapped with bows, and decorations, and holly from the market, and mulled wine, which Lisa loved to love, even though she didn't really like the taste and had to put in extra sugar, and long walks by the river, and logs in the fire that smelled of forests and spat out sap, and a huge box of chocolates, and a late tea with sandwiches and tomatoes even though they were still full from their lunch.

Lisa had always loved Christmas, but this year she was lost for words. She just could not find a word that described this feeling inside her, this feeling that seemed so much bigger than excitement. One Sunday lunch-time at the beginning of December, Lisa's grandmother had said to everyone, 'I'll do Christmas this year.'

Bill looked at May and May looked to Elsie and Elsie shook her head slightly and, although Lisa's grandmother was bent over her meal, she said, 'There's no use arguing, Elsie. I've missed thirteen Christmases with my only grandchild . . .'

Everyone looked at May's spreading belly.

'. . . and I doubt that I have that many Christmases left. I'll do Christmas this year and you'll come and enjoy yourself.'

'It's not, Elsie, Mam,' said May. 'It's me. Myself and Bill thought we'd have Christmas. Our table is bigger.'

'Did you, Bill? Did you think that?'

'Well, I did, I suppose, yes, ha ha ha.'

'So you'll have me moving about in the cold on Christmas Day? Is it that you don't like my table? Is it that you don't trust my cooking?'

Lisa's grandmother joined in with Bill's laugh, just to show that she was joking. But no one argued further and so Christmas was to be at Station Road.

Lisa was counting the days. She was going to have a real storybook Christmas with her uncle and aunt and grandmother. There was even talk of some neighbours calling in for a morning drink. She was going to have a choice of people to pull her cracker with and maybe her Uncle Bill might drink too much and maybe there might be a fight over the telly and then, when she went back to school, she could throw her eyes to heaven with all the other girls when describing her Christmas Day.

Walking home that Sunday with her mum, Lisa bounced with enthusiasm.

'Will my grandmother have a tree?'

'Yes.'

'Does she bake a cake?'

'Yes.'

'Does she bake mince pies?'

'Yes.'

'What will we buy Auntie May and Uncle Bill?'

'Why can't you just say May and Bill? I'm sure they'd rather it. You make them sound ancient with all your "Auntie"s and "Uncle"s. And what's wrong with "Granny"? What's all this "my grandmother" nonsense?'

Lisa didn't answer and didn't ask any other questions and herself, and her mother, walked on in stiff silence. They were almost out of the park when her mum finally spoke.

'I'm sorry, Lisa, love, it's just that I am a little homesick for our Christmas, just you and me. Are you? Even a little bit?'

Lisa nodded, even though she couldn't understand how you could be homesick in your home surrounded by people who had your nose and your smile. She nodded, because she knew that that would make her mum happy, but she still kept her mouth closed on all her enthusiasms. They were to be saved for her grandmother.

And her grandmother appreciated every one. During December, Lisa spent more and more time at Station Road. She called there almost every evening after school and soon settled into a routine that revolved around her grandmother.

Because she was there so often, she became an integral part of her grandmother's life. It was no longer possible for the old woman to keep her shameful granddaughter compartmentalized, and she no longer wanted to. The thirteen-year-old shame had melted into a gangly form of vibrancy and potential beauty that demanded pride. Soon Lisa was let sit in the parlour when the neighbours called. She was sent to the corner shop with her grand-mother's list. And when she walked out with her grandmother she was linked and she felt the shift of old weight on the crook of her arm. Lisa loved that – it made her feel so necessary.

But Lisa's new status brought its own problems. The whispers and the winks that her mum had warned her about started in earnest. And because her trips to her grandmother's house were purely voluntary – if anything they went against her mum's wishes – she knew that she didn't really have the right to ask her mum for explanations. Her grandmother wasn't the sort of woman you could demand information from and May was busy with her work and house and baby and husband and anyway she was more or less on Lisa's mum's side. So, Lisa began listening for answers for herself.

She used all the tricks that she had learnt in school. She sat very still in company, she took to doing her homework at the parlour table and could listen with all her being while appearing lost in her muddle of opened books and ink-covered copies. The few times she was sent out of the room, she learnt how to judge the swing of the door as she pulled it behind her. Because her grandmother's chair was facing away from it, the door was usually left open a crack. During that December, Lisa learnt a lot.

Her grandmother's callers were of her grandmother's age and the conversations they had usually dated back to their prime, to the time before Lisa was born. Lisa learnt that the town had changed a shocking amount, that the roads were busier and everyone ruder, that there were more thugs and looser morals and that Station Road was missing all the old characters.

'It's all young people now that would pass you on the road and not greet you.'

'Sure you could be dead in your bed for a week without anyone knowing.'

'A week! No, they'd know before a week was out, the smell would be awful.'

Lisa's grandmother enjoyed shocking her company

and Lisa took great pride in this. She loved to see the old ladies suck in their cheeks and glance at each other in disapproval, but they always came back for more.

It was only when these old ladies began mentioning names that Lisa would be sent out of the room. If she was sent to the shops she missed everything, but usually she was just sent as far as the kitchen to fetch more tea and then she could hear almost everything through the door that she would leave open, or through the flimsy partition wall.

She heard that the idiot daughter in number forty-three had finally died forty years later than expected. She learnt that both the Jameses in number thirteen had been alcoholics and were both dead now with it, and she learnt that Fran Burrows had not heard from James Burrows for thirteen of their fifteen years of married life and it was doubtful if he was still in the country.

'Has *anyone* heard from him?' Mrs Benson's voice was heavy with meaning.

'No.'

'Oh, he was a charmer if ever there was one. I wouldn't blame. . .'

'Blame lies where it lies and no amount of charm can raise it. Will you have more tea or must you be going?'

Lisa's grandmother tried to hold her parlour conversations within set boundaries, but invariably the talk splashed about, and Fran Burrows's death didn't help – it had left her past open for evaluation. Again and again the women returned to the tragedy of it all.

'You'd think she would have struck up with someone else.'

'You'd think, but that James Burrows – he'd cure anyone of men.'

In the kitchen, Lisa listened closer and closer to every word.

'How she ever married him I don't know. She was a sensible girl and he was not a man to marry, with his leather jacket and all.'

'Thought he was somebody, he did.'

'Thought he was above a good day's work anyway.'

Lisa always had to listen hard to catch these snippets. They were well diluted in generalized conversations. Lisa's grandmother never allowed the topic of James Burrows to develop in her parlour and soon Lisa began to guess why.

Lisa was alone in Station Road one evening. Her grandmother had stepped out to the shops and Lisa was left sitting at the parlour table struggling with the rows of numbers that, just like her great grandmother, she couldn't keep in her head, when Mrs Ryan and Mrs Benson called on their way home from town. Lisa's grandmother was due home at any minute, so the women decided to wait.

They followed Lisa into the one heated room in the house and they refused refreshment, preferring to wait for their friend. After a few polite exchanges they insisted that Lisa return to her work and when she did they paid her the compliment of flattering her as if she had dropped out of earshot.

'Isn't she a model of a girl? As neat as a button and as polite as you could wish.'

'Now, if all the young ones were like that where would be the trouble we're always hearing about?'

'And I bet she's as smart as she is pretty. Look at her there away with her books and not minding us at all. I don't know where they get the concentration from.'

Lisa kept her head down and after a short silence the women slipped into the trap of believing their own pretence and continued their conversation as if Lisa really was out of earshot.

'Do you think she has the look of him?'

'Oh, I do. It's lucky she didn't show up when Fran was around. To have to see that every day would have killed the poor girl.'

'Well, she'd go far on his looks. It's his character she could do without.'

The conversation drifted on and Lisa stayed bowed over her books with her face burning and a flutter beating against her chest. She knew now who Jim Bowles was.

CHAPTER 9

Lisa left Station Road early that day and walked slowly home through the park, even though she was forbidden to do so alone. Her mum had a city woman's mistrust of open spaces. She was a strong believer in 'safety in numbers' and saw all manner of evil lurking behind every bush. Lisa kicked the few remaining, dirty leaves and reasoned that a walk in a park was nothing compared with what her mum had done.

She plucked the image that she had created of Fran out of her head and concentrated on it. She saw a happy young girl springing along on perfect legs and then a gap and then a sad old, young woman walking in front of a bus not caring about the consequences.

Then she took out the perfection that was her dad, her mum's love for her dad, her love for her dad and bits and pieces slowly began to make sense.

The air of disapproval that hung over all her mum's stories, all the dates in the open air, all the meetings at night and early in the morning. It wasn't just because he was wild. It was because he was married. And Fran and May — they left Lisa's mum, not just because she was pregnant but because she had betrayed them. And Lisa's grandmother was consumed with shame, not just because of her daughter's pregnancy but because of her daughter's general lack of morals.

But Lisa looked again at her mum's love and she

reasoned that no woman, not even Fran, could love more and no woman could be judged for loving so much. Could the love outweigh the betrayal? Was Fran worth such denial?

Did she dare question her mum? She thought that she would. There was nothing more to hide. Her mum could tell her everything. Then she stopped in her tracks: her dad was alive. Her mum had never told her that.

Lisa arrived home, cold inside and out. Her mum was there before her with the fire lit and a stew heating up. It was Friday night, a night that was usually celebrated. They usually bathed, curled up in front of the fire, watched a video that had been chosen and discussed during the week and ate chocolate-chip cookies just like they did in the movies.

Lisa was glad of the comfort of ritual; she wanted nothing more than to have everything as it always had been and she tried to keep it that way. She tried to lose herself in the film and she managed to keep all her questions to herself.

What did those old women know? Did they know her dad better than her mum did? Wouldn't her mum want to see her dad if he was still alive?

But the hum of her questions remained, it was only silenced with a decision, she would ask her Auntie May.

And she did try to. She tried to visit May on her own the following day, but her mum had planned a Christmas-shopping trip that couldn't be postponed and May was to meet them briefly for coffee in town. Lisa's mum said that May couldn't stay long, that she had workmen in the house fixing up a room for the baby.

On Sunday they all went to Station Road for lunch

and May and Bill were there and everyone sat together and talked together and left together.

So Lisa had to wait until the following Wednesday and then try to wait until her mum was out of the room. But even that didn't work. The following Saturday was Christmas Day and May said that she had a million and one things to do and that she couldn't possibly make it on Wednesday. She had rung and Lisa's mum had taken the call.

Lisa's mum couldn't understand Lisa's reaction to the news. She spoke to her sister in the hall and then returned to the fire where they had been waiting for May and had casually repeated the conversation. 'May says she's snowed in and under. She says we'll have to amuse each other tonight and she'll see us on Saturday morning.'

'She's not coming?' It was a wail. Lisa had tried to live without thinking, sleep without letting her mind wander, talk without letting her words loose. She had tried and she had succeeded for five whole days. She had only managed to do so because she had seen an end in sight, but now that was gone and she couldn't hold out any longer.

'There's nothing bad in it, Lisa, love, it's just that she's busy. And aren't we all? We still haven't got our tree.'

Lisa and her mum usually got their tree on Christmas Eve, but this Christmas was so strange anyway that Wednesday seemed as good a day as any to put one up.

'We could get it tonight. What do you think? It'll give us a few extra Christmas days this year.'

'Mum, I know who my dad was.'

'What?'

'I heard Mrs Benson and that other one talking, the fat

one. They've been saying stuff all along but on Friday they said that . . .'

'That what?' But Lisa's mum didn't wait for an answer. 'That your dad was Jim Bowles? I doubt it, but what I'd like to know is who gave them the treat of all their information?' The indignant rise of her voice lifted her to her feet and she stared down at Lisa, drilling her questions home.

'They said that I looked like James Burrows and that it was a good job Fran couldn't see me. And they've said things before but my grandmother always hushed them up and now I know why.'

'Your father was Jim Bowles.'

'Yes, but who was Jim Bowles?'

Lisa's mum sat down again, heavily.

'Maybe you're still too young to understand but all that was and is important is that your dad was my Jimmy. Everybody becomes all sorts of things during their lives. I was your dad's girlfriend, I'm your mum, I'm my mother's daughter, I'm May's sister and all those things don't hurt each other. Your dad – he was a son and a dad and my world and whatever else he was it never harmed me.'

'Was he Fran's husband?'

'That's what everyone says and it's what Fran died believing. But Fran's husband was James Burrows and my Jimmy was Jim Bowles and that's as much as anyone knows.'

'And is he dead?'

'He's dead to you and me, love. Jim Bowles was twenty-two and so handsome, with a leather jacket and hair that licked low, almost as low as his chin. That man is gone.'

'But is he dead? Is Fran's husband dead? Did he jump in the sea after his friend?'

'God knows where Fran's husband is, but Jim Bowles is dead. He saved his friend and now he's dead. I warned you, Lisa, of what you'd have to put up with. This was the main reason I kept us separate where old stories wouldn't hurt us. What does it matter, Lisa, love? You and I, we know who your dad was, we know the stories that matter and we love him and that's all that counts. Isn't it? Isn't it?'

Lisa nodded in her confusion and allowed her heated self to be cooled and soothed in a hug. She would wait and ask her Auntie May whenever she could and until then there was comfort enough in her mum's words.

Lisa saw her aunt and took her chance on the following Saturday, on Christmas Day.

Lisa and her mum woke to this new Christmas in the same way as they woke to all their old ones, very early and very eagerly. They both sat up in their beds and nodded their heads to each other, in time to their mental count of 'One, two and three.' Then it was officially Christmas Day.

'Happy Christmas.'

They both shouted together as loudly as they could. Then they both got out of bed as quickly as they could, which was never quick enough for Lisa. Her mum always made a drama out of getting tangled up in her blankets. They came together briefly for a hard, Christmas hug before they both unhitched their stockings and snuggled back into the warmth of bed.

This was always the best part of the day, so early it still seemed like night. The room was still dark, still lit by the red glow of Lisa's mum's lamp, but outside the sky was toning up through shades of grey. The whole of the bright, blue day lay ahead. Two new Christmas outfits were waiting in the wardrobe. The toys, wrapped with bows, from Santa, were under the tree.

This year the walk would be to Station Road instead of along by the river, and the food was laid out in Lisa's grandmother's kitchen instead of her own. For the first time Lisa felt a pang of what her mum had called homesickness, but new things could be exciting too and she did trust her mum not to forget the important things like the forgotten present.

Every year Lisa's mum brightened the dullness of Christmas evening with the forgotten present. She would just casually come across it when she was checking behind the cushions for the newspaper, or looking for her glasses by the side of the fireplace and then she would say, 'Goodness, Lisa, look what I have found. It's got your name on it. Fancy Santa leaving it here instead of under the tree, he must have dropped it.' The forgotten present always cheered the night along, even if all it was was something as dull as a pair of socks.

Suddenly Lisa didn't want to go to her grandmother's. She didn't want to have to face May and whatever answers she might give. But all these thoughts were short-lived and well diluted by the joys in her stocking.

Usually her stocking was filled with bulk – oranges, a large bar of chocolate and maybe an annual squashed in, but this year what seemed like hundreds of tiny and remarkable things tumbled out on to the bed. There was a bottle of perfume, some glittery nail varnish, a tape, a diary with a key, a glass ballet dancer that twirled on her base, a necklace made with the deepest blue beads, a paperweight with a paper butterfly trapped inside and when the globe shook, his wings fluttered.

Lisa stared and stared twisting the objects about in her hands, admiring them from every angle. When she finally raised her head the room was bright with the day and her mum was smiling at her obvious joy.

'Oh, Mum! It's the most beautiful . . . the best.'

She ran over to the opposite bed, being careful not to disturb her new treasures and clumsily hugged her mum, breathing in her smell of spring-fresh fabric conditioner and night-time sweat. It was the smell of Lisa's childhood.

'So you like them, then? Or do you just like me?'

'The two of them. The both of you.'

'Well, thanks for the hug. Now go and shout thank you up the chimney to Santa.'

Lisa laughed and did as she was told. Neither she nor her mum had ever admitted not to believing in Santa. Before she went, though, she noticed that her mum had shoved her still unpacked stocking out of view. Lisa just caught a glimpse of crumpled up newspaper spilling out of it before her mum swept it aside completely.

'Don't forget your slippers and a jumper, Lisa. No present is more important than your health.'

But Lisa was already gone.

The curtains in the sitting room were drawn tight and Lisa left them like that. She plugged in the tree and under its double coil of fairy lights she began opening her presents.

She opened the biggest one first. It was a dressing gown as soft and as thick as a summer cloud, complete with a gold lining and a hood. The lining was decorated with moons and stars and to Lisa it seemed like the gown of exotic fairy tales. She put it on and marvelled at its weight and its touch of coolness on her skin. It was far too long for her and she had to pull its sleeves right back to free her hands. She had two more boxes to open.

In one was a poetry book bound in heavily tooled leather with pages that thudded as they turned and illustrations that glowed with the colours and forms of the beautiful words. And in the other was a matching book of stories.

Wrapped in her robe Lisa hugged the books tight and braced herself to face her mum. Not only was she old enough to know that there was no Santa, she was old enough to guess at her mum's finances.

'Well? What did you get? Do you like them?'

'Oh, Mum, I love them, but they must have cost—'

'Mrs Santa quite a penny.'

Lisa laughed but she didn't appreciate this reference to their shared pretence. She would rather have had a chance to thank her mum fully. Instead she just handed her her present – a scarf and some face-cream. Her mum opened it and thanked Lisa effusively. The scarf would match her new dress to perfection and the cream was exactly what she needed.

And then the bright promise of the day was over. Lisa's mum opened the curtains and the light poured in. Lisa shuffled into the kitchen with her robe trailing behind her and put on the kettle. They ate their breakfast of toast, cream cheese and smoked salmon around the comfort of their tree and they laughed between bites and flicked from station to station trying to watch as many films as possible, but still the threat of the day closed in on them.

It seemed better to hurry it along. The sooner they were there, the sooner they could look forward to coming home. So they ate and dressed quickly, and when they were ready, and after they had complimented each other fully, they wrapped up warmly and set off across the park. They took the longest route possible, because they were far too early to arrive in Station Road.

'You know, Lisa, love, I only had one Christmas with your dad and our time together on that day was spent in this park.'

Lisa nodded her head. She knew that. She knew all about that one Christmas Day.

'I had to spend the whole day at home – your grandmother was always very strict about that – but I managed to escape for an hour to be with Jimmy. I think that I did literally escape. I remember creeping out the kitchen door and running for my life down the back lane. Your dad was waiting for me at our seat with a big red box. Oh I was delighted with the size of it, but I was terrified as well, because I knew I could never come home trailing such a size of a yoke without causing all manner of arguments.'

Lisa thought of Fran, still happy on her perfect legs, waiting for James to come home to his dinner.

'To be honest, I was a little bit disappointed in your dad because normally he was so considerate, he would have thought of that. But as usual I was wrong to worry. Your dad had thought of everything. I opened the box and in it was a rose bush with a plastic bag wrapped around its roots. Your dad and me, we planted it in the rose garden in the park. Your dad said that it was a present from us to the world. He said that when two

people were as happy as we were and had so much love
between us we should give some of it back, and roses
were the flowers of love so what better way?

'Our rose bush survived your dad, which wasn't that
hard, but it died soon after. I was glad when it died. I
wouldn't like to have seen it flourish after he was gone,
because when he was gone I got jealous of all the love we
had missed. The love we had seemed so little when you
mixed it up in a whole life. I didn't feel as if I had any
love to spare any more. I hadn't enough even for one. I
probably sucked the life out of that bush. Sucked all
your dad's generosity back into myself, for what good it
did me.'

Lisa looked up at her mum. The story had never ended
like that before. Her mum had never sounded so sad
before. It was only later, in retrospect, that Lisa
recognized the emotion as either bitterness or guilt.

'But what happened when you went home?'

Lisa had never asked this before. Until this telling, her
mum's stories had always been told in romantic iso-
lation. They had never been set against the context of a
family. Lisa was surprised when her mum rose smoothly
to this new challenge and, for the first time, brought her
story home.

'Well, you can imagine. There I was in my Christmas
finery with my hair curled just so, and my nail varnish
smooth just so, and a dab of May's Chanel behind each
ear just so, down on my hands and knees digging
through frozen ground with nothing but my hands to
work with. Afterwards I fixed myself up as best I could
but when I did arrive home my mother screamed and
then, when she realized that I hadn't been attacked, she
went for me. Chased me twice around the kitchen and

once up the stairs. I stayed locked in the bathroom until she promised to leave me be. That bush ended up causing as much trouble as a mink coat.'

CHAPTER 10

Forty minutes later, when they did arrive at Lisa's grand-mother's house, they were still far too early but obviously welcome.

Lisa's grandmother smiled, a rare occurrence, and kissed them both softly on the cheek, an almost frighten-ing departure from her usual brusqueness, before ushering them into her parlour.

'Come in and get warm. The pair of you have skin that could shatter with no more than the prod of a feather. You'll have to shuffle in a little – the tree took up more room than I thought.'

Lisa and her mum obediently started to pick their way through the jumble of furniture. The whole room had been thrown back on itself to make enough space for an enormous tree and a fully extended, set and decorated table. Lisa's mum stopped midway to the fireplace, blocking the progression of her daughter and her mother.

She was staring at the tree, at all its baubles and all their old memories. It seemed as if the weight of her unshed tears drew her head down and there it stayed looking at the table, at the glass and china of every special occasion she had almost forgotten. Finally her hand closed over a battered, silver napkin ring and she turned to her mother, staring straight over Lisa's head.

'It was always kept for you, Elsie, love. It's not been

used since you've been gone and it's not been used enough.'

Lisa stayed silent. She had never heard such softness in her grandmother's voice and she rarely heard it again. A moment later her mum was sitting by the fire and her grandmother was barking away as usual.

'We'll all have a sherry.'

'Mother, it's early yet and I don't know about Lisa.'

'It's Christmas Day and it should be started with a toast, and as for the girl, a spot of a drink could be the saving of her, she's as stiff as starch. Sit in by the fire, Lisa, but not too close or you'll get chilblains.'

Lisa did as she was told after leaning across her mum to deposit their bag of presents under the tree. There were four parcels there already. That was good. That meant her mum would get another present.

'I hope you didn't waste your time or money on buying an old lady a present she'll hardly live long enough to enjoy. If you have any sense, Lisa, you'll be buying me presents that you think you'll be wanting yourself in a few years. Sure, they'll be yours for the picking then anyway.'

Everyone laughed because Lisa's grandmother looked so far from death. They raised their glasses and they sipped their sherry. It made Lisa's eyes water but she liked it. She sat down by the fire, opposite her mum, and concentrated on the strange stickiness of her drink. It clung to the glass when she swirled it and it sparkled deeply when she held it before the fire. Her grandmother and her mum watched her for a bit and then they both laughed.

'So what do you think, Mother? One sip and she's a connoisseur?'

And they laughed again and so did Lisa because it was so nice to see them happy together.

'Well, enough of this. There's vegetables need tending. If you would come with me, Elsie, we'll have them ready with the bird, and you, Lisa, keep a close eye on that fire – it took an age to catch, there's no draw in the day at all. If you can concentrate on the two things at once you can turn on the box.'

It might have been the fire, or the joy of the film she found to watch, or the memory of her beautiful presents, or the smell of cooking, or the warmth of the sherry, or everything, but whatever it was it caused Lisa to sit back in confidence and comfort. Her comfort lasted until the arrival of May and Bill.

First of all there was a great clatter of welcome in the hall, a clatter loud enough to drown out the television. Then there was Bill. May had popped her head in to say hello and blow a kiss.

'I'll give you a proper one later, but there's too much furniture between us now and I'm needed in the kitchen. I think the food is at a crucial stage.'

Her head disappeared and Bill came in.

'Isn't a fire a lovely thing, now, eh, ha ha ha.'

'Yes.'

'I've been told to stay here out of the way of the cooking. They seem to think that I'd be no good in a kitchen, but what I say is if a thing's worth doing it's worth doing well. And is it my fault that if I do the food well it turns out black? Ha ha ha.'

Lisa laughed politely, trying to keep one eye on her film, but it was useless. The room was too full of her Uncle Bill and his loud laugh, not to mention his bag of presents and his awkward fumblings around the furniture.

'If you could grab a hold of this stuff, Lisa, I could get in to the fire and thaw myself out a bit. Put them under the tree, there. Isn't that where presents go, eh, ha ha ha? And what's the film? Doesn't it look great? So, I bet you're pleased to be on holidays, eh? I always say that the best thing about school is the leaving of it, though I'm not against learning. It's just a pity you have to do it in school, eh, ha ha ha. Are you good at sports at all, Lisa?'

'Sort of.'

'Well, that could make all the difference. I always said that the lads who could play games got by a lot easier. I never was one of them. Now, that wouldn't surprise you would it, ha ha ha? I used to have a bit more hair but other than that I haven't changed much since I was your age.'

Lisa sat opposite her uncle, her sherry by her feet. She knew that to drink it would just set him off and she didn't feel generous enough to supply him with topics of conversation. They sat in silence for a while, watching the film drone on. It was just silly now, watching fairies dancing across the screen with a grown man.

'You can change the station if you want. I'm not watching this, it's a bit childish.'

'And what's Christmas for if it's not for childish things? Don't mind me at all. I'm happy with my paper. Watch what you want.'

He reached for a long out-of-date supplement that had been left by the fire, probably to burn, and pretended a great interest in it. Lisa knew he was doing it so that she would feel easy watching her film, but still she turned it off. A programme of pop videos seemed to her to be a more adult choice and it was important to her to make that choice in public. She had never really got into music. And now she saw it as almost explicitly sexual. There was nothing relaxing about watching thrusting, gyrating teenagers with her uncle. It seemed like a long wait until dinner.

But when the food did arrive, it formed a meal as pleasant as any Lisa could have wished for. Bill sat at one end of the table and her grandmother at the other. Lisa sat opposite her mum and beside her Aunt May with her back to the fire and its heat warming her through. The food came in waves, carried high by the three women.

There were three kinds of potatoes, three different vegetables, two deep-bowled sauce boats, a dish of rolled butter pats garnished with parsley, a caramelized ham studded with cloves and a stiff brown bird oozing its smell of lemon and herbs.

But the joy of it all wasn't only in the food; it was in the beauty of the ritual. The flourish in the way it was all presented and the choreography of the three women as they stepped around each other, sliding dishes along the table, tucking their elbows out of harm's way. Out of habit, the three women had swung back together, swung into the old steps.

Lisa sat still and watched with awe as her family revolved their food around her before they fluttered proudly on to their seats. Even Bill knew what was expected of him. He had slipped from his fireside chair to the head of the table and had reached for the carving knife. Lisa's grandmother waited until everyone was seated and everything poised for the centrepiece before she brought the bird in. She was almost humble as she laid it in front of the man of the house, but she had recovered herself before she reached her own chair, opposite him.

'I don't know what you may be used to Lisa, but in this house we don't hold with starters. Fiddly food that fills you full of nonsense. A dinner is a dinner and the dinner you'll get here is as good as you'll get anywhere. But for the day that's in it, I insist that we say grace.'

She suddenly sat, clasped her hands and dropped her head as did everyone else, including Lisa. There was silence for a moment. It had just dawned on Lisa that this was supposed to be a private prayer when her grandmother jerked her head forward and announced the beginning of dinner. 'As my good and God-fearing father used to say, "Amen, now carve the hen."'

Bill laughed, got to his feet and sliced open the turkey breast. The women clapped and the dishes and plates began circulating.

It was the greatest fun. It reminded Lisa of tests at school when the teacher handed the exam papers to the girl nearest her who had to peel one off and pass the bundle on, but this was more complicated because your plate was being moved as well as the dishes and everyone was constantly asking questions.

'Brown or white meat? Everyone had some gravy? Are the sprouts down your end? Who's for the heel of the ham?'

Eventually the clatter of crockery and cutlery settled down to a hum of approval and later relaxed into a flow of conversation. May started it.

'So what happened to your sherry reception, Mother?'

'I thought the better of it. Who would want their house and morning filled with the gossips of old women?'

'Well, up to last week, you did,' said Lisa's mum a little sharply, but May smoothed on.

'I'd want it. There's nothing I like more than a good gossip. It helps you work up an appetite.'

'Depends what the gossip is about.'

And everyone, except Bill, looked to Lisa, as if she had been mentioned by name.

Bill looked to the still heaped platter of meat. 'I've always been a man for neighbourly feelings, but there are certain days that just have room enough for the family and Christmas is one of them.'

'A man and an eater after my own heart,' said Lisa's grandmother. 'Pass up the plate, Elsie, and help Lisa to some on your way. That child has the look of someone who has grown out of her last meal.'

'Lisa is as well fed as . . . as . . .'

Again May smoothed things forward. 'As well fed as you never were? You should have seen your mum when she was your age, Lisa. We used to call her. . . what was it, Mother?'

'The ballooning bin.'

Everyone laughed and Lisa sat entranced by the stories that followed. These were the stories she wanted to know; these were the stories that anchored her to her life.

The talk of childhood Christmases lasted beyond the trifle and then they finally melted into the heat of the room and the lethargy brought on by too much food. But by then Lisa wasn't listening any more. Despite herself, her eyes kept darting over to the tree and the bright packages underneath it.

During their last journey, her grandmother caught them and smiled her stiff smile. 'Why, I had nearly forgotten, but I have a little thing for you all. Bill, you're the nearest. Can you stretch down and reach me up those blue parcels?'

He did, and with a nod to May he fetched their parcels as well. And Lisa, red with excitement, ducked under the table, the quickest way to the tree, and bobbed up again, laden with boxes decorated with bows. She had seen too many picture books not to insist that presents must always come in a box with a ribbon. It was like the serving of dinner all over again, except now parcels were touring the table instead of dishes. There was a frantic and loud five minutes when everyone tore at paper, rustled it aside and tried to outdo each other with their gasps of delight.

Lisa got a top from her Auntie May, one that she knew would change her life. It was the sort of top that couldn't help but attract friends and give confidence. And from her grandmother she got a post office book with an amount of money in it that she just couldn't understand. She read the balance and held it up to her mum, who read it and turned to her own mother for an explanation.

'It's thirteen years' worth of Christmases and birthdays and Sunday tips and cheap at the price. I've never forgotten her birthday, Elsie, and I've never forgotten her at Christmas. I knew this day would come.'

Lisa saw her mum nod and glance sadly at the wool-mix cardigan her mother was holding.

'And where did you find this, Elsie? Did I tell you that

I was looking for this exact colour? I've a skirt waiting for it upstairs.'

But even Lisa knew not to ask to see the skirt.

The present-opening sapped the last out of everyone. They sat in satisfied silence for a while and then broke apart. Bill slipped back into his fireside chair and his dated supplement and Lisa's grandmother settled herself opposite him and dropped her head and droned her breath through her nose. Lisa's mum, Lisa's Auntie May and Lisa were left facing each other over a mound of dirty dishes.

'I'll do it,' said Lisa. 'I didn't help before.'

'Well, that's fair,' said Lisa's mum. 'But be careful. These things are older than you and far less replaceable.'

'I'll be careful.'

'And I'll help you. I need to walk about and digest a bit or this poor baby will be suffocated in Christmas dinner.'

It was just as Lisa had hoped. She and her Auntie May together with the washing-up. She had guessed that that would happen. Three people in the kitchen would just get in each other's way and May liked exercise as much as her mum loved the afternoon film.

Her mum did put up a show of resistance. She did her share of clearing the table and she hovered about in the kitchen until May and Lisa were settled about their work. Then she left them alone and they could hear the television and the rumble of Bill's laugh. Although Lisa felt that she had a limited amount of time to question her aunt, she wasted a lot of it wondering how to broach the subject. Initially May took charge of the conversation.

'That was some dinner. Your grandmother always excelled at Christmas time.'

'Yes.'

'I think I've eaten far too much. It's one of the perks of pregnancy. You can eat and eat without fear of bursting and there's always the hope that the baby will eat all the extra calories and bring them out with him.'

'Yes.'

Lisa was standing by the sink, beside her aunt wringing her dishcloth in her hand, occasionally drying something from the wet, heaped pile in front of her. She was obviously not listening to a word that was being said.

'Are you all right Lisa?' May stopped her work and turned to face her niece. Her question had been asked seriously and straight into Lisa's face. Lisa had no choice but to answer honestly.

'Not really. Auntie May, who was my dad?'

'You should ask your mum that.' May briskly plunged her hands back into the soapy water filled with dirty dishes.

'Did you ever meet him?'

'Oh yes, I knew him.'

'And his name was Jimmy Bowles?'

'Well, I think that was just a nickname your mum had for him. You know the rhyme don't you?'

'The rhyme?'

'The skipping rhyme. You must have heard it:

> *J is for Jimmy*
> *I is for is*
> *M is for my*
> *M is for man*

Y?
Why?
Y?
Why?

Because his name is Jimmy.
Jimmy Bowles is the best.
He loves me more than all the rest.

More than Tom?
Yes, more than Tom.
More than John?
Yes, more than John.'

May stopped, breathless and laughing. 'Goodness, I didn't think that I could remember things so well. The game goes on from there. Whoever is turning the rope turns it quicker and quicker and they ask as many boys' names as they can in time to the rope. If they miss a question they lose and if whoever is skipping trips over or misses an answer they lose. You never played that?'

'No.'

'Me and your mum and Fran used to play it all day long out on the street and before we used to go to sleep at night your mum and I used to make up stories about Jimmy Bowles. You know, white knight and shiny horses – that kind of thing.'

Lisa had stopped drying. The draining board was full, and so her Auntie May paused in her washing.

'So who was my dad?'

'You must ask your mum. Come on, dry up or we'll be here all night.'

'All she ever says is that he was Jimmy Bowles. Did my

dad sing in a pub? Did he die trying to save his friend?'

'I don't know. He could have, but I doubt it. I didn't know him very well and all this is to do with your mum and not with me.'

'Was he Fran Burrows's husband?'

Lisa waited for an answer and none came. Her aunt had started drying now. She was clattering the dishes together, pretending that she couldn't hear.

'Mrs Benson says he was. I know he was so it's all right for you to say.'

'Say what, Lisa? I'll say anything if you start drying again. Come on, I want to see that film.'

'If you don't tell me I'll ask Mrs Benson out straight. I will.'

'Ask her what?' May stopped her pretence of work and of deafness and of urgency. She seemed to surrender to the inevitability of the questions.

'If my dad was James Burrows.'

'You'd knock on her door and ask her that?'

'Maybe not, but I could ask her when she came here and she would tell me. I know she would.'

'And you'd not ask your mum? You'd ask Mrs Benson before your mum?'

'I've asked my mum and I'm asking you. If you both don't tell me then I will ask Mrs Benson. He's my dad. I have a right to know. Everyone else does.'

'And would you believe everything the likes of Mrs Benson would tell you?'

'Unless I'm told different.'

There was a long pause. Lisa was looking at the knot of her dishcloth. She could feel her aunt's eyes on her as they considered her and considered the situation. But even after the length of silence and even after Lisa's confidence in her information, her aunt's answer was sudden and shocking.

'All right then, he was.'

Lisa surprised herself by crying big, wet tears for her mum's shame and Fran's sadness and her own living dad.

'Hush, Lisa. There's more to it than it sounds. James Burrows was as cold and as charming as the devil himself and Fran wasn't bold enough to keep him. She tricked him into marriage in the first place telling him she was pregnant. Their marriage was over long before he and your mum struck up and by then your mum wasn't even that friendly with Fran. Fran had started going a bit weird even then. It was a bad, nasty mess but some good came out of it. You did, and the love that your mum had for your dad did. I know that she loved him deeply.'

'How do you know?' Lisa wiped a hand across her face. She didn't want her tears interfering with her concentration.

'The way your mum was about him. She never said his name, not even to me. She always called him Jimmy Bowles, even when it became obvious that he owed her some sort of support. Whenever she was questioned her eyes would cloud over with the happiness of remembering and she refused to name him.'

Lisa understood. She knew her mum's stubbornness, and she knew that expression her aunt was talking about.

'If she never said his name, how do you know for sure?'

'Because everything else said his name loud and clear.'

Lisa stayed listening, even though her aunt had turned back to her dishes.

'Lisa, it's a long story and one your mum should tell you.'

'But she won't, and I've no one else. If you don't tell me, Mrs Benson will.'

'All right then, but don't tell your mum I told you. When I get a chance I'll tell her myself. We can't risk any more family rows, now, can we?

'Your mum started going about with a boy. We all guessed that much. She was going out at night all dressed up, but she refused to bring the lad home and she would never admit, not even to me, that he existed. Well we let her be, thinking that she was just shy – it was her first steady boyfriend.

'The first we – your grandmother and me – the first we knew about trouble brewing was one night after there was some scene down the docks. This is what your mum might have meant about your dad saving someone's life. A friend of James Burrows fell off the pier or was pushed off for a lark and James jumped right after him. I think the water was a bit deeper than either of them thought it would be and they both had to be fetched out. It sounds like a small affair, but there was great excitement about it at the time. The news was all over the town and exaggerated beyond belief before the event was even over. Bill was there. I was going about with him even then. He and another lad stripped down and dived in and hauled the two messers out. But between you and me, I think they did that for show. There was no need for such heroics. It was more a jetty than a pier and an outstretched arm would have done as well.

'But that's all beside the point. I only remember it because it was that night that your mum came home, streaming with rain and looking like the wits had been frightened out of her. I was home and so was Bill, still a bit damp behind the ears but acting the real hero, and in burst your mum, crying and wailing and asking over and over, "Is he all right?" I heard her in the hall and went out to her. Mother was with her already but she pushed past us both. Well, the sight of Bill must have embarrassed her into silence, because she stopped her wailing, but she still looked the colour of death. I followed her in and I must have caught her off guard, because it was the only time she ever said his name.

'"Is who all right?" I asked.

'"James Burrows," she said, in front of me and Mother and Bill. "I heard he had an accident. I heard he was dead."

'And she was nearly off again.

'Your grandmother just ignored her crying and said, "He's all right, whatever that means to you."

'She must have known immediately what was what, or maybe she had guessed already, because I remember thinking that she was terribly sharp with Elsie. And that was that.

'James Burrows must have barely dried himself off before he was packed and gone. Myself and Bill left soon after. Bill got his job and we rushed a wedding within a month and left. Everyone's still expecting the baby they thought was on the way then. I'd say that they never met with such a long pregnancy as this.' Lisa's Auntie May patted her belly. 'But it wasn't me that was pregnant. It was your mum.

'After the state I saw her in that night, I had no doubt who Jimmy Bowles was and everyone else soon put two and two together. Almost as soon as she started to show, you were dated to James Burrows's disappearance. I missed it all, but I heard that they came knocking and they came asking and all your mum would give them was some old nursery rhyme.

'Fran didn't come knocking or asking, though. She came banging and screaming and so your mum upped and left. Your grandmother would have stuck close if your mum had been honest with her, but she must have felt too ashamed to admit to the truth and she was always too proud to ask for help. It would have been better if I was here, but Bill needed me too and a woman has to choose her man sometimes. I wrote, though. I drove your mum mad with letters, but she soon stopped writing back and I don't blame her. She was busy being poor and she must have felt that I had sided with the world against her.'

'But you stayed away so long.'

'Yes. Time loses itself when you get a bit older, Lisa, and time lost itself for me and probably for your mum and probably for your grandmother. But I never forgot you or your mum. I'm not saying this so you'll thank me, just so as you know that I've always loved you and thought about you. For years, me and Bill sent whatever we could afford to your mum and for years your mum sent the cheques back saying that she was managing. And I thought she was. I thought that she wanted nothing of or from me and that broke my heart.

'Now get busy, or you'll have me in tears and we'll be stuck doing this washing-up all night. Just remember, Lisa, that all this mess is ironed out now and we have all the time in the world to make up for all the time we lost.'

Lisa nodded and dried the wet delft and felt her emotions and her dinner churn through her body and her soul.

CHAPTER 11

When Lisa and her Auntie May returned to the rest of the family, Lisa felt as if she had been away for an age. She was an age away from her mum. She had taken her first adult step. But everything was still all right.

The sound of the parlour door shutting alerted Lisa's grandmother, who woke with a snort and immediately talked over Bill's laugh. 'And about time. I never knew I had so many dishes until you started washing them. And now that they're clean is there anyone interested in dirtying them again? I'd kill a cup of tea myself.'

There was a muttered acceptance of the offer and Lisa's grandmother left. The others stayed watching the end of the film, Lisa's mum swamped in a tissue and red about the eyes.

'He never knew she loved him,' was her excuse and everyone laughed at her tears, breaking the spell for her, and so she laughed as well.

It was nearly time to go home then, but they stayed on, drinking tea and playing the word games that had been a fireside tradition when Elsie and May were children.

It grew darker and darker outside and the family sat warmer and tighter around the fire and Bill laughed all the time and everyone surprised themselves by eating some sandwiches and then Lisa and her mum got up to go.

It took them a long time to get through the front door. Lisa kept dragging behind. She went to the bathroom and lost her glove and insisted on watching the end of something on the television and bid a long goodnight to everybody, before finally walking up Station Road with her mum. They walked slowly, laden down with the food they had eaten, the gifts they had received and the leftovers Lisa's grandmother had forced on them.

Lisa had intended to confront her mum, in spite of what she had promised her Auntie May, but before the words could form themselves, her mum wrapped an arm tight around Lisa's shoulders and squeezed hard.

'Wasn't it lovely, Lisa? Was it as lovely for you as it was for me?'

Suddenly Lisa understood the sacrifice her mum had made. Whatever wrong she had done, she had punished herself enough. She had wrenched herself away from that fireside and had kept herself apart for years.

'Wasn't it lovely and tasty,' said Lisa.

'Wasn't it lovely and tasty and cosy?' said Lisa's mum.

They quickened their step in time with their game and in their eagerness to be home from the cold that was burning their faces and cutting through their flimsy, Sunday shoes. Lisa trotted by her mum's side and her need to talk about the past faded. Her mum was right. Her dad was Jim Bowles and if some people called him James Burrows what did it matter? Her mum had loved him and he was the best man around to love – all her mum's stories proved that. He had tried to save his friend and after that he had disappeared so it was like a death of sorts, but he wasn't dead and some day Lisa would meet him and that would be the right end to all her mum's stories and that was the only piece of her mum's story that needed to be mentioned and that could wait at least until they were at home.

But when they got home and after they had lit the fire, and after they had prepared some hot chocolate, and after they had settled down with a box of chocolates, Lisa's mum found the forgotten present and this year it was a board-game that kept them occupied until bed-time. There just wasn't time to talk about fathers, alive or dead.

As time went on and the days passed, Lisa found it harder and harder to phrase her question. Conversation never seemed to touch off any trigger for such a thunder-bolt and the clear blue sky of disconnected chatter offered no inspiration. Eventually the worst happened and the whole affair was blurted out in an argument.

It was late in January, when Lisa was back in school. Her new-found family and the solid respectability of her grandmother's house had given Lisa a new breadth of confidence when it came to socializing. She had always maintained the standard of popularity that pretty girls assume but she had never demanded more, not until now. Not until she had her family behind her, her new-found wealth in the post office and her Christmas top that made her look so sophisticated. Now she began visiting girls after school, staying out for meals and disappearing on Saturday afternoons.

Lisa's mum was pleased with her daughter's new interests and new friends. She just got angry when she found the cigarettes squashed under Lisa's pillow. Lisa knew she was in the wrong, she knew that her mum was only cross because she was worried and she knew that she hated even the sight of the things after she had forced

herself to smoke three of them with Jane Blake, but
something inside her snapped when she saw her mum's
tight-lipped anger and the cigarettes in front of her, on
the kitchen table.

'I didn't even finish them and you've no right to be
snooping around my things.'

'How many times have we had this talk?'

'Enough times for me to know what you think, but I
wanted to know what I thought.'

'I suppose it was that Jane Blake put you up to this?'

'She did not. I can think for myself.'

'Well, you've been thinking differently since you've
been friendly with her. And I thought I could trust you.'

'You *can* trust me!'

'Trust you to smoke and God knows what else. What
do you do on Saturdays for instance?'

'You know, just hang about.'

'Well if you're hanging around street corners smoking
I won't stand for it. In future you're staying home.'

'You can't do that to me.'

'Oh yes, I can, and I will until I think I can trust you
again.'

'Yeah, and I suppose people can trust you? I suppose
Fran thought she could trust you?'

'Lisa!'

But it was too late. Lisa couldn't stop. 'She trusted you
and you went away with her husband and I trusted you
and you told me my dad was dead and he isn't and
you've done me out of a father for thirteen years.'

Lisa slammed out of the kitchen and into the bedroom
where she sat waiting for her mum. She was waiting a
long time and the silence from the kitchen terrified her.
There should have been a clatter of dinner preparation,

but there was only the oppressive sound of nothing doing and everything developing.

She wanted not to have said anything except, 'Sorry about the cigarettes but I had to find out that I hated them.' She had intended to tell that to her mum anyway.

She wanted not to have sounded so dramatic about her dad, all that nonsense about being done out of a father. She had never really felt done out of anything. She hoped her mum didn't realize that she had copied her sense of loss from American soap operas.

She wanted, more than anything, for her mum to come in and hug her, and say everything was all right. Eventually the bedroom door opened and her mum stepped in, but she didn't reach out for Lisa and she didn't say everything was all right. She just stood and then she spoke. 'Who has been talking to you?'

'Auntie May told me but only because I made her. I knew because Mrs Benson told me, not on purpose, but I heard her.'

'Then you know as much as every gossip made it their business to know.'

'But I don't, Mum.'

Lisa's mum sat down on Lisa's bed and Lisa put her arm around her and Lisa's mum patted the hand on her shoulder.

'Despite all they say, trust me, Lisa, love. Jimmy Bowles is dead.'

'But James Burrows isn't.'

'No, he's tough as old boots. He'll last for ever. But me and your dad, we made a pact. We knew that we couldn't be together, that too many people would get hurt, so we decided to act as if we were both dead to each other. The accident down the pier was as good a starting point as any for me. I buried Jimmy Bowles in my heart and your dad went away and we neither of us knew about you. When I did hear about you, I didn't see the point in telling a dead man, and your dad couldn't have done anything if he had known. You would only have been a torment to him, knowing he couldn't be with you. He always loved children. I meant to tell you, Lisa, love and I would have told you when you were older. It's only a bit of the story that I left out, a bit of an epilogue after the accident.'

'Auntie May says that the accident was nothing except a bit of messing.'

'Your Auntie May always knows her own truth about everything. Who told her about the accident?'

'Bill. He was in it.'

'And there's your answer. If Bill were any less self-seeking he'd still be looking for himself in his pram. Of course Bill told her it was nothing. Why would he be wanting to worry his fiancée? But it was something, Lisa. It was close to the drowning of four men. One idiot and three with less brains than bravery.'

'Where is my dad?'

'Where he wants to be.'

'Will he come back?'

'No. My Jimmy Bowles is dead and I'm past grieving for him. I'm lucky though, Lisa, love. I've all my memories and that's a lot more than most women have.'

There was nothing more to say and the cigarettes were thrown away and some ice cream was bought for after dinner because, as Lisa's mum said, 'My nerves need soothing and your temper needs cooling and that's a job for ice cream.'

They sat by the fire eating it and flicking through the

stations on the television. A football game was on most of them and so they turned it off and listened instead to the click of their spoons against their dishes.

'Do you want to know the real ending of your dad and me Lisa?'

'Yes.'

And she did, more than anything. It seemed to her like it was the first real story, told to her adult to adult.

'I arranged to meet your dad for the last time just after the accident. It was about two days after, I think, and we met in the park as usual. Your dad was waiting for me by our tree. It was nearly summer and the park was open late. I think he knew that it was the last time as well as I did, because he wouldn't let me speak for ages. He said that he didn't want to hear the words that he could see in the air around us.

'He took me down to the river. He said that he had found the loveliest walk, and he had. It's that walk through the woods, a little way up from the water. It was the first time I had gone that way. Your dad talked all the way there telling me stories of our life together and how it would be. For the first time he didn't say if only and I didn't remind him to. We were both just pretending.

'Well, we got to the woods and they were lovely – quiet and still and smelling gorgeous, the way they do when the day's sunshine is oozing out of them. It made it worse that we were in such a beautiful place, but I had to speak and I did try to. But your dad talked over me again. He whispered close to my ear, "Hush, there are fairies about." And I was going to laugh, but he looked so serious that I didn't, I just looked to where he was pointing. And do you know what I saw?'

Lisa shook her head.

'A fairy peeping out from behind a leaf halfway up the height of a tree! When I saw it, my mind gasped, but by the time that gasp had reached my lips I knew that it was a trick and I laughed instead. Your dad stepped away from me and I could feel him watching as I looked about me, suddenly seeing that the whole place was alive with little faces, half-hidden, and little bodies astride branches. There was even a little teaset laid out on a tree-stump. It was made from leaves bent together and walnut shells.

'Your dad had done it all. Lord knows where he got the dolls. I recognised the little faces from the Sunday comic strips. But it was the teaset that broke my heart. To think of your dad and his big work hands concentrating on a leaf to wrap it into the shape of a cup. It made me want to cry. And I think I did, though I tried to hide it from your dad. He told me that he had wanted our last afternoon together to be magical and that was the first time either of us had said that word, "last".

'We spent hours in that wood by the teaset under one of the magic trees and we mapped out how it would be. I was to believe that he had drowned and he was to believe that I had died of appendicitis. We picked on that for me because the previous year I'd had a very bad dose of appendicitis that had ended up with an emergency operation. We thought that if we picked things that had already kind of happened, we wouldn't be tempting fate. Then we both cried a bit, but we promised to be as strong as we could be and then we both went home.

'Your dad left soon after that and I think I was only one of the reasons, but after he was gone, it was so much easier to think of him as dead under the sea and by the time I was telling you the story, it was almost as true to me as if it had happened. I'm not that good a storyteller, Lisa, love. If I didn't believe in what I was saying, who would?'

'And was Fran very upset? Did she love him very much?'

'Of course she was upset when her husband left her and she was upset when her husband was with her. She was just glad that she had someone to blame. Is it over now, Lisa? Are we friends again?'

And they were.

In time, Lisa looked upon Fran as nothing more than an added dimension to her mum's romantic adventure.

CHAPTER 12

Lisa's cousin was born the following March. She was a little girl and May insisted on calling her Elsie. Bill had offered a few alternatives, but May wasn't prepared to discuss the matter. She said that she would be home with the baby all day and she would call it Elsie no matter what was on the birth cert, so Bill agreed, and he laughed when he rang with the news.

'There can't be too many Elsies in the world, eh, ha ha ha.'

It was five in the morning and Lisa and her mum were sharing the phone, so that they could both hear what was to be heard at the same time. Their ears were crumpled up together, fastened over the receiver.

Lisa's mum said, 'I thought you'd have wanted a fresh name. Families are confusing enough without adding complications.'

Bill laughed, but Lisa thought that her mum had sounded more cross than flattered, but that was often the way with her mum. She was never very good at saying thank you.

Lisa got a day off school for the occasion and her mum took a day off work and they were both in town almost before the shops were opened.

'This is the only birth day little Elsie will ever have,' said Lisa's mum. 'Everybody has only one birth day. All the other ones are just anniversaries. So the present we give little Elsie today has to be the best she ever gets.'

They looked and they looked and they finally bought the softest teddy bear they could find and the one with the kindest face.

'Every child needs a teddy bear,' said Lisa's mum, 'and the sooner you get your teddy bear, the better friends you become.'

Then they bought flowers for May and two fat, glossy magazines and some chocolate and a nightie with buttons down the front and then they went to the hospital.

They found May at the end of a long ward. She was sitting up in bed looking very happy and Bill was sitting on one side of her and Lisa's grandmother was sitting on the other. As they got closer, Lisa could see that there was a little bundle, wrapped in white, on May's pillow and for the first time she realized the enormity of what had happened.

'And where have you been?' asked Lisa's grandmother. 'The child was nearly walking out to see what had kept you.'

'We thought that we would give May a chance to rest,' said Lisa's mum.

'Rest! The girl has done nothing but rest for the last nine months. You should have been here as early as I was. I needed help waking her up.'

Everyone laughed and Bill laughed harder than them all. He hadn't even heard the joke. He was shuffling around the neighbouring cubicles trying to find chairs. He found one for Lisa's mum, and Lisa sat on the bed.

Before Lisa's mum sat down she hugged May, a big, deep, hard hug, and then gently pulled the blanket away from the child's face. 'Let's hope she has more sense than her namesake.'

'I'd be happy if she grew in to half the woman you are.'

The sisters smiled at each other and then Lisa's mum straightened herself. 'Are you calling me fat, May Gaskell?'

And everyone laughed again.

'Lisa, dear,' said May, beckoning her over and raising her cheek off the pillow slightly, gesturing for a kiss, 'would you like to hold your cousin?'

Lisa nodded. It seemed to her like a silly question. She sat squarely on the bed and her Auntie May laid the small bundle across her lap and her crooked arm.

'Hold her firmly. Make her feel secure and support her head. My, but you're a natural.'

Lisa was awestruck. She sat quietly for the whole visit with her precious charge balanced between her knee and her arm, which, towards the end, began to stiffen into numbness. Every now and again one of the adults swooped the baby up for a moment, but mostly they just let it lie and they looked and marvelled at the serenity, the perfect beauty of baby Elsie and Lisa's competence and complete concentration.

'You've the makings of a great little mother,' said Bill.

'With any luck, by the time Lisa gets to being a mother there'll be nothing little about her at all.' Lisa's mum snorted her reply, and though it was a funny answer, it was said too sharply to inspire any laughter, even from Bill.

'Of course. I didn't mean . . .'

But Lisa's grandmother didn't give him time to retract. She obviously thought that no form of apology was necessary. She glared at Lisa's mum and May smoothed the conversation on as she usually did.

'Do you know, but that baby Elsie has a strong mark of Lisa about her.'

'Oh, how can you tell?' said Lisa's grandmother. 'The child is only fresh into the world. You have to give her features a few hours to settle.'

'Yes, May.' Everyone listened because Lisa's mum was taking sides with Lisa's grandmother. 'You're jumping ahead. You should be just happy the child looks like a child.'

The two sisters giggled and Lisa joined in her grand-mother's look of disapproval.

'That reminds me,' said Bill. 'What's the difference between a keen swimmer and a person who abandons their closest sibling?'

No one answered. They just stared at him in confusion.

'One's for taking a swim and the other's forsaking a twin.'

There was some polite laughter and under its cover Lisa saw May reach out for her husband's fat little hand and heard her whisper to him, 'With a father as good-hearted as you, the child is blessed.'

They were still holding hands when Lisa's mum stood up suddenly. 'Well,' she said. 'I think we should be off. You must be tired, May dear. We'll be back later. Kiss your cousin goodbye, Lisa.'

'Would it be silly, Mum, if I called her my sister? She's nearly my sister, isn't she? She'll be as close to me as you are to May, won't she?'

'Except for thirteen years, Lisa. She'll be as close to you as a cousin should be.'

'Don't you mind your Mum, Lisa, love.' May sounded as cross as Lisa had ever heard her. 'Of course she can be your sister, and I know I am right. Baby Elsie *has* the look of you. She has your chin and your far-set eyes.'

'I'm sure baby Elsie will want a sister,' Bill added. 'And if you're not going to be it, she's not going to get one, because I don't think we could pull this off a second time.'

'Bill!'

'Bill!'

Both May and her mother hushed him up sharply, but he just laughed.

Lisa and her mum left then, leaving the others behind.

'Why do we have to go so soon, Mum?' asked Lisa breathlessly. She was running to keep up with her mother. 'If my grandmother is staying and Bill, then Auntie May won't be resting. I'll be good, I'll be very quiet. I was good at holding the baby, wasn't I?'

'You were very good and we'll be back later. Too many people breathing around May will tire her now. Anyway, a husband and a wife need some time to themselves on occasions like this. Your grandmother should know that much, but she never was one for tact.'

'Wasn't she lovely? Are you so proud she is Elsie too? Wasn't that really nice of Auntie May? Do you think she really looks like me? Do you think people will believe that we are sisters?'

'Yes, Lisa, she's lovely. Yes, Lisa, I'm proud. Yes, it was nice of May. Yes, Lisa, she looks the wrinkly image of you. And yes, people will always believe what you tell them.'

Lisa didn't ask any more questions. Her mum sounded too tired to answer them.

They never did go back to visit. May sent word that she was too tired for evening visitors and the next day she discharged herself, much against her mother's wishes.

Lisa's grandmother opened the door to Lisa and her mum when they came to call on May the following evening.

'She's sitting up by the fire, pretending as if she's fine. A woman May's age needs healing time after a baby. If she's trying to prove to us all that she's seventeen, she's starting at the wrong end. She has the face of a thirty-five-year-old woman and I'm sure she has the nether regions to match. Excuse my farmyard plainness.'

She talked them down the hall and, just as she opened the door to the sitting room, Lisa's mum said loud enough for May, bent low over her bundle, to hear, 'A body mends better at home and a child settles better in its own bed. Isn't that true, Mother?'

'It is, but a woman sleeps better when the child is at the far end of a corridor under the care of a nurse.'

'I'm all slept out,' answered May.

And she looked it. She looked younger and happier than before. Lisa had never believed her to be old and had never seen her sad, but now there was something deeper about May's satisfaction. Her contentment stretched soul-deep. Lisa wasn't to know that baby Elsie had taken ten years to arrive, that she had been given up on, that May had been grieving for the loss of her unborn family.

'Can I hold her?' Lisa asked, her eyes sliding from her aunt's face and down to the child in her arms.

'If you sit down with her.'

'Where's Bill?' asked Lisa's mum.

'Work. I shooed him off. You can imagine how he is, far too happy to bear. I think he was hoping for a daughter and so was I, to be honest. More for Bill than for me. He'll just love to have a daughter to dote on, and baby Elsie is going to have a daddy from a Disney film.'

All eyes settled on baby Elsie and there was a breeze of gentle sighing and then Lisa's mum got up.

'I'll make us all a cup of tea, and then perhaps we should be going. We only came to check up on you.'

In answer to Lisa's pleading look, she continued in a slightly sharper tone, 'You know you have homework to do.'

Lisa knew no such thing, but she knew not to argue when her mum's eyebrows started to converge. She just nodded and held tight to her charge for as long as she was allowed.

Baby Elsie was still tiny and red and wrinkled, but Lisa saw what her aunt meant. The baby had a chin that ended in a blunt point just like her own, and the baby's eyes were far flung from her nose, just like her own. Thirteen years weren't so many. Some families had longer gaps. Lisa didn't care how silly her mum thought her, she was going to claim this child as a sister and they would be friends for all their lives, every thirteen years for as long as they both lived.

She woke suddenly from her pledge and looked up and tuned in to the adult conversation. It had taken a turn worthy of her attention.

'Do you remember how seriously we took wishing presents?' Lisa's Auntie May was asking Lisa's mum.

'Yes.'

The answer was abrupt and left no room for the usual lurching jump into the past that Lisa's mum loved to share with May. May might have chosen not to pick up on her sister's tone or she may have been too intent on her memory to register it. Either way she continued with enough enthusiasm for them both.

'Do you remember the ritual of wishing we insisted on for each other and Fran?' She paused to laugh. 'Do you know how it started? I bet you don't. It was my idea, being the most imaginative and the smartest.'

Catching Lisa's eye she shifted the weight of her explanation on to her. 'It was what we used to do for birthdays and Christmas for each other, instead of buying each other presents. We would wish each other good things, like in Sleeping Beauty. It was a sweet tradition. Remember, Mother, you used to encourage it, but I'm afraid it came from bad motives. I figured out at a young age that wishes were much cheaper than presents.'

May paused to allow some time for laughter before continuing. 'The nicest ceremony we had, though, was for Ruth Murdoch. You must remember that, Elsie?'

'Yes, I do. And now we really have to be going.'

'But what did you do?' asked Lisa.

'Oh, we'll tell you another time.'

'What's your rush, Elsie?' asked Lisa's grandmother. 'Leave the girl be for the five minutes this will take. If you need that time as much as you say, you'll make it up in good grace or you'll lose it twice over in resentment.'

Elsie could think of no argument to counter her mother's and so she sat, and May continued in a slightly different vein.

'I only remembered Ruth Murdoch because I want us

to do the same thing for baby Elsie. Don't you think it would be lovely, even if it is a little silly?'

Elsie opened her mouth to answer, but Lisa talked over her mother's unspoken objections. 'What about Ruth Murdoch? What did you do to her?' she asked.

'You'll probably think this is so dumb,' May answered smiling at her sister, trying to draw her into the warmth of the memory. But Elsie looked away and so May smiled at Lisa instead and continued, 'but we brought her out to the woods just beyond the river. She was a baby at the time, about six months old, and we wheeled her out there with her two older sisters, and Fran was there and your mum and me. Your mum and me had gone out earlier and we had decorated the trees with little cut-out dolls that were supposed to look like fairies and we had propped up some of our dolls around the place, dressed in leaves, with daisies for hats, that sort of thing. And then we had made a type of bed throne out of a heap of weeds decorated with more weeds, but it did look pretty. Didn't it, Elsie? Then we went and fetched Ruth and the others and we laid the baby out on her throne bed and we all wished her spells of happiness for her future. You see we were all the good fairies, we had twigs for crowns and twigs for wands and Fran said we had air for wings and we were delighted. Then we all took turns and wished the baby well with all our might. We wished her health and wealth and beauty and probably a lot of toys.

'I know it sounds silly, but I would love us to do that for baby Elsie. So many heartfelt wishes must count for something. What ever did happen to Ruth?'

'All I remember about her is her hockey legs.' Lisa's mum rose as she spoke and made to go for the second time, and this time Lisa didn't argue. She waited until they were well away from the house before she drew breath to ask the inevitable, but her mum got to it first.

'I'd forgotten about those games we used to play. It's funny, isn't it? I must have told your dad all about them. That must be where he got the idea from and all I remember is your dad's idea and I forget the inspiration behind it. He had that way about him, your dad did. He blocked out everything that went before him and he kind of overshadowed everything that came after him. Everything except you, of course.'

CHAPTER 13

May never got her wishing ceremony. There never seemed to be a day that suited everyone and so the plan was forgotten. But in spite of that, baby Elsie grew into all a mother could wish for.

She was pretty in the way of all the Gaskell women, though Lisa's grandmother attributed the family's good looks to the Fitzgibbons. She had May's nose and May's smile and the same finely squared chin that Lisa had and the same far-set eyes. Her hair wasn't as dark as the other women in her family but it didn't quite have the thin, mousy look of Bill's. The Gaskell women still had hopes that it would thicken and darken with age.

Lisa didn't, though. She delighted in the differences between herself and this child just as much as she revelled in the similarities. She believed the former to highlight the latter. She loved her cousin as fiercely as she imagined sisters to love each other and as sincerely as life friends grow to. It was largely because of baby Elsie that Lisa's growth away from her mum was accelerated.

It began as soon as baby Elsie was old enough to be baby-sat. Lisa would go directly to her aunt's house after school to play with her cousin, while her aunt worked or entertained or rested or even shared in the game. Lisa loved her Auntie May's house. It was as big as her grandmother's, which was big in Lisa's experience. It had two bedrooms, an upstairs bathroom and toilet as well as a downstairs shower room, and one big sitting room as well as one big kitchen, just like her grandmother's house.

But it was lighter than the house in Station Road. It was only newly built and hadn't yet gathered its share of the weight of age. Everything in the house was new. Everything gleamed with fresh polish and chrome fittings, and every room smelled of the freshness of baby Elsie. The floors were wooden and the walls were painted. Every corner was exposed and every piece of furniture was light and portable.

There was no room here for forgotten mementoes, or dust-laden cobwebs or stilted, censored half-conversations. Here, amongst the bright tumble of baby Elsie's toys, was nothing that needed questioning or nothing that wasn't soon focused on the baby and turned to laughter. Here Lisa became an integral part of the bright, plastic world of television families, and she wallowed in it.

She began to stay later and later with her aunt. Soon a bed was bought for her, and at weekends she was invited to sleep over, sharing the brightness of baby Elsie's nursery. Lisa expected these invitations more and more frequently. When she was away, she did miss her little house, and her shared room, and the glow of her mum's red lamp, but she missed these things only as much she missed her fading childhood, and not as much as she welcomed her new position of maturity and responsibility.

Her mum watched her pack her overnight case and sometimes accompanied her to May's house and sometimes waved her away on her own and never once asked her to stay or mentioned her own obvious loneliness.

The only thing that bothered Lisa's new routine was the presence of Bill. He worked long, irregular hours and most of the time was safely in his office or, even more securely, out on the road. When he was gone, Lisa and May and often Lisa's mum would sit and laugh, and tell silly stories, and play with the baby, but once Bill was heard in the hall, things changed. Lisa's mum would make an excuse as soon as she could and Lisa's Auntie May would focus all her charm on her husband, and Lisa and baby Elsie would sit forgotten until Bill acknowledged them and that was even worse.

'How's school?' he would ask. Or, 'Doing any exams this year?' Or, 'Won any medals in your swimming lately?'

Lisa would answer, but though she tried, she could never stretch her replies beyond the basic required monosyllable. And then, as if to highlight her uselessness, Bill would swoop down on baby Elsie and absorb himself in her. May would look on happily and Lisa would feel the exclusion that Bill's politeness had been intended to dispel.

Lisa never could understand her aunt's obvious love for her husband and though she often tried to broach the subject with her mum, she always ran into the same conversation. Her mum would answer any question Lisa posed with, 'Bill Graves is a very good man.'

'Yes, but he is dull, isn't he?'

'Dull is neither here nor there. He is a very good man and if you do half so well you'll be doing twice as good as most.'

'But he's boring, isn't he?'

'He's steady, and steady is what a man should be.'

'And he's not very handsome.'

'He treats May as she should be treated and there's few husbands that can say that. He works as hard as he can and he manages to stay cheerful with it and he dotes on baby Elsie. What more could you want from a man?'

But Lisa's mum didn't fool Lisa for a minute. Lisa knew that grown-ups were duty-bound to stick up for the virtuous and the moral amongst them, but duty was something other than fondness. Lisa's mum obviously found Bill as dull as Lisa did. Her endless remembered appointments and abrupt departures were proof of that.

Lisa knew that her mum expected more from life and more from men. She expected just as much as Lisa hoped for and Lisa hoped for it all. She knew herself to be her father's daughter. She could sense his wildness in her blood, and like him, she was aiming beyond security.

As time went on, Lisa managed to glean quite a lot of information about James Burrows. Most of it came from her mum's eagerness; some of it came from neighbourhood gossip; some of it was drawn from her reluctant aunt; and a little was researched in the newspaper archives of the local library.

Her mum continued with her stories, the same old ones and some new ones, like the story about the midnight scooter ride. Lisa and her mum were watching the news and listening to a horrific tale of horror against the elderly, when Lisa's mum was reminded of the night Lisa's dad borrowed a scooter and came calling.

'It was April, but it was still cold and I didn't want to get out of bed even though I recognized his call from the garden. He used to hoot because he thought that people would just assume he was an owl. It never dawned on either of us that an owl around Station Road would be an event for the newspapers.

'Well, he hooted and hooted, so eventually I had to go or he would have woken the house. I met him out front and he had a scooter with him, a lovely one that was bright white – even in the darkness I could see that much – and he had with him a spare parka and a gleam in his eye. Of course, I couldn't resist, so I didn't even pretend to. I just climbed on board and hung on to him. I thought that he was going to spin me around the block and drop me back to bed, but I should have known to ask. Your dad never did the expected.

'We took off and, without a word, he drove straight out of the city. Well, *he* didn't say a word – I said plenty, but my words all blew back at me and soon I gave up and just relaxed into his strong back and the force of the wind on my face. We drove for about an hour out along the coast and then, suddenly, turned off the road and he switched off the engine and, taking my hand, walked me up a rough kind of avenue that led to a tiny little tattered cottage. Once we got there, he pulled out a small wrapped parcel and an envelope and left them both on the doorstep and then we crept away again.

'As we drove home, he explained to me that an old aunt of his, whom he was very fond of, lived there and that the next day was her birthday. She was a strange old woman who had never married and had never had any attention from men. But every year your dad made a point of leaving an anonymous birthday present on her doorstep with a card signed with love but with no name. I'm sure it must have done that woman a wonder to find herself with a secret admirer so late in life.

'And do you know that your dad didn't even bring me to show off about his good deed – he brought me because I was for ever whining on about wanting a go on a scooter. We drove home immediately because he had to get the bike back. I don't think his friend knew that he had borrowed it. I can still remember that ride and how the wind pressed at my back, pressing me in close to your dad. It was as if nature itself agreed with our being together.'

Armed with such stories, Lisa was well able to confront and adapt the gossip she heard over the years. She knew that the Mrs Bensons of Station Road were only talking about the James Burrows they saw. They knew nothing about the poetry of the man. All they had seen and all they spoke about behind Lisa's barely turned back was the cruelty of the boy who played away from home and finally left a miserable wife and a disgraced mother to further his own selfishness.

'And the state of him, with that ridiculous hairdo of his and the pair of surly eyes behind it.'

'She didn't get his manner anyway.'

They would stare at the retreating Lisa.

'She has the manners of her grandmother. But Maud Gaskell wouldn't stand for anything else. I remember that Burrows lad had no respect for his elders. He pushed me once out of a bus queue, nearly out of my standing.'

'I remember pulling him up once on his use of language and he blew a bubble of gum in my face.'

Lisa's Auntie May was hardly more charitable towards her memory of the man. Her compliments were always superficial and her omissions were heavy with insult.

'He was very handsome,' she would admit when pressed. 'And he could be charming when he put his mind to it. He was good at parties, he could sing quite well, though he never had as good a voice as Bill.'

If Bill was there he would laugh and Lisa would join in. The image of her uncle as crooner was laughable.

But as Lisa pressed harder for information, her aunt guarded her replies and picked the words of her sparse answers with caution. 'It's not that I didn't really like him. I didn't know him.'

'Well, you must have known him a bit.'

'Yes, I did.'

'And did you like what you knew of him?'

'No. But then Fran did and your mum did, so I may have missed something.'

'Why didn't you like him?'

'I didn't trust him.'

'Why didn't you trust him?'

'Oh, Lisa, he just wasn't very nice.'

As Lisa probed, and her aunt evaded, both their tempers began to fray. Eventually May blurted out what she knew she shouldn't. 'He was nothing but a criminal and a thug and he dragged his poor mother's name through the papers more often than once.'

After that May closed her mouth for good and James Burrows was rarely mentioned between herself and her niece again, but Lisa was happy. She had something more to work on.

She avoided her aunt's house for a while and instead spent her free time at the library. There were a lot of papers to get through. She eventually found what she was looking for towards the back of one of them and again, on the front pages of two of them.

Local man charged with assault and battery, was the heading on the first. It gave an account of a fight outside a bar in which a nose, two ribs and an arm were broken and only one man arrested. Mr James Burrows, of 14 Station Road, was fined and released on parole.

The second one was more serious. It gave an account of the trial of two men charged with breaking and entering. They both got off due to a lack of evidence, but the judge issued a warning to James Burrows.

Lisa read the two accounts with a certain amount of pride. She had faith enough in her dad to know that he would only hit a man if he had a good and moral excuse and she knew for a fact that he would never break into someone's house.

All these accounts did was prove her mum right. People always judged by appearances. They none of them took the time to get to know her dad. They just allowed themselves enough time to condemn him. But Lisa knew better. She and her mum could see clear through to the soul of the man.

CHAPTER 14

Lisa's mum hoped that Lisa would go on to college. Lisa's grandmother assumed she would and Lisa's Auntie May encouraged her to, but Lisa had no intention of doing so. She had liked school – bits of it she liked more than others – but by the end of her years there, she felt full of words and theories and stifled by the tedium her teachers exuded and the dead institutional air they breathed.

Lisa had felt herself compressed by school. There was something young and large in her, waiting to burst out and live, and a more adult institution didn't seem the place to nurture such emotion. Her stance obviously caused arguments. Sniping, darting comments had been following her through her final year at school and, after she took her final exams, they burst out into the volume of Lisa's first real extended family row. Despite her anger at the time, Lisa quite enjoyed it.

It happened one Sunday, over lunch in Station Road with Lisa's grandmother presiding.

'So you have finally left school then?'

'Yes. Finally.'

'And have you decided on a suitable course?'

'A course of action or just a course?'

'You know well what I mean, girl. I am too old to waste my time playing word-games, but an answer to either question will do me.'

'I'm going to work for a while, save as much money as I can and then travel around the world.'

'Nonsense.'

'No, Mother, she's serious.'

'And what if you only earn sufficient money to take you halfway around the world?'

'I'll stop off for a bit and work some more.'

'And then what? You'll face into a life without training, without any opportunities. You'll end up in a place like Mitchell's, working for the wages they'll spare you, unless you can find yourself a good man.'

'It worked out all right for Mum.'

'It never did, Lisa,' said her mum. 'We never had a holiday, a heated bathroom. You never even had a bedroom of your own. Everything was a struggle.'

Lisa's grandmother coughed, but thought the better of reminding Lisa's mum that that was largely due to her own pride.

'But remember, Mum, we always had what we needed and never bothered about what we wanted.'

Lisa's mum didn't answer. She just looked away and May took over.

'Your Mum's right, Lisa. Once you have a degree you can travel, and your education will be an asset, and when you come home you'll have a bright future.'

'I'll travel and make my future. I'm not going to depend on a piece of paper for my future happiness. Anyway you can't do anything to stop me, I'll be eighteen next week.'

Her tone rather than her words evoked the full anger of the women of her family.

They shouted at her and then soothed her. They shouted over each other and then fought to calm each other and Lisa toyed with her food and lowered her head and promised herself that she wouldn't cry. Baby Elsie, still called baby despite her five years and still cursed with mousy brown hair, sat under the table playing with Lisa's shoes. Bill sat quiet and smiling, ready to make a joke at the first presented opportunity. None came, but eventually he laughed anyway and surprised everyone into silence. He finally sobered himself sufficiently to explain the joke. 'Oh, you're a funny group.'

'Funny? Could you please explain?' Although she sounded politely interested, May's eyes bored into her husband's and, as plain as letters can spell, they said, 'You had better have a damn good joke to share with us.'

'Do you think you can bully the girl into learning? She's not ready, she knows she's not ready, she's told you she's not ready and still you lot think that if you bully her away from what she wants to do she'll do what you want her to do and take the time to do it happily and well.'

Lisa looked up and caught her uncle's eye and watched it close over on a wink. She was astonished by his insight and, as he continued, her astonishment grew.

'You are all desperate to make that girl into something you never were, but sure she's that already. She went to the convent for starters, she looks like a queen and she has the accent of a lady. You've already primed her for a job with a shirt and collar. No offence, Elsie, but that girl of yours will never work on a factory floor and, if she takes the time to travel well when she's young, she'll learn a sight more than any of us at this table. Of course I'm not including those of us that are sitting under it.' And he finished back where he started, with his habitual laugh.

May was the first to speak. Her words drowned his last few chuckles. 'I suppose there is nothing we can say that will make you change your mind.'

'No.'

'You'll learn that we were right, though, and hopefully you'll still be young enough to do something about it.'

Lisa just nodded at her mum. She knew how much the dream of university and medical training had meant to her.

'Where will you work to earn the fortune to support this plan of yours?' asked her grandmother. 'The world is a very broad place. You'll need a lot of money to see yourself around it.'

'I don't know yet.'

Lisa didn't have the nerve to tell her grandmother that she had already accepted a job in Moran's bakery. She had – they all had – enough to digest for one mealtime.

Lisa was a little frightened about this new responsibility that she had assumed, and she was a lot frightened about the inevitability of her first job.

In the comfort of her classroom, this plan of hers had sounded broad and beautifully exciting. It had dazzled her classmates and it had swept Lisa's imagination far into the corners of the world and the wild wisdom she would find there.

Driven by this ever-growing dream of hers, she had approached the local businesses looking for work, and even before she had sat her exams she had been offered the counter job at Moran's.

Mr Moran himself interviewed her, though Lisa had initially approached his wife. Lisa's heart sank when

Mrs Moran referred her on to her husband. Lisa didn't see much hope for herself in Mr Moran's deep-set eyes, lost in flaps of flesh, or in the downward turn of his tight, overly moist lips. At least not as much as she saw in his wife's large bosom and homely way of talking. She sat opposite him in a room over the bakery and, out of nerves, began talking almost before he began questioning.

Mr Moran had looked hard at her and barely seemed to be listening to her complicated reasons for thinking herself ideal for the position he had advertised. Finally he interrupted her mid-sentence and Lisa was too relieved to be insulted. The sentence he had cut across was nervously leading nowhere.

'. . . and I'm punctual which will be useful here, although of course punctuality applies to every job, but bakeries open earlier than most other places, so even if I'm needed earlier than when the shop opens I can be just as punctual for that, I mean the bakery itself . . .'

'Do you object to a uniform?'

'No.'

'Black with a white apron. We will soon be expanding and providing a small café service. Do you believe that you can wait tables as well as take care of the counter?'

'Yes.'

'As this is only a trial for us, we want initially to take on only one new member of staff. Of course your salary will reflect the extra work expected of you.'

He mentioned a salary that made the young, inexperienced Lisa suck in her cheeks and feel her first adult wave of greed.

'Our premises, we hope, will be up and running by August and by then you should have the results of your final exams. We will expect you to prove yourself in maths and English and if you do so I will be delighted to offer you this position.'

He stood and so did Lisa. He extended his hand and Lisa took it with a slight shudder and she left and the deal was closed. As Lisa walked home, she computed that with such a wage she would be free to travel after ten months of employment. It was that that had scared her, but it had also encouraged her to study hard at maths and English and geography and French and she even threw in a little history. She thought that it would help her to find her cultural bearings as she travelled.

Lisa never told her mum about her interview. She had hinted at her plans and she had refused to apply to any college, but her mum never knew how far Lisa's plans had developed and she watched her daughter lose herself in her books and she couldn't believe that such industry would not eventually pave the way to a profession. Her secret hopes were shattered on that Sunday, over that lunch, and six weeks later the debris from the crash of her dreams was swept away.

'I've got a job, Mum.'

'Where? When? Has the post come?'

It was a weekday morning and Lisa had joined her mum for breakfast. She had got her exam results the previous day and to celebrate their greatness she and her mum had gone out to dinner.

It was such a happy evening, Lisa hadn't the heart to say that her excellence in maths and English had secured her future away from further education. Her mum had hinted at late applications for certain courses and, for one night, Lisa had let her. But this morning she would go to Moran's and some morning soon she would start work there. It was time her mum found out.

'No, I got it before. I was waiting for my results.'

'Where? When did you get it?'

'Moran's bakery—'

'Moran's! You can do better, surely! That place is just a food factory.'

'No, I'll be out front. I'm not baking, I'm serving. They're opening a café and I'll be serving as well as being on the counter.'

'Two jobs?'

'But they pay two salaries. It'll be tiring, but it'll be worth it. I'll be able to go away before next summer and it's good experience. There'll always be restaurants wherever I go, and I'll have been trained and . . .'

'Why were you waiting for your results?'

'They wanted good marks in English and maths.'

'They want a lot without giving much.'

The two women sat in tense silence for a moment, both staring at the black teapot between them and then Lisa's mum pulled herself up by her shoulders and forced her head back to look hard at her daughter.

'I think that if you had stayed studying I could have pretended to myself that you were staying young, but you wouldn't have. No matter what you do now, Lisa, love, you'll be leaving me . . .'

'No, Mum, I'll not. I'll only be away a bit. I couldn't leave you and Auntie May and baby . . .'

'You're right, Lisa, love, and I'm silly. Now give me a hand up or I'll be late for work.'

'I'll give you a hand up and clear the table.'

'Give me a hand up and clear the table and get some potatoes.'

'I'll give you a hand up, clear the table, buy the potatoes and make the beds.'

Lisa had followed her mum into their tiny hall to continue the game, but Lisa's mum at the opened hall door had the last say. 'You can give me a hand up, clear the table, buy the potatoes, make the beds and arrange with Mr Moran for a tenner extra a week, a strict procedure for tips and a definite rate for overtime.'

Lisa laughed with the joy of her mum's blessing.

CHAPTER 15

Lisa started in Moran's before the week was out. The café wasn't ready yet, but a makeshift counter had to be manned. Lisa's uniform wasn't ready for her either, but because of the amount of dirt lying about, Mr Moran thought that it was better that way.

Mrs Moran, dressed in powder-blue lambswool pulled tight over the huge spread of her middle-aged chest, greeted Lisa on her first morning and all her subsequent ones. She took her place early every day, presiding over the makeshift counter that had been pushed to the front of the shop. It was the position Lisa had been hired to take.

Mrs Moran always wore a powder-blue lambswool jumper, even in the heat of the shop, in the added heat of mid-August. The colour of her skirts and her blouses changed daily but her jumper was always powder-blue and always V-necked. The shade of blue varied slightly and the cut varied slightly but only to the experienced eye. To the customers, Mrs Moran always looked reliable in the same powder blue, but Lisa could soon recognize at least five different jumpers.

Behind Mrs Moran, builders and carpenters and painters were loud with muted clatter. They were warned daily to work as quietly as possible so as not to disturb the customers. On Lisa's first day she was thrown in with these men who were referred to by everyone as 'the crew'. By everyone except Mr Moran that is – he called them 'my crew'.

Lisa stayed with 'the crew' day after day for almost two months. Her job, Mrs Moran told her, was to keep the dust down and she tried to, while all around her a collection of men worked hard at creating as much dirt as they could.

Behind 'the crew' were 'the men', or as Mr Moran said, 'my men'. These were the bakers who worked from pre-dawn to noon over large flaming ovens or elbow-deep in thick pats of unyielding dough. The men were largely left alone, even by Mr Moran. They were a law unto themselves. They worked through the early morning dark, rarely conversing with anyone other than themselves. Few of them were married and even fewer were under fifty. They had worked for old Mr Moran and they were working for young Mr Moran and they knew the feel of bread and the lightness of pastry. They knew the power of yeast and the joy of cinnamon. They had firm, toned arms with flabby torsos and soft legs and Lisa could hear the muffle of their jokes when she came in in the morning and she could hear their goodbyes by the back door before she took her lunch. She never knew how many men there were – she rarely saw them, and when she did, they all looked the same to her. All old and red and stooped. She was very much afraid of the back room with its welcome warmth and its wealth of deep, golden smells.

She wasn't too fond of the front area either. Every now and then when Mrs Moran needed to do a 'jobby' or had to 'pop away for a wee while' Lisa was called in and left in charge of the breads and the cakes and the pastries and the till and the sandwiches, and invariably Lisa got something confused.

No one had ever taken the time to talk her through the types of bread, or to show her the quickest way to make a sandwich, or even to teach her the trick of folding the cardboard flats into firm boxes with just a flick of the wrist. Eventually Lisa learnt most of what she needed herself, but only after failing continuously before her public.

But on Lisa's first morning, all this horror was as yet unexplored. She arrived for work, a perfect ten minutes early, with a beautifully framed picture in her mind's eye of herself, dressed as neatly as an Edwardian upstairs maid, weaving in and out of tables with a silver-plated coffee pot in one hand and a plate of dainties held high on the other. She would serve the gathered well-dressed elderly with such nibbles before weaving her way back to her counter and her waiting customer who, for some reason, wore a feathered hat, a bustle and had a big wicker shopping basket hanging from her arm.

Of course the reality of Moran's was nothing like Lisa had imagined. Mrs Moran in her blue lambswool jumper opened the door for her and pushed her through to the back room.

'Welcome, welcome, and I hope you get on here as well as we hope you get on. Mr Moran, my husband, told me to be expecting you. Of course I said to Mr Moran that we wouldn't be needing you quite yet but he insisted. He said that I had enough on my plate and I said that wouldn't I be sad if I didn't in this business? But that's Mr Moran all over and this is the crew. Lads this is . . .'

'Lisa.'

'Miss . . .'

'Gaskell.'

'And lads, this is Miss Gaskell. We like to keep a distance between our staff – a friendly distance, but a distance. Mr Moran says that it avoids unpleasantness in the long run.'

The latter part of Mrs Moran's speech was whispered loudly at Lisa and the building crew politely waited until she was finished before they chorused their greeting. Lisa could count five men. She was later to learn that there were only three continuous ones and a host of occasional ones. Even after her two months among them she didn't know all their names.

She answered their chorused greeting as happily and as enthusiastically as she could. She was too young to sum the men up by their reaction to her and she made the mistake of smiling her broadest at those who smiled their broadest at her. Then she followed Mrs Moran up to the room above where she had been interviewed. As she passed it, Mrs Moran pointed out the door to the bakery beyond.

'Now, in there is not really your business and the men don't like to be disturbed. I do all the stocking of shelves, but if you ever need anything from them I'll fetch it for you or else if I'm not around be sure to knock. You can leave your coat and bag up here. They'll be quite safe – the crew are a trusty bunch – but just to be sure, I carry my readies with me.'

She paused to wink and pat her cleavage. Lisa left her coat and bag on the chair she had been directed to and, under Mrs Moran's nodding, urging head, she fished out her five-pound note and tucked it under her bra strap, since there were no pockets in her skirt. Then she followed Mrs Moran back downstairs.

'Mr Moran said for me to train you up and I will, but there's plenty of time, eh lads?'

They growled.

'We're all running a little behind and, trust me, you'll know everything by opening day. Oh, your uniform is one of the things that's running behind and a good job too, eh? So hike up your sleeves and set to.'

She pointed to a mop and a bucket and a few cloths stacked against the wall of one corner of the room in between a much-used workbench, a pile of still-uncut planks, a selection of paints and brushes and the start of the curve of the new counter.

'But where will I clean?'

'Why here, of course. We have to keep the dust dampened down. We can't have the customers complaining of grit in their bread, now can we?'

'No.'

Mrs Moran left, and Lisa, with her head bowed and face red, picked up her mop and looked to fill her bucket. It took her a full day to realize that the work was totally unnecessary, and it took her longer to make the connection between Mr Moran's infrequent visits and Mrs Moran's 'jobbies' and so she always greeted Mr Moran from the front counter. And because his greeting was always so brusque, and because his eyes always took the time to run over the tangle of her hair and the dust on her clothes, she never got the courage to complain to him about her work in the back.

It was Joe who pointed her in the direction of the sink. A slightly plain, overly tall young man, he was one of the youngest of the continuous crew, but obviously held a senior position – the rest of the men were always calling to him for directions.

He had nodded her over to the sink without saying a word and she had walked past two surly backs and two smirking faces to get there. Over the din of the gushing water drumming into the tin bucket, she could hear a quiet scuffling, a few fierce grunts and some stifled laughter. Her face burned to the tips of her ears and the bucket filled up and finally she had to turn around. The crew's eyes were suspiciously lowered and then casually, one by one, they turned to her.

'So you're the new face of Moran's,' said one of the formerly surly ones.

'Yes.' She tried to say more by smiling as hard as she could.

'Well, I hope you like it here.' He turned back to his work.

'Here, there and everywhere and we'll be in luck.'

There was a scuffle behind her and before she could turn to reply, a darkly handsome man was pushed at her.

'A Beatle song that was. I'm for ever singing Beatle songs. Do you like them? Hi, my name's Larry.'

'Hello, Larry.'

She shook his hand and then took up her mop. There seemed to be nothing else to say.

That first morning was a nightmare. Whenever Lisa turned, there seemed to be movement and sniggering behind her, yet in front of her everybody was always calmly occupied. Conversations started around her occasionally, but they always came to an abrupt halt due to their content. It was worse, though, when they made a smart attempt to include her.

'The ref was blind. Sure he was way offside. We were there! We saw it!'

'Offside, me arse! Sorry. And even if he was, they were the better team. They'd have qualified by now except for that penalty.'

'And they'd have qualified yesterday except for that offside call. Face up to it, man, they're crap.'

'Crap, eh? Well, we'll see about that. Let's ask the lady. And what do you think, Miss Gaskell? Would you say that it was a fair game?'

'I didn't see it.'

'Oh, I understand. One dahd not get to view that pahticular match.'

'Ah, leave off her.'

There would be a scuffle of words and silence again.

'Saw your sister last night.'

'At work?'

'Yeah, she was working all right.'

'You're asking for it now.'

'That's what I said to your sister last night.'

Larry was so delighted with the opening presented to him that he almost shouted his answer. But the laughter that followed was uneasy and was soon followed by a snarl from one of the surly men, and Lisa could feel Larry's resentment at the loss of his joke. It all came to a head just before lunch, when Larry approached her with what seemed to be a genuine offer of help.

Lisa had been cleaning a corner as far away from the men as she could get. She had washed the floor and had polished some tiles and was removing the excess grout from them when Larry pointed out a bit she had missed. 'Up there, love. You'll need a stool to reach it. Up you get, and I'll hold it steady.'

His voice was soft when it was low and directed just at her, and his expression had lost its glint. He looked humbled, standing before her, holding a paint-splattered high stool. He sounded sorry for her and for his previous behaviour.

'Thanks' she said and she went to climb on to the stool that he had placed in front of her. He held out his hand to her and his strength pushed her high and held her safe. And then, under his direction she stretched to where he directed her.

'Over a bit, love, further, further, now up a bit.'

She turned suddenly, dropping back off her tiptoes to hear his directions. They had suddenly become less distinct, and when she turned she saw why.

He was talking to his mates. Still holding her hand he had turned to the roomful of men. They were all smirking, Larry's directions had been orchestrated to expose more and more of Lisa's leg. She wrenched her hand free and wobbled dangerously in doing so. Suddenly his smile froze, and before the stool decided to topple, he had pulled her off it, holding her high to his chest. As she slid to the floor, she noted the worry in his eyes and the sheer beauty in his face and the ripple of his muscles as they steadied her weight, and she smiled despite herself and forgave him.

'Will you leave the poor girl alone, Larry.' Joe pushed him aside before Lisa was fully balanced and she tottered against the legs of the fallen stool.

'The poor girl was fine until you hit her over.'

'Oh, she was fine, was she, being made a fool of by you?'

Lisa didn't need reminding of her shame. She left the two men at it and walked straight out of the bakery, past the rest of the staring or smirking or indifferent men, past Mrs Moran thankfully engrossed with a customer, and thankfully into the fresh air and thankfully into her own company for a full hour.

She sat in a crowded rival café eating a rival sandwich and tried to keep her mind as blank as possible. She knew that if she thought too much about the coming afternoon she would just go home to her mum and failure. So instead she concentrated on the softness she had seen in Larry's eyes and the feel of his chest as he steadied her on the ground.

Lisa had never had many dealings with boys. She'd never had to prove her popularity with them – her looks were proof enough – and so she had rarely bothered with them. Her school had been an all-girls' one and though her friends had brothers and though the local boys from the local schools hung around the gates of the convent every evening, she had never really been tempted by anyone.

She had kissed a few out of curiosity, but she had never enjoyed the broad wetness of their mouths or their subsequent clawing attentions. Then, during her last year at school, she had found Michael, because to avoid the other boys she had to produce someone. Michael was perfect. He kissed neatly when the occasion arose and accompanied her to all the farewell parties and the break-up dances without once mentioning their future together. Lisa hadn't seen him since the last results dance and she knew that she probably wouldn't see him until the next reunion dance.

Lisa knew her friends thought that she was a little odd or a little cold but she didn't mind. She didn't expect them to understand. Their dreams of romance were based on their childhood stories and their teenage films. Lisa had seen and read the fuel those dreams were driven and limited by, and she knew that she had so much more. She had the glory of her mum's legacy to live up to and she had her dad's sense of romance and drama to drive her. None of the boys she had known had the ability to move her. None, that is, until now, until Larry – but he was a man.

Lisa's afternoon, when she finally faced into it, was easier than her morning – it could hardly have been worse.

It started with the blue lambswool block of Mrs Moran stretching across the door into the back. 'Where were you? You looked so upset running past I thought that we had lost you for good. Were the crew at you? If they were, I'll tell Mr Moran and he'll have words with them. I warned Mr Moran. Mr Moran, I said, a pretty girl like that, what do you expect? Why don't you wait until the crew are away before you bring her in, but oh no, Mr Moran knew better, no, he said, we need her now, he said you needed training. Training with a mop? I said but no. . .'

'I was only at lunch.'

'Ah, you pet, and I was hoping you'd have a spot here with me, keep me company and taste a bit of the produce, eh? Perk of the job, I say, but not to Mr Moran, eh? Not a word to him, but we'll do that tomorrow. Just you and me and a bit of a girl-chat and maybe you'd be able to give me a hand with the lunch-time rush.'

Then there was Larry and the crew to face. Already they had separated into Larry and the rest. Lisa smiled around, avoiding Larry's eye, but she blushed anyway, before returning to her mop. As before, there was a scuffle behind her and then the sound of someone clearing their throat and a voice, trembling with uneasy nonchalance, said, 'I saw a pretty good film last night, just opened in the Savoy.'

'Really, what was it?'

A decision to act politely had obviously been reached during Lisa's absence. The conversation that had started as a badly rehearsed play soon melted into realism and a healthy, clean, accessible topic. When they were safely in the flow of an argument about Bond movies Lisa was called in.

'Yeah, but let's ask an expert. Eh, Miss Gaskell, you're a woman . . .'

There was some laughing and Lisa turned in time to see Joe glare Larry back into respectable behaviour.

'I want a woman's perspective is all I meant. Would you think, Miss Gaskell, that it is believable that Sean Connery could pull birds of the calibre he was pulling at his age?'

Lisa took a breath and glanced to the plain kindness of Joe's slightly gaunt face before answering. She knew that Joe was doing his best for her, but ultimately she was the only one who could save herself.

'Sean Connery could wait until he was eighty and still pull me backwards through a bush.'

There was a great roar of surprised laughter and a lot of calling to Larry.

'Put you in your place, what?'

'That'll shut you up.'

Larry laughed the lads off, but looked quite differently at Lisa.

'You can call me Lisa. I'm not old enough to be anyone's school mistress.'

And there was more laughing and more nudging of

Larry, but he didn't come out with the expected clichés and so the others did it for him.

'I'd go back to school for you any day.'

'Bet you could teach me a thing or two.'

Lisa listened, propped up by her mop, and laughed. The comments were easy to fend off once she knew that she had intentionally instigated them. She could hardly feel intimidated by something she could control. She was smiling at Larry, who was smiling at her, when Mrs Moran banged heavily on the door and scattered everyone back to work.

CHAPTER 16

Lisa arrived home that evening stiff and tired and dirtier than she had ever felt before. She had spent the whole afternoon cleaning, and watching her work sink under a new layer of dirt almost immediately, and she had been forced to spend her afternoon break with Mrs Moran at the front counter.

At half past three, Mrs Moran had popped her yellowed head around the door to call firmly for Lisa. 'Just us two girls and a bit of a chat. You bring the coffee – milk, two sugars – and I'll fish us out some nice apple slices.'

Lisa did as she was told, laughing at the crew's warnings.

'Make sure she takes a bite out of both sides of your apple slice, the witch.'

Then she leant against the makeshift counter, listening to Mrs Moran for fifteen minutes. She had to move whenever a customer came in, but Mrs Moran didn't even pause her flow of speech and the customers usually knew just to call their orders out over her before settling to join in with the conversation.

'It's the standing on my hips I don't like. My mother had bad hips and I can feel I have the same so I insisted on a stool. Of course Mr Moran said no, but I said, Mr Moran, I said . . .'

'A Vienna roll, Mrs M., a half-dozen doughnuts and a cream slice.'

'. . . you'll have me crippled and what use will I be to you then and sure can't I reach most things from here. Lisa, love, the slice there like a love, no, beside it, no, with jam.'

'And who's this Lisa? Is this your daughter, Mrs M.?'

'Daughter! Lord no! Wait till I tell Mr Moran that for a joke. I was never fit to carry children. Me W-O-M-B never up to P-A-R . . .'

'I'll take a large batch.'

'The doctor warned me and of course it broke my heart and there's your one pound ten change. If it wasn't for me hips I'd have adopted. The batches are to your left, Lisa, and would you hand us a bag like a love?'

Lisa fled back to Larry and the crew at the first opportunity. They didn't hurt her head like Mrs Moran and her customers could.

At five on the dot the crew dropped what they were doing. There was actually an audible clatter of them downing tools. They yawned and stretched, pulling themselves alive for their free time, and over all this Mrs Moran called to Lisa. The crew and Larry tramped upstairs and Lisa went through to the front.

'And how did you get on on your first day?'

'Fi—'

'They're a rough lot, but harmless, and don't you mind them, but remember to keep a distance like Mr Moran says, and I agree with him, so I called you out here. Those men up there could be getting changed or anything and I owe it to your mother to keep you out of harm's way. Be a love, will you, and pull down those shutters and then if you could give us a hand with these trays, they'll have to be washed down with hot water. Ow, but do you know what, I think my ankles have swelled, the pain in them would shock you. No, I'm all right, well, I will be if I just sit for a bit.'

So Lisa carried and washed the trays and one by one the crew walked past her, every one of them still dressed in their work clothes. Joe stopped to say goodnight and Larry paused to wink, and Lisa, under Mrs Moran's directions, locked the door behind them and swept the shop and wiped the glass of the counter. It was a quarter to six before she was let go.

'You're an absolute doll, Lisa, a treasure. Now for your trouble – I won't hear of a no – you're to take this cake home for your tea.'

Mrs Moran held out a slightly squashed cream cake.

'Oh and Lisa, not a word to Mr Moran about my ankles. Our little secret, eh. I don't want to worry the man when he has so much on his plate. But you know what I say?'

Lisa nodded, but was ignored.

'You'd be in a sad state in this business if you had nothing on your plate, eh?'

It was half six when Lisa arrived home, stiff and tired and an hour late. Her mum was waiting for her with a half-cold plate of dinner and a pinched look of worry.

'You had me scared. You should have rung. What happened to you? Did you like it?'

Lisa groaned in reply, privately forgiving her mum for all her years of grumpiness during that crucial first half-hour home from work. Lisa's mum heard and obviously recognized the pitch of her daughter's answering groan.

'The water's hot and the bathroom's ready for you.

Your dinner will taste all the better for the wait.'

Lisa smiled and left to lock herself away with the bath. Her mum called after her, 'And then you can tell me all about it.'

After a wash, and after a mound of food, and after two mugs of hot tea and a fat slice of squished cream cake Lisa did want to tell her mum all about it. In her eagerness to she started in the middle and tried to work sideways.

'. . . but I don't think he meant to be mean 'cause he did look sorry and it was Joe that made me trip and anyway he didn't say anything mean all afternoon . . .'

'Who?'

'Larry.'

'Enough of Larry. Tell me about the work and the customers and Mr Moran and did you put in for overtime for tonight?'

So Lisa said it all, skirting her cowardly refusal to demand her rights, and after a moment's consideration, a less exaggerated description of her workplace than she had rehearsed, but even so it sounded all rather horrible to her mum. It was a far cry from medicine.

'So it's cleaning.'

'For now.'

'Did you explain that you weren't hired to clean?'

'Well, it's cleaning or nothing at the moment and I need the money. It'll get better, Mum. My uniform will come and the café will open, and anyway, it's kind of fun.'

'It's cleaning.'

'Tell me, Mum, about the first time you met Dad.'

'What, that old story? Now? Why?'

'Just tell me, please.'

So Lisa's mum told her. She never needed much encouraging. The two of them sat facing the empty summer grate and Lisa's mum started.

'I met him first in November. It was a very cold November that year and I had just started working in Mitchell's . . .'

Lisa listened happily, right down to the last.

'And do you know what?'

'He never sang *Moon River* to anyone except you, ever, ever, ever again.'

'Amen. Happy now?'

'I am, Mum. I think I met someone and he makes me feel just the way your eyes look when you tell that story. I wanted to hear you say it again just to make sure and now I am.'

'Let me guess. Your knight in shining overalls, Sir Joe?'

Lisa just laughed at the suggestion. Joe hadn't the face or the shape to start a girl sparkling. But before she could correct her, her mum continued, 'He also sounds like a perfect gentleman and that's a sight more important than anything else. I always say if you limit yourself to faces you'll miss out on a lot of good hearts.'

'I suppose you listened when they said that about my dad?'

'That was different.'

'No, Mum, it wasn't. You never felt you were limiting yourself.'

'No, I never did, and you never should either. What I meant was good faces shouldn't influence you. So does this man of yours have a good face? Or need I ask?'

Suddenly Lisa didn't want to share what she felt about Larry. Her mum's romantic priorities seemed to have shifted towards responsibility. So Lisa answered as casually as she could. 'He's handsome enough.'

'Handsome enough to make your eyes twinkle?'

'Handsome enough to make my eyes twinkle and my feet curl.'

'Handsome enough to make your eyes twinkle, your feet curl and your knees go weak?'

They laughed and settled down to their own separate silences and their shared television programme, Lisa's mother happy with the new clutch of hope that this boy would keep her daughter at home.

That night in bed, under the rosy glow of her red lampshade, she sat up and said to her half-sleeping daughter, 'Don't put too much store by my stories, Lisa, love. They're all remembered from far away and when you do that you always remember the best bits. Things weren't always that perfect.'

'But you loved my dad?'

'Yes.'

'Then that's as perfect as it gets.'

'Yes, I suppose so.'

Lisa was still stiff when she climbed out of bed the next morning, and she was still tired. She could feel the pull of sleep tug at her gut as she forced herself up.

It'll get easier, she thought to herself as she staggered into the bathroom and, facing her bleary self in the mirror, she shook herself and said aloud to her image, 'He'll be there.'

She dressed with casual care – jeans, a T-shirt, mascara and a couple of curls worked free from her pony-tail and balanced along both cheek-bones.

She arrived for work eagerly and punctually at nine. Mrs Moran let her in.

'Are we a little late today, dear? Not to mind, though, the traffic is awful.'

'No, it's just nine. Mr Moran said nine.'

'Did he, indeed? It was just that yesterday you were here to be ready and working at nine. Did Mr Moran make that distinction, love? To be here at nine doesn't mean to be working at nine, now does it? You need a bit of time to get your coat off, say how do you do and wet your mop now, don't you?'

Lisa listened on and didn't start work until almost a quarter past.

As she walked past the crew Larry called out, 'Hey, if it's not Lisa the poshest char since Sooty and Sweep went into business! I thought we'd lost you to a dinner party.'

There was a little laughter, a few hellos and a muttered rebuke from Joe.

'You'll not lose me so easy.'

Lisa stood her ground staring up at Larry, and he slowly stepped back and ran his eyes down the length of her and back up the height of her before letting them settle on her now burning face.

'Baby, I'm not even trying.'

Lisa went back to her mop. She was out of her depth and her heart was racing.

Larry left that morning, though. After only one or two more comments, he was gone. He was a painter and there was nothing left for him to paint until the new plaster had dried, so after a few words with one of the older, burlier men, he left and Lisa's day flattened out in his wake.

She was made to take lunch with Mrs Moran and, as expected, she was made to work through the lunch-hour trade and somehow the onus was on her to thank her employer for the opportunity.

'Just a little girl-chat, just you and me, if we ever get the chance to be alone. I don't know what you do all day, says Mr Moran. Well, I say, I'd do a lot more if we weren't so busy. How's that for a joke, eh? If you move over a bit, you could get me the butter, there's a love, and there's the bread, wouldn't it be an idea if you had some slices buttered and ready? Now, not a word to Mr Moran, but you take your pick, girl, and fill yourself a sandwich fit to bust with whatever you fancy and however much you want.'

'Thank you.'

'Not at all, dear, but if you could just wait until this crowd is out of the way first, and could you just hand me a box there and get the door, that lady looks a bit stuck in her shopping. Now, missus, what can I do you for?'

Afterwards, even more tired than before her break, Lisa returned to her cleaning, but she was beginning to clean a little wiser now. It was more boring but far less tiring to spend most of her time half-perched on a stool and half-heartedly moving her mop about.

The only unused stool was one close to Joe's bench where he was planing the surround of the new counter. He acknowledged her presence with a smile and a nod and let her settle before he cleared his throat to talk. When he did speak it was with a tremble of uneasy nonchalance. 'So where were you before you came here?'

'School. This is my first job.' To put him at his ease, Lisa continued, 'I never even had a summer job before. I

suppose I was just lazy, but I'm making up for it now.'
She gestured at the mess surrounding them. He laughed
and his voice was firmer when he spoke again. 'You
shouldn't let Mrs Moran get the better of you. Her old
man's bad enough, but she's a right weapon. She'll run
you ragged for a joke, take my word for it.'

'I think your word came too late. I've already been run
ragged. But it'll be all right when the café opens. I'll be
on my own then.'

'And that's okay?'

She laughed at his incredulity.

'I suppose it will be better than us lot, but you're not
to mind the crew. They're only bored.'

'Oh, I don't mind, not at all.'

'And that Larry, well, there's always a bad one.'

Lisa smiled to herself, a glowing secret smile, because
she knew that it was the bad ones that hid the finest
hearts. Her smile was spotted, though, and there was a
flurry of nudges and winks.

'Hey, Joe, working hard, are we?'

'If that's work, mark me down for overtime.'

Joe snarled to cover what he imagined to be Lisa's
embarrassment, and Lisa hopped off her stool and into the
fray to cover what was, in actuality, his own discomfort.

'It's a full-time job talking to me all right. We were
talking metaphysics there.'

There was laughter, even from the burly, surlier men.
They were beginning to think of Lisa as all right and
then Mrs Moran popped her yellowed head around the
door.

'I'm just nipping out for a quick wee jobby, Lisa, love.
Could you keep an eye on everything up front like a
dear?'

And she was gone.

Lisa could hear the front door close and she had to run through. She couldn't imagine anything less professional than an empty shop.

'Run ragged,' Joe called after her, but she didn't have time to answer. Already there was a customer waiting and behind that one the door was opening on another one.

Lisa began serving immediately, her hair still dull with dust, her hands black and her skin crawling with grime. She was careful not to touch any of the orders and she tried her best to keep her hands palm-down with her filthy nails curled under. She managed it – at least the customers didn't complain about anything. They were too busy chatting amongst themselves. They asked after Mrs Moran, relayed their orders, and then turned towards each other, and Lisa was left guessing at the names of loaves and cakes and randomly piecing prices together from what she had seen of Mrs Moran in action.

A kind-faced woman was questioning her change when Mr Moran came in.

'I think there's an extra two pounds there, love. I wouldn't want you to get into trouble even though I do appreciate your generosity.'

Those behind her in the queue laughed, but Mr Moran, who had heard, didn't. He looked long and hard at Lisa before enquiring after his wife.

'I don't know. She stepped out.'

'When she comes back, have her relieve you. I want to see you upstairs.'

Mrs Moran came back soon after and Lisa went to meet her fate.

'Ah, Miss Gaskell, I would ask you to sit down, but I don't expect this to take too long.'

Lisa stood in front of Mr Moran, with her hands locked behind her back and her head bent low, the apologetic stance she had learnt from the nuns.

'I cannot have you in charge of the tills if you are incapable of giving the right change. That is why I insisted on a result in maths.'

'I wasn't sure of the prices.'

'You should have made it your business to know them before you took charge. Did you not learn them yesterday?' He didn't wait for an answer. 'Obviously not. And I wish I didn't have to say this and I suppose it may be partly my fault for not providing you with your uniform, but when you are behind a counter representing a business you must dress accordingly and when you are dealing with food certain levels of hygiene must be maintained.'

'But I didn't have time to wash.'

'That is no excuse. You must just get up a little earlier in the morning.'

'No, I meant . . .'

'That will be all. You can report back to Mrs Moran and remember that you are only on trial.'

Lisa did as she was told and stood by Mrs Moran listening to her attempts at comfort and handing her everything she needed that lay beyond the reach of her stool.

'Was he at you, love? Well, you don't mind him. I'll have a word. Mr Moran, I'll say, she's the greatest little worker I've seen. Once she comes in, she sets her mind to work and I'm sure once she learns what she needs to know she'll not forget it. Slow learners are like that, slow to learn, slow to forget. That's what I say. . .'

As usual, she spoke loudly and in front of her customers. Lisa was finally relieved after about half an hour when Mr Moran passed out through the shop with hardly a glance to his wife or to Lisa.

'Well, enough of my blab, you pop in the back and give that dirt another run for its money.'

Lisa did as she was told. She went back to her stool, her mop and Joe, who almost made her cry with the kindness of his smile. 'So you've met the real Mr Moran?'

'Yes.'

'Think of the hell he's in, married to her, and think of what she has to put up with married to him, and you'll be able to forgive them both.'

Lisa laughed, and at five o'clock on the dot she downed her mop and ran through the shop, where Mrs Moran was dealing with a customer. Lisa was out the door before she heard her name called and away down the road before Mrs Moran had lumbered off her stool in pursuit.

CHAPTER 17

After a week, Lisa felt as if she had been in Moran's all her life. It had been an exhausting week but by the end of it she felt that she had learned how to manage a little better and so her evenings were suddenly her own again, no longer just periods of recuperation for the next day. But still, by Friday, she was ready for nothing except rest. She didn't visit her Aunt May on Saturday and she was reluctant to face her grandmother for Sunday lunch. She thought that with the insight of the old, the woman would be able to smell the exhaustion off her, but her mum convinced her.

'You look fine, love.'

'I don't. Look at my eyes, and my nails – I'll never get them clean again.'

'No one will be looking at your nails.'

'I know they won't be looking, but they'll have to notice them.'

'If you don't turn up they'll imagine the worst and you look a sight better than the worst your grandmother is capable of imagining.'

That settled it. Lisa dressed with care and accompanied her mum for their weekly family meal, and her mum rose to the occasion as splendidly as if she had never dreamed of a doctor for a daughter. As soon as they were settled to eat, Lisa's grandmother started.

'And how is the world of commerce?'

'Fine.'

'Fine! Is that all I am going to hear?'

'Oh, Lisa's too modest to say more.'

'And being a mother, I assume that you're not?'

'Not a bit.'

Lisa sat silent and listened to her mum's flourishing tale of her daughter's success in the catering trade. Bill and May and her grandmother listened as intently if slightly less incredulously. Even baby Elsie was quiet under the table.

At the end of her mum's speech, Bill laughed his approval and May applauded hers.

'Well, that deserves a toast to my favourite niece. Fancy them trusting you to order stock on only your third day. It looks like you made the right decision and found your calling, doesn't it, Mother?'

'It's not much of a career if it can be learnt in a week.'

But despite her words, her pride rang through. Lisa felt horribly guilty about and slightly amused by the picture of competence her mum had drawn, but she got over her discomfort by raising her glass in answer to her mum's wink and vowing to herself to prove her mum's speech in time by devoting herself tirelessly to the cause of Moran's.

By the following day her intention had dimmed a little, but she arrived at work early and eagerly and managed to keep her mood intact for most of the day. She knew now, a little better, how to deal with Mrs Moran's continuous demands. On Joe's advice, she just ignored the woman. Mrs Moran was so used to being ignored she took no offence.

Lisa also learnt how to deal with the crew. As the days went by, they separated more and more into individuals.

There was the crew leader, a big scarred block of a man in his sixties. He treated Lisa much as he treated every-one – he was polite to her but he largely ignored her. He presided over and coordinated a full complement of about ten men and a core group of two – Joe, his second in command and a high-pitched, weedy, giggling apprentice. The other eight, including Larry, came and went as the work dictated.

They were large, loud, healthy lads who took pride in their work, especially the plasterer, who worked his medium with artistry and complete concentration. He never seemed to hear the comments flung at him; he just mixed his plaster and applied it with controlled, uniform sweeps of his arm and the surfaces that he finished looked deep and dusty brown before hardening into a smooth grey.

Lisa loved to watch him work and, although she knew it was a shame to paint over such perfection, she looked forward to each newly dried wall, knowing that it meant that Larry would be needed.

On that second Monday, Larry was there before her. She blushed immediately she noticed him and he paused his conversation to notice her reaction. 'Hey, Posh, have you been running or are you just pleased to see me?'

There was no answer to that, so Lisa ignored it and went to leave her coat upstairs. When she came down she bravely chose to clean within conversational distance of Larry.

'So, did you miss me then, love?'

'I wasn't aiming for you.'

'Aiming or not, I think you've scored a bull's-eye. Hey lads, I'm in love.'

'Leave her be, Larry.'

'I didn't touch her,' he answered, with an exaggerated grimace of innocence and then softly, just to Lisa, he continued, 'There's none of us would have a chance to touch you with Joe around. I'll have to get you later.'

'And before that you'll have to catch me.' Lisa laughed off the comment, but she lived on it for the rest of the morning. It sounded to her like the promise of a date, as did a few of his later questions.

'So, do you like dancing or do you rather just skipping to the main event?' and, 'If I were to walk you home one night, keeping you dry under my umbrella and warm under my coat, would you ask me in for coffee?'

Lisa was finding it more and more difficult to keep her composure. Every question was muttered low, just to her, and was accompanied by a smile that bared his teeth and crinkled the flesh that framed his eyes. Finally, Lisa mopped her way back to the comfort of Joe and her high stool and the easy scraps of dialogue that had grown to pass for conversation between them.

'You're not to bother about Larry.'

'Oh, I don't.'

But she blushed, wondering if Joe had guessed her secret.

'Once he finds that he can't bully you he'll drop trying.'

Lisa relaxed.

'Good weekend?'

'All right, bit dull.'

'Better than here, though.'

'Oh, yeah, much.'

The day wore slowly on.

The following day, May called in, despite Lisa's warnings not to.

'I'm not there long enough. I won't be able to talk and I'll look a mess and . . .'

'Okay, okay, I won't.'

But May couldn't help herself, especially not after the glowing reports she had heard from Elsie. Anyway she needed bread and it was only right to support what was now almost a family firm.

So, on Tuesday afternoon, Lisa's Auntie May and her cousin Elsie queued up to face Mrs Moran.

'Ah look at the doll! Aren't you a doll? Have you got a hug for me? I'll give you a biscuit for a hug?'

Elsie clung tight to her mother.

'Are we shy then, eh? Is she shy? Never had any of my own, but that's God's own plan, eh? Something wrong with my W-O-M-B. It's a burden more to me than Mr Moran, I'd say, but it's no picnic for him . . .'

In the end, May did what those who knew better did immediately. She shouted over the continuous stream of words that were being flung at her. 'I was looking for Lisa.'

'. . . and if it wasn't for my hips I might have adopted . . . Lisa, you say? Now, you wouldn't be her mum would you? Because if you are, let me tell you that I've taken to that girl. Like the daughter I've never had she could be . . .'

Eventually word was passed back to Lisa and she appeared out of the back room looking worn and grubby and quite unlike the picture of executive competence that her mum had painted. May smiled so hard it was almost a laugh and baby Elsie, seeing a familiar and well-loved face, flung herself at it.

She was scrambling up Lisa's legs and cooing for a

hug when Larry walked past, and on out to another job. Lisa smiled at him and then, self-consciously, buried her attention in baby Elsie.

'Look at you!' she said, and, 'Did you come to visit?' and, 'How's my baby today?'

Larry seemed a little shocked but he didn't pause to ask any questions and Lisa didn't notice any change in him. He seemed his usual self, cocking his finger and winking at Mrs Moran and May beside her.

'See ya, ladies.'

Lisa didn't see Mrs Moran's answering simper or her Auntie May's slight shudder. She was still too engrossed in baby Elsie.

'Do you know what you should do? You should take your break now, Lisa, and take as long as you want. You can always work up the time. Now, you all go upstairs and you can have a nice cup of whatever and not a word to Mr Moran.'

'But . . .'

'I insist, Lisa, and you can take these cakes up with you.' She handed Lisa a random selection of what was within reach of her stool.

'Thank you.'

'Not to worry. We can settle up at the end of the week.'

And she turned, directing her flow of conversation at an incoming customer. Lisa had no choice. She led her aunt through to the filth of the back room and the staring crew. Once they were upstairs in the storeroom-cum-office-cum-locker-room, May gave in and laughed.

'Oh, Lisa, I should have known! No offence, but I did think it was a bit too much that they were planning on sending you away to a trade fair.'

'Mum went overboard a bit.'

'A bit! You were going to double up as the company accountant!'

'It was for my grandmother's benefit really.'

'Oh, I know, I know. What kills me is that I fell for it in the first place. I had just forgotten what an amazing storyteller your mum was.'

'Was she?'

'Oh, yes, and she obviously still is. When we were at school, I had to deal with all sorts of stories. At one stage we were supposed to have a helicopter pad on our roof because we were on an army fly-over route and our family were mostly living off the compensation the government gave our mother. All completely untrue, but believable and great fun. A bit like a daughter who single-handedly saved a business in a week. So what are you really doing here?'

'Cleaning.'

They both burst out laughing, holding their sides and snorting and finally frightening baby Elsie, whose whimpers sobered them up.

'I'm cleaning the back room while the crew are working.'

That set them off again.

May had the good grace not to let on to her sister that she had discovered the full extent of Lisa's role in Moran's. May still called every Wednesday evening bringing baby Elsie with her and the following day was no exception.

Lisa had already told her mum that May had called to Moran's and that she had stayed for coffee but, as was discussed with her aunt, to save her mum's face, she didn't elaborate. The following evening May said only just about as much as Lisa, though she did probe a little further just to tease.

'I hear you called to Moran's yesterday?' Lisa's mum asked when they were all settled around the still-empty grate.

'I did and I don't know how they could have managed before Lisa.'

'I suppose not very well.'

After one warning glance at her aunt, Lisa settled back with baby Elsie and let the sisters battle it out.

'They couldn't have, the amount of work she has already got through! In just a week, sacks of it.'

'There must be a lot of paperwork.'

'There is, which is surprising, seeing as they're not even using wallpaper.'

May left it at that and Elsie allowed her the last word. They just smiled at each other over their coffee mugs and happily changed the subject.

CHAPTER 18

After just a short while, Lisa thought of work only in relation to Larry. He usually worked on the café on Monday and Tuesday, sometimes he did a bit on Friday and he called in for his pay on Thursday. He always took the time to notice Lisa and sometimes made an issue of paying her attention, but he never again hinted at any dating and Lisa was giving up hope. It was after one especially dispiriting Tuesday that Lisa finally gave in to Joe's persistent and subtle invitations.

He had started by asking her about her weekends and then had asked her about her interests and then her haunts and he had likened all her answers to his preferences.

'No, I just stayed in on Saturday watching telly.'

'Me too. I hate pubs on the weekend.'

'I went for a walk on Sunday.'

'Me too. I love walking, especially after a big lunch.'

'I don't really go to pubs, but the crowd from school go to Byrne's, so I go there sometimes.'

'So do I, but just sometimes.'

Lisa never pursued these conversations. She knew that Joe was always just a flicker away from suggesting a meeting and she didn't quite know how to refuse him. However, after that dispiriting Tuesday she encouraged him sufficiently to secure herself the invitation that she had finally decided to accept.

Larry had arrived for work that morning a little later than Lisa and a lot later than the rest of the crew. The foreman had rounded on him as he swung through the door and behind her Lisa could hear and almost feel the rumble of the older man's disapproval. Larry, though, just swung on past it.

'So dock me some hours. You can dock me the whole day and she was still worth it. Hey, lads, do you think it's love? She's already cost me the price of three lagers and an hour's pay.'

'And you're still smiling. That's love all right.'

There was a ripple of laughter, but the crew were busy and maybe a little used to Larry's stories and maybe a little jealous of them, so all they spared him was one reply and a ripple of laughter. It wasn't enough for him.

'Hey, Posh, would you say it's love or was I done?'

'Three lagers is cheap. I'd say you got what you paid for.'

She immediately bowed her head, hot with the realization of what she had said and the obvious implications that could be got from her answer.

'Ooooh.' Larry came close with his lips pursed tight in a camp exclamation. 'So my girl is cheap is she? And how much would you cost?'

'Larry, leave her alone.' The pitch of Joe's tone alerted the whole room to a listening silence.

'A posh girl like you, would I have to pay you in margaritas?'

'Enough now.'

It was the foreman that brought the incident to a close, but he couldn't stop Larry brushing his mouth close to Lisa's ear and whispering, 'If I thought you were worth it, I wouldn't be wasting my time haggling.'

She didn't lift her head to register the insult and she didn't trust herself to stay dry-eyed under Joe's kindness. Even though she could see him beckoning her over to his corner, she moved her mop away from everyone and calmed herself with her own reasoning.

She felt mean and dirty and used and cheap and angry and she hated Larry and she hated the way his close words had tingled down her spine and how the glint in his eye showed that he saw them as they went.

She hated that he could talk about another girl like that and she hated that he had another girl and she hated that she had shown him how she cared and she was angry with herself for showing him and her anger dried away any threat of tears and she turned to where Joe was still beckoning her and mopped her way over to him.

'You're not to mind Larry. No one else does.'

'Oh, I don't.'

'And you were right – the sort that go with him are always cheap.'

'Well, they'd have to be.'

'So did you do anything last night?'

'No, just stayed in. I called to my grandmother for a bit and then just stayed home.'

'Me too, watched a bit of telly. And tonight, any plans?'

'No. Boring, eh? Are you doing anything?'

'I thought that I might go to a film.'

'That sounds like a good idea.'

It was that easy.

Lisa met Joe that night outside the Savoy at half past seven. Her mum was delighted with the arrangement and her Auntie May was told over the phone and she was delighted. They had both agreed that a girl as young as Lisa would be a danger to herself travelling alone and a boyfriend would either keep her home or else accompany her. Either way a boyfriend was what she needed and this Joe sounded so nice it was a bonus, but Lisa wasn't playing.

'So what are you going to wear, love?'

'Jeans, I don't know. It's just a film.'

'Nothing "just" about a film. I'll run you a bath and you get yourself something to eat. Half seven is very early isn't it?'

'The film starts at eight, and stop fussing, Mum. He sees me every day looking as big a mess as I can. He won't recognize me if I'm too done up.'

'I don't care. Wear your blue skirt, Lisa, and do your hair properly. It's only respectful to the man.'

And so, despite herself, Lisa arrived at the Savoy at twenty-eight minutes past seven looking as well as her beauty, her youth and her wardrobe allowed, which was very well indeed.

Joe was already there. He had been there since a quarter past, preparing himself for the worst. He was so lost in imagining the horror of work the next day, after she didn't turn up, that Lisa had to reach out for his shoulder before he noticed her.

They smiled happily and shyly at each other. It was different out of Moran's. It was very different in the evening when they were both dressed up.

'You look marvellous,' he said.

Lisa laughed because the word sounded so strange and archaic coming from him.

He turned away on her laugh and she followed him

into the cinema. It was an uncomfortable start to the evening. She never got the chance to tell him how well groomed he looked and she was left with the uneasy feeling that he had interpreted her laugh as an insult.

He insisted on paying for the tickets, but in a clumsy way. Lisa had queued with him to keep him company. She had had no intention of paying for herself – he had made it obvious from the formality of his invitation and the stiffness of his shirt collar that he was following a strict code of date etiquette and any offer of payment would be viewed as an affront. At least that is what Lisa thought until they came to pay for the tickets.

'Well, then, I suppose I'll get these.'

Lisa, shocked into a new role, guiltily reached for her wallet. 'No, no, let me pay half.'

'No, I'll pay for the tickets.'

'Well, I'll get some popcorn and stuff then.'

'None for me thanks, but if you want some I'll get it, I just have to wait for my change.'

'No, I don't want anything.'

'Are you sure?'

'Yes.'

'I might have a Coke after all. It's a thirsty business I'm in.'

'I'll get it.'

'No, I didn't mean that. I wouldn't have said it if I thought you'd get it. But you'll have one yourself?'

They were both red and damp with embarrassment by the time they sat for the film. It was the least threatening, most innocent film showing. A light comedy that Joe had chosen very carefully. He didn't want to be embarrassed by any sexually explicit scenes and he also made sure to avoid any violence in case Lisa was looking for any personality traits in his choice. He knew to steer clear of kids' films as well just in case she thought him weak; art films were pretentious; and girls universally disliked westerns. His final choice, though thoughtful, was deadly dull and that led to its own problems.

They were seated in their numbered seats both holding the popcorn and Coke that they didn't really want. Thankful for the cool and settling twilight of the theatre, they soon relaxed into a discussion about work. By the time the film started, they had found each other again, and after ten minutes of tedious on-screen jokes, they caught each other's eyes and smiled at each other to register the fact that they both felt the same – it was a bad film but they were happy to be there, and then they stared straight ahead again.

It was a small cinema and only about half full but the seats had been sold in a block and so the centre seats in the centre aisle were almost totally filled. Lisa and Joe were wedged into the centre of a full row, behind a full row and in front of a full row.

About fifteen minutes into the film the boredom from the screen filtered through the crowd and the people around Lisa and Joe rustled and muttered and whispered in waves of movement. Then the majority of them settled down to each other.

What had been just rows of people fused into rows of couples. Hands were joined, then arms were entwined, then faces were lowered and lips were sealed, except, of course, for the occasional big, slurping, adolescent noises that managed to escape. Lisa and Joe watched on and didn't look at each other again.

Afterwards they had to wait until the credits had fully rolled into a blank, bright screen before the couples around them had disentangled themselves sufficiently to put their coats back on.

They waited in silence and Lisa read the names of the third bell hop and the gaffer and wondered what a best boy was actually best at. Once outside she wanted nothing more than just to go home, but to leave the night on such a note would make work in the morning unbearable. They both knew that, so Joe had the courage to suggest a drink and Lisa accepted without hesitation.

'Will we go to Byrne's?'

'It's a bit of a walk, isn't it? Here looks fine.'

'Here it is, then.' Joe agreed happily and swung open the door Lisa had pointed at enthusiastically, but Lisa knew that she had answered too quickly, too sharply, and he was smart enough to know why. She was almost tempted to lie and say that her friends only met on a Wednesday night but then she thought that to mention them might solidify the insult.

'Well, isn't this lovely?' was what she said instead.

The pub was comfortable and that was a help and the drink filled their hands and that was a help and so they stayed for a second drink, which Lisa insisted on paying for, and began to talk quite naturally to each other. They spoke about work and did impersonations of Mrs Moran and Joe told tales from some other jobs and they didn't mention Larry and they managed to laugh quite a bit and then Joe caught Lisa's eye and said, 'It was an awful film.'

They both laughed with relief.

'Next time, it'll be my choice,' said Lisa and they neither of them thought that that was too presumptuous a thing to say.

Soon after, they left to go home. Lisa was walked to her bus-stop. She declined the offer of a taxi or a chaperone on the bus. Drink had made Joe easier in his role of dater, but she allowed him to wait until she was safely on the bus. And that was all he did – he waited. He stood beside her with his hands in his pockets and she stood beside him with her hands in her pockets and they talked about their favourite childhood films and when the bus came they both said, 'See you tomorrow,' and then they both groaned and laughed and that was that. Lisa decided that it had turned into quite a pleasant evening. But, unfortunately for her mum, not one that she thought merited discussion.

As soon as she got home, Lisa almost tripped over her mum, who was waiting, filling their hall with her eager enthusiasm.

Elsie had heard the turn of Lisa's key in the lock and had sprung out of bed in the hope of tea and confidences. Neither was forthcoming.

The cramped hall-space was far too cramped for the swing of the hall door, the bedroom door and two adults. With difficulty, Lisa was manoeuvred into the bedroom and put sitting at the end of her mum's bed.

'Well?'

'Well, what?'

'Well, you know what.'

'Well, I know what I'm not going to tell you.'

'Oh, you ungrateful child.'

They laughed.

'But really, Mum, it was nothing very special. We went to a film that was awful, we had two drinks each and then, like a gentleman, he walked me to my bus.'

'And what did you talk about?'

'Just what we talk about every day – work, television, nothing much. It was the same as it always is.'

'Did he pay?'

'Yes.'

'Then it's not at all the same, but if he did pay and it felt as comfortable as it usually does then it's something special.'

'No it isn't, Mum.'

'So he left you to the bus?'

'Yes.'

There was a long silence where the two women stared hard at each other. Lisa's mum was forcing the question out and Lisa was willing her to stay silent and they both knew what the other was up to. Eventually they both laughed and Lisa gave in.

'We didn't even shake hands.'

'He didn't even try?'

'Didn't even try to try.'

'Who could ask for anything more? A gentleman Romeo.'

'I'm getting ready for bed.'

When Lisa came back, dressed and ready for sleep, her mum was almost asleep and the room was only lit by the soft red light that still shone from under her shade. Lisa snuggled herself down into her bed opposite and called to her mum in her night-favour voice, the one that matched the light, 'Mum, tell me about your first date with my dad.'

But Lisa's mum didn't answer in her usual night-story voice. She spoke in a jarring tone, one suited to bright daylight. 'You know it well enough and I'm tired.'

But Lisa wasn't to be put off. 'He asked you out for a meal, didn't he?'

'You seem to know it well enough.'

'And you got dressed up for a restaurant because you didn't know he was as poor as he was . . .'

'Or as mean.'

'What?'

'He may just have been mean. I'd only his word that he was broke.'

'Mum!'

Lisa's wail pulled her bolt upright. Her mum had never spoken about her dad's memory with such cruelty or such hardness before. Almost by reflex, Lisa's mum sat up in answer to her daughter's pain and automatically she began to soothe.

'I'm just tired, love. Lie back down and don't mind me. Yes, I got dressed up in what I thought was the height of sophistication – a black sleeveless dress, and it was November. I wore a cardigan with it that I was going to take off as soon as I sat down and I wore a huge, ancient, smelly but very warm overcoat belonging to your grandmother that I planned to take off as soon as I got into the restaurant and not put back on until we were outside. That way I figured your dad wouldn't see too much of it.

'Your dad said we'd meet at the restaurant and it was a very swanky one. When I arrived, I was glad of my black dress even though I was still cold . . .'

'But he was outside.'

'Yes, he had picked that restaurant because it was the closest landmark to his favourite chip shop. That's what he said as innocently as you like, but he knew what he was at. It was all a bit of devilment. I fancy it was his way of testing a girl. He'd have found out straight away that night if I had been only after him for what I could get.'

'And you got the best chips in town.'

'Yes, and we ate them in the bright, smelly chip shop 'cause it was too cold outside, and me in my horrible coat.'

'But he liked you anyway.'

'Yes, I suppose it was a good test on my part, just to check if he was only after a dolly-bird.'

'And he walked you home by the park and got you flowers.'

'Well, twigs. It was November. He picked them off the ground.'

'And he kissed you.'

'Yes.'

'And he said that your face fitted his.'

'Yes.'

'And he sang *Moon River* to you and promised it to you as your very own song and he said that the gift of a song was a very happy and a very sad thing and that it was happy and sad for the very same reason, because it lasted for ever.'

'Yes, he said that.'

'Joe just walked me to the bus-stop.'

Lisa settled to sleep again. Her mum was almost there and so she spoke heavily.

'Bus-stops are very good places.'

But Lisa wasn't listening.

CHAPTER 19

The next day at work was easy. Lisa didn't know what she expected, really, but she was pleased when Joe nodded his usual hello along with the rest of the crew. There was no sniggering, no nudging, no winking at Joe. She walked past and upstairs and thought that really she hadn't expected anything less.

There was a lot of work to get through that day and Lisa was kept busy, so Joe's ability to be discreet was not overly tested. The café counter was being fitted and a constant scattering of loose shavings gathered around it as it was being fine-tuned and hand-sanded, and, that afternoon, Mr Moran came in to spend a few hours upstairs with the accounts. Lisa had spent her lunch-hour with Mrs Moran as usual, and when she was just about to return to her mop she was called back.

'Would you ever be a love, dear, and have a look after this lot. I've a little jobby that just can't wait.'

'All right.'

'There you go, then, a nice white apron. You know how Mr Moran likes to see you. I tell him, I say Mr Moran, I say, that girl would look a picture in a sack and he says that I'm to tell you that that is no reason to come to work in one. Now, you slip on your apron and maybe wash your hands, especially your nails – the ladies won't mind waiting – now will you?'

Two of the three waiting ladies left, but Mrs Moran didn't seem to notice.

'Just hurry back, Lisa, love. I can't wait all day and remember to keep a steady head when you're giving back the change. Now, what can I do you for?'

As Lisa left to clean herself, Mrs Moran turned to her one remaining customer. Lisa heard her continue her continuous speech hardly pausing for breath.

'Oh, she's a right little dinger and I wouldn't be without her, the daughter I've never had and as sweet as you could want, not everything is down to brains, now is it?'

Lisa didn't see much of Joe that day or the next. He was too busy to spare her much time. By Friday she almost missed him and his easy talk and slow, kind jokes so, when he passed her and her mop on Friday morning and asked her out for a drink after work she accepted happily.

As the day wore on, Lisa's enthusiasm for the arrangement grew. She smiled over at Joe a few times too many and hovered near him with her mop even when he was too busy to talk. She didn't allow herself to equate any of these actions with the presence of Larry.

He came in early in the afternoon and spent his time painting the skirtings. The paintwork was nearly all finished but Lisa, mopping with her back to Larry, made sure that she didn't even notice him. By four she was satisfied that her indifference was beginning to annoy. Larry, on his way to some unnecessary bottle of turps, took the time to walk in front of her mop.

'Hey, Posh, how about a shoeshine?'

'Leave her be, Larry.'

'I'm just being friendly, saying hello. Amn't I, Posh?'

'It's all right, Joe.'

Lisa looked up and into Larry's eyes. She was hoping to be defiant, but the intensity of the stare that met hers confused her intention. She forgot everything except those eyes. Slowly they crinkled into a knowing smile and she was reminded of herself and thankfully of her mop. She lowered her head and applied herself to it. Larry lowered his head as well.

'Maybe I'm ready to haggle. Could I afford a girl like you?'

But Lisa just mopped around him and avoided answering.

She rang her mum after work, from the upstairs room, well within earshot of the most of the crew, to say she was going to be late.

'Is it him again?'

'Yes.'

'Just him or the whole crew?'

'The first one.'

'Will you be late home?'

'No, not at all.'

'Oh, please be, just a little, don't want you drinking too quick and getting the hiccups.'

'Goodbye.'

For her mum's sake, Lisa was almost beginning to wish it was love.

Unfortunately, the time it took to make the phone call allowed Mrs Moran time enough to organize Lisa's capture. She was caught just as she stepped off the stairs.

'Ah, Lisa, would you be a dear and give us a hand washing these down? Isn't it well for you, off tomorrow?

If I had the luxury of a day off, perhaps I wouldn't be crippled so bad with my hips.'

It was quite late when Lisa finally made it to the pub and a very worried Joe. She saw him first, sitting alone, away from the bar, with his head low over his nearly empty pint. She ordered him a fresh one before she went over to him and she smiled when she saw the change in his expression when he saw her.

He stood up, but his whole body seemed to have melted with relief.

'I had given up. I didn't think you were . . .'

But she didn't let him finish. She just laughed.

'I never saw a man so happy to see a pint.'

'Oh, I didn't . . . is that for me? But you shouldn't have . . .'

'Oh, go on, pretend innocence. I saw your eyes light up when they saw the drink.'

They both laughed and he let the joke pass. It made for a much easier start to the evening. They stayed late enough to please Lisa's mum and they drank too much on an empty stomach to allow for reserve. They had a very pleasant time.

Joe walked Lisa to her bus-stop again and they put their hands in their pockets again but the heat of the drink and the warm evening breeze thawed them while they waited for the bus.

First they fell silent and then Joe took one hand out of its pocket and stretched it towards Lisa. She smiled and so he took out his second hand and, putting them both on her shoulders, took a step forward. She closed her eyes and he bent his head and pressed his dry rounded lips on hers.

Afterwards he immediately straightened up and she

opened her eyes and they both smiled and then, what Lisa remembered as the only magic of the evening occurred. The bus came with cinematic timing. She had only time enough to say goodnight and get on.

Later that evening, over a cold chop dinner, she told her mum all she could about Joe. It may have been a small kiss but Lisa knew by it that Joe would be around long enough to meet her mum and so her mum had to be told what to expect.

'He's older than me.'

'A lot?'

'No. About four years.'

'That's just about all right.'

'And my dad was how much older than you?'

'This is not about your dad. This is about your Joe, so go on.'

'He's tall and thin and eats a lot and has brown hair and kind of bucked teeth but you don't notice unless he smiles. And he's very sweet and kind and I doubt there's a puppy dog's tail in him.'

'When will I meet him?'

'I don't know.'

'I'll call into Moran's, that's what I'll do. I can get off early on Monday and—'

'You will not.'

'So when will I meet him?'

Lisa's mum didn't meet Joe for a few weeks. Lisa saw no point in trailing him home after working with him all day.

'Things will be different,' she said, 'after the job is done.'

The job was very nearly done. Out of the chaos of dirt

and wood and paint and smells, and out of the hours of seemingly meaningless toil, a café was forming, and a very lovely one at that.

The counter was curved and blond and planed satin smooth. The walls were perfectly plastered and painted in shades of white. The floor creaked with the character of its old boards and the ceiling dripped with ten individual glass bowl shades, one to hang over each table. The tables hadn't come yet, but they were to be round with glass tops and metal legs. The chairs were to be blond like the counter with a suggestion of the same curve in the shape of the seat.

Lisa was surprised that the Morans were capable of such taste, as was Mrs Moran.

'Well, I never, I said to Mr Moran,' was how she frequently greeted her customers. 'What an idea, spending all that on a chair. And what's the point of a fancy seat when it's just for seats, eh? What a joke, eh? If our customers' seats had eyes, I said, they'd be impressed, but as it is . . . but he knows best, Mr Moran, and he says so and he says he'll settle for nothing short of it.'

From Joe Lisa learnt that Mr Moran had had the good fortune to hire the crew and the good sense to take the advice offered to him by the gaffer. He had spent more money than he had expected, but he had bought himself more style than he could ever have imagined and was sensible enough to recognize this and be thankful for it.

As the café took shape and as the crew fine-tuned the finer details, the Morans relaxed into good humour and the whole place took on a festive atmosphere. Occasionally, even the men behind in the bakery could be heard laughing and humming. It was out of this good humour that the idea for the party was born.

It was the crew's last week and Lisa's eighth. The plumbing was rerouted and boxed in, the room was extended and its ceiling heightened, the staircase was redirected, the tiles were grouted and the varnish on the floor was sealed. The doors to the cupboards behind the counter were attached and the display cases were fixed into position. The menu board was blackened and decorated with a painting of grapes and loaves, and the fridge was expected by Friday. Lisa had cleaned and polished and rubbed and burnished, and by Wednesday the effect was dazzling.

The last and only thing left to be done was the demolition of the partition into the front makeshift shop area of the café and that was not going to be started until Saturday, when Moran's was closing for a day. A momentous decision on Mr Moran's part, as Mrs Moran explained to her customers.

'He says that his dad never closed a day except Christmas Day and his granddad never closed a day at all, but as Mr Moran says when a thing needs doing it needs doing well and how would the crew be able to go about their business with a lot of ladies the likes of us in their way?'

The tables and chairs were due to arrive on Saturday and the crew were to work all day Saturday, and the crew and Lisa and the Morans were to work on the Sunday for as long as the finishing touches took to finish. On Thursday morning, Mr Moran gathered them all together, including the men from the bakery with their white arms and flushed faces, to explain this to them.

He started by clapping his hands together for attention and then he worked them harder, slapping them off each other at a faster and faster pace, applauding the men, his workers, who slouched before him.

'I applaud you all,' he shouted over the noise of his hands, in case any one failed to understand what he was doing and then suddenly he stopped and the muttered aside from the back was plainly audible.

'Clapping his hands costs him nothing. You'd think he'd run to a couple of beers.'

'You've all worked very hard and I'm pleased to say that our opening date that was fixed for Monday still holds. We originally planned to open in August but as I always say a job worth doing is worth doing well and if well means a delay of nearly two months who am I to argue? October is as good a time as any to launch ourselves. But to do so I'll need you all here on Sunday. We want everything shipshape and toes out for early Monday, eh? Of course you'll all be paid time and a half.'

His last sentence was added hurriedly – he had seen the bulk of the gaffer shift into a more upright position. But even after Mr Moran had spoken, that bulk continued to tense itself for speech, so Mr Moran spoke on. 'I mean, double time.' His eyes flickered to his left again. 'Double and a half.'

The gaffer relaxed and the crew cheered and Mr Moran smiled. Lisa didn't know such subtle threats could work so well in an auction situation and she cheered the gaffer along with the rest. Mr Moran's smile ended with a nod. He obviously meant it as a dismissive smile but no one was going anywhere. No one had much work to be going to and everyone had heard the muttered aside from the back and everyone agreed with it.

'Well, I'll not be keeping you. I'm sure we all have things to be doing.'

But still the men stayed. They looked to the gaffer and the gaffer, knowing what was expected of him, spoke for them. 'Will you be having a grand opening then, sir?'

'Nothing grand but something suitable to mark the occasion.'

'And what's your idea of suitable, sir?'

'A few free tasters maybe. We might run to a couple of bottles of wine.'

'And would there be an open invitation to this . . . wine tasting?'

'Well, yes, open to customers.' Mr Moran was beginning to lose his composure.

'Well, we're all of us meaning to take our custom here, aren't we, lads?'

They all muttered in agreement.

'So we'll see you Monday, Mr Moran, sir, for a glass of wine, maybe.'

The gaffer lumbered upright and went to lumber back to his work. The crew followed his lead, shuffling as if to disband, but Mr Moran stopped them. He saw that he had no choice.

'Well, I must say I'm touched that you would all bother to take time out of your day to pay us the compliment of drinking to our good fortune. As I always say, though, if a job is worth doing at all it's worth doing well so I'll stand for no half measures when it comes to that drink. Tomorrow afternoon I'll stand you all a drink and a slice of our best pie.'

Once he had finished his announcement the men

cheered and began to melt back to their positions, but Mr Moran knew that he had been had and he needed to re-establish some proof of his authority before he could return as easily to his accounts.

'Miss Gaskell,' he called, loud and clear, and Lisa turned. 'Your uniform is due to arrive tomorrow. I have ordered two outfits for you and it is your responsibility to keep and clean them. And please remember that you are working with food. Now that I have supplied your wardrobe you have no excuse but to turn up to work looking neat. I'll no longer stand for your half measures in hygiene.'

And he left.

He left behind a shocked silence that suddenly returned to a full and completely different range of con-versations. The crew's tact hurt Lisa more than any barbed comments that they could have flung at her. She couldn't bear to look at Joe's kind face so she just lowered her head to her mop and tried to control the tears that she could feel collecting. It was Larry who came to her rescue.

'Hey, Posh, what was all that about? Don't you wash behind your ears where you come from or are you afraid that you'll wash away the Chanel?'

Joe answered with his usual, 'Leave her Larry.'

But Lisa spoke over him. 'Yeah, and when was the last time you smelled of anything other than turps or paint?'

'Never had any complaints.'

He was moving closer now and talking low in that way that always dissolved Lisa, but she stood her ground.

'Lager is known to affect a girl's sense of smell.'

'Maybe, but when a girl's with me her other senses make up for the loss.'

He was close up to Lisa now and getting closer. She stepped away from him, swishing her mop back and forth between them and he just laughed and turned around, but by then Lisa had forgotten about Mr Moran.

CHAPTER 20

That evening, the evening before the party, Lisa had arranged to meet Joe. They had seen all the films worth seeing and they had drunk too much over the weeks they had been dating so, that night, they decided to meet for a meal. Joe had offered an expensive restaurant but Lisa had insisted on a cheap one. She didn't know why but she couldn't imagine Joe comfortable in a luxurious setting. So they met and ate a pizza and talked.

Well, Lisa did most of the talking. She talked about work and Mr Moran and her Auntie May's recent holiday and her evening babysitting for baby Elsie and then she finally ran dry and a little irritated. Joe didn't even seem to be listening and listening was one of his main virtues. If he lost that, well . . .

Lisa was thinking of telling him as much when he smiled his odd, bucked little smile at her and reached for her and awkwardly stretched his arm across her shoulders. She smiled back. She always responded to his smile, it was so kind, but she didn't respond so well to his touch so she just squeezed his hand and drew hers away. He didn't seem to notice.

'Lisa . . .' He spoke low, in a voice that really was more suited to those who sat hand in hand. 'I have a favour to ask.'

'What?' Lisa replied cheerily and very loudly, but he didn't follow her example and his answer was still muted.

'I would like if you and me could be at the party tomorrow together.'

'Of course we'll be there together. Were you thinking of separate rooms?'

But Lisa knew what he meant.

'No I mean together like a couple. Not that I'd be all over you – it's just that when we're at work . . . well, I keep having to stop myself looking at you or talking to you as much as I want to.'

Lisa stayed listening and stayed smiling but the effort must have strained her because Joe noticed and continued in a slightly sterner tone.

'I understand why you didn't want the crew to know about us seeing each other. I understand how it might have been a bit awkward for you with us all working together, but I do think that it could have saved you some bother as well. But now, well, we're finished. Tomorrow is a farewell party, so what's the problem?'

'No problem.'

Lisa knew that there shouldn't be a problem. She knew that Joe was a good man and was well liked, that she could handle any teasing that would be dished out and that she would never see Larry again after Sunday.

'No problem,' she repeated in a firmer voice with an accompanying nod.

'That's such a relief.' Joe reached for her hand again. 'It's such a relief, it calls for a celebration.'

He stopped a passing waiter and ordered two large helpings of ice cream.

'You had me so worried,' he continued. 'It wasn't only the crew I was worried about either. It was everyone – your friends and your family. You keep talking about people but you've never asked me to meet them and you've never come home with me when I've asked you.'

'I'm sorry. I thought you were just being polite.'

Lisa disentangled her hand in readiness for her dessert and remembered her mum's story about her dad and the ice cream.

He had found a shop that still used its cone machine in December and for a week he had made himself sick on ice cream. He loved to saunter down the road licking his cone and all the people around him wrapped up and huddled into the cold would take the time to uncoil and stare at him. Lisa's mum had tried to do it too but she said that she wasn't as good at pretending nonchalance and she felt that she was ruining Lisa's dad's style. So, she just walked behind him and admired the effect he was having.

Work the following morning passed easily and lightly. The crew and Lisa cleared the biggest table they could find for the pies and then lined as many chairs as there were up against a wall in case of tiredness. The radio was tuned in to a music station and someone produced some balloons. The place looked and felt strange but festive. A little after one, Lisa was called away.

'Just a wee jobby that I don't think can wait. Be a love and step in for me. Oh, and Lisa, dear, comb your hair out. You know how Mr Moran likes to see it dust-free.'

Lisa was just positioned behind the counter when Mr Moran burst in. He pushed the street door open with his back and trundled on past Lisa as quickly as he could. He was bent low over a box filled with beer. Lisa could hear his arrival being welcomed with a cheer and then the door closed behind him and everything else she heard was muffled.

She heard the door to the bakery open and she heard

the rumble of greetings as the men came through. Later she heard louder and heartier goodbyes as they left, and in the meantime she heard the continuous and ever louder screech of Mrs Moran's laugh. Soon it was accompanied by some deep guffaws.

There was also the sound, ever more frequent, of glasses knocking off each other and occasionally hitting the ground and, as the afternoon wore on, there were bursts of loud and louder conversation. Words seemed to claw over each other, any sense in their content lost in the effort to be heard. With everyone talking and no one listening, the noise level would climb and climb until it eventually burst in a surge of laughter and then it would start again, at conversational level.

It was almost four when Lisa was relieved. Mrs Moran popped herself back behind the counter. She looked soft and moist and red and her breath smelled of a heavy earthiness.

'Did you think we had forgotten you, dear?' she asked and then she answered, 'We'd never forget you, would we? The daughter I never had, how could I forget you?'

Lisa left without waiting for more, but she saw Mrs Moran turn to the waiting customers and she heard the inevitable, 'Never can have children, the doctor says there's something wrong with my W-O-M-B, if it wasn't for my hips . . .'

The party, when Lisa finally joined it, was in full swing. The room was messy and smelly and dense with smoke and the men in it filled it to breaking point. They seemed unnecessary to Lisa. They were unnecessarily loud and unnecessarily large. She stood before them, momentarily uncertain, and that's where Joe found her.

He was suddenly before her, calmly, palely, holding

his glass of orange juice and that, for some reason, annoyed Lisa further. When in Rome, she thought to herself, and briefly imagined the gathering before her dressed in togas. She smiled back at Joe's bared bucked teeth.

'It was Mr Moran's fault. He insisted the shop had to be open and he assumed you would do it. You haven't missed much, though. I saved you a beer and a piece of pie. It's good, it's worth eating.'

And then, finally, words failed him and he paused for a bit before he reached out for her hand.

'Come with me. I left them over here.'

He led her through the crowd of men, which parted before them and began a low whistle after them and then the comments started. In the middle of the room, Lisa leaned back on Joe and let him fend them off. It was easy enough. Joe was popular and Lisa fancied herself fairly well liked. The crew were happy in drink and they were delighted with this extra gift of gossip.

'Go on, Joe, you lad, you. I suppose your excuse is that you never hold hands and tell.'

'You lucky dog. I'd be holding her hand myself if only my old dear would let me.'

'I know what you mean. I'm in the same boat. Sure I'd be holding her hand if your old dear would let me.'

'You're asking for it.'

'That's what I said to your old dear last night.'

'And I'd want her hand if it was legal.'

It was the last comment that got a rise out of Joe. 'What do you mean by that?'

'Nothing. Just that you catch them close to the school yard don't you?'

Then Larry stood forward.

'Ah, leave Joe alone.' He said 'If there's any cradle-snatching going on here, I'd say it was the other way around. It's a wonder what these women can do with make-up these days.'

In reply, Joe stepped forward and announced, 'Not that it is any of your business, but I am twenty-two and Lisa is eighteen. There is no one snatching anyone here.'

His words were greeted with laughter, just for the sake of it, and everyone returned to their own conversation. The fun was over. Lisa got her drink and her pie and decided that it hadn't been at all bad.

'So you told him that you were eighteen?'

The words were whispered low and close and she could feel them tremor down her spine. Joe was off refilling his glass, so she gulped back a swallow of beer and turned.

'I am eighteen. I'm still too young to have to lie about my age.'

'Well, then, you should learn to lie or that daughter of yours will be very disturbed. She must be six. What are you – in the Guinness Book of Records as the youngest mum?'

'I have no daughter.'

'So you haven't told Joe about her either. And I thought the man's main appeal was his worthy father look.'

'What are you talking about?'

'Don't worry, little lady. I won't make any trouble. I don't go busting up nests, but you can at least be honest with me. After all, I've seen her.'

'Who?'

'Your girl. I saw you out there.' He gestured to the

shop beyond. 'I saw you cooing and oohing and holding her with a "my baby" this and a "my baby" that.'

'Baby Elsie! She's not my daughter, goodness no. She's my sister, I mean my cousin.'

'Hey, steady now. You're running out of female relatives.'

His confusion allowed Lisa enough time to calm herself and describe her relationship with Elsie.

'So I am eighteen.'

'And you don't look a day over.'

And his hand snaked low while his eyes fixed her rigid. And his hand toured around her waist and rubbed itself across her lower belly.

'I never believed that such a figure could have carried a child.'

And his head bent lower and lower and his mouth breathed into her ear, 'Some night soon I'll buy you two lagers and you'll beg me for a third.'

Lisa pulled away from his words and his hand as soon as she could, but both of them knew that it was sooner than she wanted to. Larry smiled as he left. He was gone before Joe reappeared with his juice.

After their conversation of the previous evening, Lisa had decided that the time had come to introduce Joe to her family. She had broached the subject with her mum and her mum had been delighted and before Lisa knew what was happening, events had accelerated beyond her control.

Joe was expected for tea that very evening. Her mum had arranged to leave work early and was probably at home already trying to arrange a casual and haphazardly delicious meal.

Lisa had no doubt that Joe would accept her invitation. All she had to do was ask him. She had been postponing the inevitable all day and now it seemed even harder, but it had to be done. Joe was already talking about plans for later.

'So would you like to walk past the cinema and see what's on, or . . .'

'We could go to my house for tea.'

'What?'

'If you want to, I thought that maybe we could go to my house for tea.'

He didn't answer but his eyes lit up and before he realized where they were he bent his head to kiss her. He remembered himself before his lips met any part of her and he straightened himself and they smiled at each other. Lisa remembered her mum's story about her dad kissing her when they were both standing up on a crowded bus, and the kiss was so loving and he was so handsome and her eyes sparkled so much afterwards that the people around them had all sighed with the sweetness of it. Then she remembered Larry's hand.

Lisa had been right about her mum. Although she arrived home with Joe about a half hour earlier than usual, her mum was there before them and, by the look and the smell of the house, she had been there a long time before them. She greeted them in the hall, wearing a white frilled apron, just as Lisa pushed the door open.

'Hello, dear,' she cooed and kissed her daughter's cheek. 'I see you've brought a friend home. Aren't you going to introduce us?'

Lisa battled the urge to introduce this new maternal cliché as Mrs Lucille Ball. Instead she just glared at her mum and said, 'This is Joe. I told you that he might be coming.'

Her mum glared back.

'Did you, dear, and I clean forgot. Forgive me, Joe.' She took his hand. 'But luckily, I have a roast in the oven that will do three as well as two. You two go on through to the fire and warm yourselves. Dinner will be about another half-hour.'

She disappeared into the kitchen as she spoke and Lisa led Joe into their sitting room. He sat on the couch facing the fire. He seemed to know that the two armchairs were for Lisa and her mum.

'Your mum is lovely,' he said enthusiastically. 'Just perfect. I bet she bakes and everything.'

'You know she's only trying to impress you or embarrass me or something. She's usually not home until after me and on Fridays we usually have a take-away.'

'But she is perfect, isn't she?'

'Yes, she's perfect for me.'

A voice floated out from the kitchen. 'Why don't you show Joe our photographs?'

Lisa rolled her eyes and all three of them laughed and then Lisa shouted back, 'Why don't I show Joe our photographs and our bank statement?'

'Why don't you show Joe our photographs, our bank statement and that cake you baked last night?'

Joe joined in. 'Why don't you show me the photographs, your bank statement, the cake you baked last night and that jumper you've just finished knitting.'

Dinner was an enormous success. They ate beside the fire and carried the table from the kitchen in so they could do so in comfort. Lisa's mum took off her apron and relaxed into normality and Joe soon lost the high, nervous edge to his voice.

They talked about the weather and the coming Christmas and the food and then work. Joe had an aunt who used to work in Mitchell's and Lisa's mum nearly remembered her, but trying to place the face reminded Lisa's mum of all sorts of old stories of devilment, stories that Joe could well match from his experience on building sites. Lisa threw in her few tales of customers and Mrs Moran and then sat back and watched the other two compete. It was a lovely, friendly meal that lasted a perfectly polite length of time. At nine, Joe stood to leave and no amount of persuading would change his mind.

'It was a lovely evening but I'm not here to take up your whole night. I hope to see you again very soon.'

'Elsie' Lisa's mum prompted. 'I hope you will. Now that you know where to find us, you've no excuse not to sit through another ordeal of a meal.'

'Oh, I never think of anything as an ordeal once I'm being fed.'

'I'll walk you out.'

Lisa got her coat with the intention of walking him as far as the bus-stop, but he didn't allow her further than the hall door.

'This will do. Thank you for a lovely evening. I should have known your home would be as lovely as you, but it was nice to see for myself. Will you meet me tomorrow night? We could walk past the cinema and see what's on.'

Lisa remembered her mum's story about her dad and the picnic in the park.

'Can you think of anything else to do?'

He thought for a while and Lisa could see the options flit through his mind – a drink, a meal and then blank.

'We could maybe go and listen to some music?'

'Yes, that would be nice.'

'I'll see you tomorrow then.'

'Yes.'

'Hall's clock at eight?'

'Yes.'

He placed his lips on hers and she pushed hers against his and then watched him down the road and closed the door. His walk affected Lisa in much the same way as his smile did. It filled her with an echo of his kindness. But there must be more than films and meals and drinks and bands and she needed someone to show her. She closed the door slowly, and slowly returned to the sitting room and her mum's inevitable enthusiasm.

'He is lovely Lisa. You never said how lovely he was. Of course I always trust your taste, but if I had found him I'd be mooning about him day and night.'

'He is lovely and kind and funny, but he's not very handsome is he?'

'Handsome is nothing much. He's intelligent and kind-looking and that's far more important.'

'Maybe it's not handsome then. It's just he doesn't have that . . . something.'

'Don't make the mistake of clouding your judgement of reality with some half-baked dreams. Your grand-mother will love him. Do you think you could bring him to Sunday lunch sometime? I know everyone would love to meet him.'

'We'll see.'

Lisa didn't pursue the subject. She didn't want to have to try to picture Joe in Station Road. She guessed that she would be terrified by how easily he would fit in.

Lisa's mum knew exactly what 'we'll see' meant and she let the matter drop. Perhaps Lisa was right. Perhaps a family affair so soon would scare the young man away.

They both let the conversation die there, and when they started talking again it was about the practicalities of the day, the basic relaying of information. It wasn't until they were in bed and safely under the red glow of Lisa's mum's tasselled lamp that Lisa broached the subject she had been aching to explore.

'Tell me the story about my dad and the picnic, Mum.'

'You know it as well as I do. Tell it to yourself.'

'Please, Mum, or tell me about him dancing with you in the park.'

'I've told you too many stories, Lisa. You shouldn't pay so much attention to an old woman's stories. They're only worth the air they're carried on. It's time you started making your own stories.'

Lisa didn't know how to answer the sadness in her mum's voice, and so she didn't. She just said goodnight and dreamed her dreams of Larry.

CHAPTER 21

Lisa arrived in Moran's on Sunday morning for her last day working with the crew. There wasn't much to do and whatever there was was done almost immediately. Mr Moran was obviously distraught by the number of men working for double and a half times what they were worth at their best. He hounded them and barked at them and allowed no conversation to hinder their complete concentration.

By twelve it was as if the makeshift partition had never been. The rubble that had been strewn all over the place when Lisa first arrived was in a skip outside, the join in the wall had been plastered over, the floor was newly varnished and the tables in place. By lunch-time the crew was dismissed and Lisa was given the sizeable job of the last clean. Mrs Moran was to stay with her to supervise and to unpack and arrange the extra crockery and cutlery.

Lisa took up her mop and the crew trooped upstairs to their coats for the last time and then they filed out of the café for the last time. Lisa was very touched by their sincerity as they queued to shake her hand and wish her well even though she wasn't capable of focusing on what they were saying. She was waiting.

Larry waited until the end, until even Joe had gone, before he approached her. She finally heard him just as the street door swung closed on Joe, just as she had returned to her cloth and bucket, just as she was beginning to tune in to Mrs Moran's stream of conversation.

'Lovely boys, all of them. I'll miss them something dreadful. Some of them had grown as close as family to me and Mr Moran. I was just saying to him just this morning, Mr Moran, I said, if ever I had had a son. . .'

Lisa heard a clatter of boots on the stairs and she stopped listening to everything else.

'So, Posh, this is it then, this is goodbye.' He was standing before her, looking as serious as he ever had, with his hand humbly extended. 'I know that I may have given you a bit of a hard time now and again, but you must have guessed that it was only because I liked you. I'll miss working with you, Posh, so let's shake and part as friends.'

He had spoken in a controlled, public voice and he had stood at arm's length from her. Lisa was disappointed, but she wasn't blushing when she took his hand.

He shook it once, firmly. Then he pulled it sharply towards him and Lisa, attached to it, fell forward. He caught her, swept her downward and kissed her long and full on the lips. When he righted her, she was purple with emotion and Mrs Moran was screeching at the wit of it all.

'I'll see you tomorrow,' said Larry. 'I'll be in to finish that last bit of painting.'

He pointed to the new plaster and Lisa felt even more foolish. She should have known that.

'Cheerio then, Mrs M.'

'Toodily pip.'

He turned to go and, with the same movement, brushed his lips against Lisa's ear.

'Tomorrow, we'll arrange a night for that drink.'
And he was gone.

He left Lisa annoyed, indignant, embarrassed and uncontrollably smiling. It was a relief to her that she wouldn't be seeing Joe until Wednesday at the earliest. He was overdue on a new site that was running way behind schedule.

Lisa worked right through the afternoon, not pausing for a break. She rathered it that way – a break with Mrs Moran was too big a contradiction to bear. Anyway she was due in her grandmother's that evening. Sunday lunch had been held late for her and she wanted to be hungry enough to do it justice. By four she was starving and the café was sparkling and so she was dismissed by a grudging Mr Moran.

'. . . and here are your two promised uniforms. I have enclosed a packet of hairnets and I want your hair in them and not in the food. Oh, and you'll have to be here by half seven. We are going to open at eight with breakfasts.'

Lisa all but snatched the uniforms that were balanced over Mr Moran's arm and, finally infuriated by his continued references to her lack of hygiene, asked firmly, 'When am I to finish?'

'Five as we discussed.'

'Then I presume that from half seven to nine I am to be paid at the overtime rate of double and a half, the same rate as I am due for today.'

'Now, steady on.'

But Lisa didn't respond. She was hoping that her threatening silence would have the same effect as the gaffer's, and it did, up to a point. It was finally arranged that she would work from half seven until four with an agreed increment added to her basic wage. It was more than Lisa had hoped for and it meant that her trip could start a couple of months earlier than planned. She mentally blessed the gaffer and hurried on to Station Road.

The lunch was much as she expected it to be. Her mum had been there about an hour before her, certainly long enough to brief everyone on the details of Joe. When Lisa did arrive, Joe's name was on everyone's lips and they all agreed amongst themselves that his spirit was obviously in Lisa's smile and in that sparkle in her eye. With every blush and every grin, Lisa's mum saw her daughter's plans to travel diminish. But Lisa wasn't thinking of Joe.

'So, Elsie tells us that she has finally met this man of yours and that she likes him.' Lisa's grandmother's voice was weighed with sarcasm as she spoke on. 'Elsie's approval of the man sets all our minds at rest.'

'Mother, there's no need for all this.'

'Well, you can't deny that you could never straighten the virtue from the charm.'

'But Joe has no charm.' Lisa spoke defiantly from her mum's corner and everyone laughed that she would use such a strange boast about her friend. Bill, as usual, laughed on and, as usual, the conversation politely waited for him to stop. May started it off again with a string of safe, interested questions.

'How old is he? What does he look like?'

'Where does he live? Who with?'

'Where did he go to school? Who does he know?'

'When will we meet him?'

Lisa answered every question and then, because his

name was spilling out of her mouth and his kiss was burning in her mind, she brought Larry into the conversation.

She just had to talk about him, but everyone thought that she was trying to hide the sparkle of her love by changing the subject, and they all, to their satisfaction, thought that she couldn't. That even when she was talking about someone else, her bright little secret smiles kept breaking through. May nodded over at her sister. She agreed that Lisa might yet decide to stay at home.

'Hey, Elsie.' Lisa kicked her feet and ducked her head under the table to attract her cousin's attention.

Baby Elsie looked up from the puzzle of her father's laces. She wasn't used to being addressed during adult mealtimes.

'A man in work thought that I was your mum.'

Elsie laughed because Lisa was smiling, and Lisa righted herself, back on to the adult level.

'That's not so nice,' said May. 'How old did he think you were?'

'A lot older than I am. But it proves that me and Elsie do look alike, doesn't it, Mum?'

Lisa's mum nodded.

'This man, how does he know Elsie? Is he from here, and if not I would have you steer clear of him, he may be following you. Stalkers seem to be terribly fashionable these days.'

Even though Lisa's grandmother had spoken sternly and from her heart, everyone laughed at the thought of a fashionable stalker. But after Bill's laughter had died away, May pursued the question.

'When did he see Elsie?'

'When you were in the shop that time. He walked past, remember?'

'Oh, him. He looked a bad sort. He had that cheeky, brattish look that some men don't ever grow out of.'

'Oh, Larry's all right.' Lisa tried to sound nonchalant. 'He's just having a bit of fun most of the time.'

Lisa was happy to let the conversation lie there. She had said his name and that was relief enough for the time being. She didn't want to betray herself by giving too much away, but her mum already knew enough to ask, 'And the rest of the time what does he do?'

'Oh, I don't know, paints mostly.'

'Does Joe like him, this Larry?'

'How should I know?'

'He's not that chap that you were complaining about when you started there?'

'Probably, but that was before I knew him.'

Lisa's mum stopped probing. She knew as much as she wanted to.

The following day, Lisa arrived at work at half past seven in her black uniform dress with her starched white uniform apron and her hair tight in a bun in a hairnet. Her face was clean and make-up free and her nails were scrubbed pink and white. Her tights were as dark and as thick as decorum dictated and her shoes were sensible, but had enough of a heel to highlight the curves of her leg.

Mr Moran was delighted and Mrs Moran seemed rather alarmed at his enthusiasm and talked over his compliments as best she could.

'Well, Miss Gaskell, I must say I am very favourably impressed. You've really made an effort and you look quite the part. Yes indeed, and, even more than that, you look—'

'A lot cleaner than we expected, eh, Mr Moran? I was just saying to Mr Moran last night that he was not to worry. You are not to worry, I said. I said that I am sure that that Lisa of ours will scrub up a treat . . .'

'Let me assure you, Miss Gaskell, I never—'

'Now, Mr Moran, if you want us to serve breakfasts you'll have to let us cook them and to do that you have to be out of our way.'

Mrs Moran turned decisively towards her four-ringed cooker and her four waiting frying pans and Lisa turned to everything else. The setting of the tables, the positioning of chairs, the arrangements of cold foods and the brewing of the first pot of coffee. Mr Moran obediently left them to it.

The café was to serve hot breakfasts and cold or microwaved everything else. Mrs Moran was on duty to help with the breakfasts but from eleven she was supposed to leave Lisa alone in order to buy and prepare the food for the next day.

The lunch menu was mainly limited to pre-prepared sandwiches with only one hot option a day, usually quiche, and the afternoon menu was just made up out of the leftovers.

It was thought that Lisa could deal with all this on her own. The tables were to be waitress-served and from behind the counter Lisa was expected to deal with the usual takeout trade as well as making the salads and replenishing them on demand. She was also to make up sandwiches to specifications and there was talk of introducing soup on to the day-long menu.

Mr Moran was fully occupied with 'the salaries' and

'the VAT' and 'the invoices' and the excuse of the busy world of business that men of his generation use to veil their activities from their wives. He couldn't be expected to help at all.

In theory all this had seemed somehow feasible, but once the doors opened at eight o'clock Lisa realized her mistake and the extent of her exploitation.

The breakfast trade started immediately the doors were opened. Lisa wondered where all the shoppers, the chattering ladies, the labourers and the suited men and women had eaten last week and every week before that. They seemed so securely at home in Moran's, it was impossible to imagine them elsewhere. The ten tables were filled in as many minutes and they stayed filled long after Mrs Moran had made her prompt escape. She left at eleven on the dot. Lisa could have sworn that it was only nine.

For three hours she had been running from table to table to counter to till. Her head was reeling with lists of orders and her face ached from smiling. And her feet! She didn't want to think of her feet. The pain was working itself up her calves.

It didn't help that the fan over the cooker only worked at its lowest setting, or that the majority of customers smoked, or that Mrs Moran began to feel pressurized. At first Lisa would shout her orders above the noise of fifteen conversations and Mrs Moran would shout back a variation that was close enough to the original to confuse the matter entirely.

'One all-in special, one all in without the egg and extra bacon, one sausage, bacon and beans and one sausage, bacon and egg and four rounds of toast.'

'What was that, dear? An all in, an all in with extra

bacon, two bacon and beans and one sausage and egg?'

Lisa, halfway through a till transaction and making a pot of tea, would have to take the order again and even then it often came back to her confused. By nine she was writing the orders down and leaving them in numbered stacks beside the cooker but even still the plates were passed to her with a random heap of food on them. Sometimes Lisa doctored the plates. Some customers didn't notice the mistakes, some didn't care, but some complained; and though Lisa fended them off, some complaints reached Mrs Moran.

As Lisa guessed, that just flustered her further. She got redder and redder and damper and damper and her powder-blue lambswool jumper wilted from the heat and the amount of grease flung up at it.

'Well, if he wanted an egg why didn't he say so?'

'Shh, he did.'

'Don't hush me up, girl, and tell him if he ate it, he's to pay for it.'

'He didn't eat it.'

'Well, tell him to, and while he's at it to say a prayer for the souls of the starving millions. Now, there you go – three specials all without toast and one with two eggs.'

But even still, everything got that little bit worse after Mrs Moran had left. Lisa just couldn't put a stop to the breakfast trade. They kept coming and coming and ordering and ordering and, when Lisa said that the breakfast was over, they would point at the diners around them, still eating their sausages and bacon.

Some customers demanded the same, and some asked for it quite sweetly, and it took until almost midday before Lisa learnt how to put her foot down with a resolve, inspired by exhaustion, that couldn't be shaken.

'Breakfast is off.'

'But that man has . . .'

'Ordered long before you. Breakfast is off. If you would care for a sandwich . . .'

'He couldn't have ordered long before me – he's just starting.'

'He is a slow eater.'

'He is not. I've been watching him.'

'Then I am slow at cooking. Either way, he ordered long before you.'

'Well, I'll just have an egg then.'

'Breakfast is off. I can get you an egg sandwich.'

'You can have a boiled egg for lunch, I often do.'

'Not here, you don't.'

It was during this altercation that Mr Moran chose to come back. He glared at Lisa in passing and she glared back at him. It may have been that he realized the hugeness of her workload, or it may have been that he just never got the chance but, for whatever reason, Lisa was never reprimanded for her treatment of the customer and, heartened by that, she made her life that little bit easier by being a little bit tougher with the clientele.

The lunch-hour passed in a flurry of sandwich-making and counter service and the afternoon sped by in an effort to keep the chaos of rising dirt and disorder under control. It was a quarter past four when Mrs Moran returned and she hadn't appeared to cover for Lisa's two o'clock break.

Lisa's anger was well fuelled by adrenaline and when she had finished with her employer she had demanded and been granted an hour's overtime pay and a promise of future punctuality. Once that had been arranged, Lisa left. She walked straight through Mrs Moran's grating apologies and pleas for help.

'You wouldn't believe how sorry I am, love, but I haven't been resting myself, not a second. On my feet all afternoon I was, what with shopping and the amount of lettuce I washed, and the amount of eggs I hard-boiled, where's the extra tea, love? Are there any more knives, dear? Mr Moran, I said, I'll need more help with the food and now look I've spilled the milk, could you be a love and pass the mop?'

It wasn't just anger that marched Lisa out of the café, slamming the door on her employer's request. She was driven by the image of her bath and then her bed.

She was deep under a layer of bubbles, her head resting on the pillow of her hair and her skin purifying itself under a hardening layer of cosmetic mud before she remembered the lack of Larry. He had never come back to finish the painting and he probably wouldn't now. The smoke and grease from one day's business had camouflaged the join that had needed touching up and, anyway, there was no way he would be able to work around the customers. No, Lisa thought, he wouldn't be back. Mr Moran would put him off if he hadn't done so already, and Lisa would never see him again.

Her sense of loss at this realization shocked her. She saw her imagined youth of wild glamour fade out of reach. It was only now that she admitted to herself how many dreams she had manufactured out of their one kiss. Travelling alone didn't seem to have the same appeal now, not after she had plotted her trip around

Larry and all the adventures he would provide for her.

She lay in the bath until it got cold and then dressed herself in slovenly comfort and sat in front of the television with the intention of staying there for the evening. Her mum, when she did come home, had the good grace to serve up some dinner silently and withhold her taunts and bubbling 'I told you so's.

The next day was much the same, except that it started with the weariness of the previous day and then miraculously got better. Lisa knew now to check every plate as it was handed to her and she knew that for survival she would have to bark back at Mrs Moran and stand firm with the customers. Breakfast ended at eleven on the dot and though that lost the Morans a lot of trade, it gave Lisa time to organize herself for the lunch rush. And the lunch-hour passed more smoothly because Lisa had an idea of which sandwiches to stockpile and which salads were the more popular. Mrs Moran reappeared at two on the dot and Lisa rested for half an hour over a large mug of coffee and a towering sandwich that she had assembled for herself.

By four she was tired and she ached, but only superficially. The tiredness did not extend to nausea. A nap and a snack and she would be fine. She smiled to herself on the bus and once she got home she sang.

She was bursting with pride. She had got herself a difficult, arduous job that was very well paid and she had already amassed a surprising amount in tips. Of course Mrs Moran would demand her share of them, but still she was earning enough to be able to keep herself, help her mum, buy everyone the most wonderful

Christmas presents and then travel and see everything and meet all sorts of people and learn all kinds of things and do it without the thrill of Larry's kisses or the strong security of his broad shoulders or the wit and knowledge that lay behind the crinkle of his smile. And then she stopped singing.

CHAPTER 22

The next day was Wednesday and Lisa had arranged to spend the evening with Joe, but getting up on Wednesday morning was that little bit worse than getting up ever was before. Her bed seemed to be just serving to remind her body of the joys of sleep. It threw her into each new day aching for rest.

Lisa's mum found her palely stumbling around the kitchen.

'You look wrecked, Lisa, love' she said.

'I look wrecked and shattered.'

Lisa answered automatically, but it was too early for games and her mum didn't join in.

'The first days at a job are always the worst. Once you get used to a routine it does get better.'

'Oh, it's getting better already.' Lisa roused herself to sound animated. She was so pleased with her mum for not saying the obvious and opening up the old college argument. 'It's just that it's so early. I'll be much more awake by the time I get there.'

'All the same, though . . .'

Lisa tensed.

'. . . you should take things easy over this week. Maybe you shouldn't go out tonight. When you meet Joe after work the two of you should just come back here for tea.'

Lisa, relieved, agreed.

*

She arrived at work as usual at half past seven and as usual was let in by Mrs Moran. The first thing Lisa noticed was that Mrs Moran seemed giddy and flushed and the second thing she noticed was Larry in a white T-shirt and a pair of soft blue jeans balanced halfway up a ladder. He was turned away from his work, grinning, and Mrs Moran was obviously laughing at something he had said.

'Well, hello, Posh,' he called out. 'Me and Mrs M. here were having a bit of a chat about sausages.'

Mrs Moran started giggling again. Larry winked at Lisa from behind Mrs Moran's back and continued innocently.

'I only asked her if she preferred cocktail sausages to frankfurters and she was off laughing. I can't get a straight answer out of her. What about you, Posh? Which do you rather?'

Lisa had been stunned by his sudden presence, but the shock was wearing off now, giving way to excitement and nerves and shyness and a complete inability to function socially. She was barely listening to the question, let alone the innuendo, so she answered plainly. 'I like all kinds.'

The room exploded with Mrs Moran's laugh. Larry just smiled and stepped slowly down from his ladder.

'Well, then, I must be in with a chance.'

He was beside her, now, with his lips brushing her ear and his words rumbling low. 'What time do you get off?'

'Four.'

'At four I will be outside waiting for you.'

'But I'll still be in my uniform.'

It was Lisa's only concern. She forgot everything and everyone else.

'I like a girl in uniform.'

He stepped away and looked her up and down and smirked, in a way that proved his words, before raising his voice to banter level. 'That's it, then, Mrs M. Last bit of paint painted. If any of it falls off, I'll be seeing you, and if not, good luck.'

'Goodbye.'

He was gone and so was Mrs Moran's good humour.

'You seem to have made a bit of a conquest, but look out for that one. I'd say he's got more girls in trouble than the taxpayer can afford.'

She sniffed and went about her work in uncharacteristic silence that, unfortunately, didn't last.

Lisa tried to reach Joe during her ten o'clock break but he wasn't available and she couldn't try again until two. He was working on a big site and it took almost ten minutes to locate him. She had to call back twice.

When she finally did talk to him, his voice was high with concern. She had never rung him at work before. No one had. Especially on a site as large as the one he was on. It was a long walk to the site office and a long climb back up the scaffolding. Joe assumed that he wouldn't be called on to make such a trip unless it was an emergency.

'What's wrong?'

'I can't make it tonight.'

'Of course, of course, what's wrong? Is everyone all right?'

It was only then that Lisa realized her mistake.

'I'm sorry, it's nothing like that. It's just that I'm so tired.'

'Tired? You're not sick?'

'No.'

'Well, why couldn't you have said that when I saw you or just left a message with Mrs Moran?' He sounded almost cross. His voice had plummeted from its original pitch.

'I'm so sorry. I just wasn't thinking. I'll see you tomorrow maybe. I'll call you tomorrow evening.'

'All right. Goodbye.'

He hung up before Lisa could answer. She stared at the receiver in shock. He was either in an enormous hurry or she had been hung up on.

It made her feel a little easier about meeting Larry. As did so many clichés:

She and Larry were just friends.

She and Joe were just friends.

She hadn't promised anyone anything.

She had never told Joe that he was the only one.

And at the back of them all was that one fundamental truth that Lisa's mum's experience proved: all's fair in love and war.

The day passed quickly. Sometimes Lisa willed it along, pushing the hours by, and sometimes she longed to step in front of each flying second, needing to block its way. Her stomach was alive with anxiety and her face flushed with each imagined scene.

The coming evening was something she longed to run from, but she strongly felt it to be her destiny. Larry had the look of a lifelong love and he also had the look of transience. In Lisa's romantic vision, those two traits were interdependent.

At four Lisa left Mrs Moran in charge of the café,

went upstairs for her bag and coat and stayed up there for almost a quarter of an hour. She washed herself free of grease and tried to wash herself free of exhaustion and then, with just the help of a comb, she tried to tweeze herself into perfection.

When she finally left the café she had convinced herself that he wouldn't be waiting and she was desperately relieved by the logic of her argument. But when she stepped out on to the street, and after she had furtively glanced to her right before turning left towards home, after she had proved herself right, she was devastated with disappointment.

And then there he was.

'Hey, Posh, were you giving up on me?'

'I was just on my way home.'

'You're a fast worker. But it suits me. Home we go then.'

'Home to my mum.'

'And home's the place to keep your mum. You and me, we're out on the town.'

He grabbed her arm and spun her around and her coat swirled and her shoulder bag arched itself free and fluid and Lisa felt like she was walking on set on to a musical extravaganza, or a romantic comedy.

'So, Posh, I was thinking of dinner, maybe a show, a few cocktails for starters and a few snifters for finishers, and then I remembered that I'm nothing but a common labourer, so how's about a bag of chips?'

'I love chips.'

'Oh, do you? Do you just adore them? And do you eat them sometimes for a lark?'

Lisa laughed at his elaborate imitation of her accent, though there was a hardness in his tone that frightened her. But the fear melted into the heat of her excitement. She was only momentarily aware of it as a separate emotion.

Larry steered her down the road, across the street and through some estate. Soon she was in a totally unfamiliar part of town and she found herself dependent on Larry's guiding arm. She had been walking a little ahead of it, but, as the houses grew tighter and the roads got darker, she fell back into it. Larry noticed the change and tightened his grip on her far shoulder.

'So where's Joe tonight? Is he joining us later or should I not mention this evening to him?'

'He's not . . . he doesn't know.'

Suddenly Lisa felt mean and nasty. She hadn't stopped to think that Larry would be working on the same site as Joe, that he would be smirking at Joe tomorrow.

'I won't say a word.'

But Lisa didn't trust him. He was even smirking as he spoke.

'Honest, not a word.'

Lisa had stopped walking. She was deciding whether to leave now before things went any further.

'What do you take me for, some kind of fool? Why on earth would I tell Joe about this when Samantha is in and out of that site more often than a—'

'Who's Samantha?'

'My girl.'

'Your girl?'

'Yeah, like Joe's your man. There's a pair of us in it, eh. And here we are.'

He swung her into the welcome heat of a chip shop. She had no time to respond.

The owners knew Larry and he shouted his order over

the waiting crowd before he motioned Lisa into a seat. There were three booths to the back of the shop. Lisa chose the one furthest from the crowd. She had settled herself before Larry turned from the conversation he had started with two of the queuing men to call over to her. 'Not that one, love. Too close to the smell of the gents.'

The men laughed and Lisa got up and moved one booth up. She was tempted to leave, but that would be petty and anyway, what did she expect from such a rough diamond? The manicured manners of Joe, or the thrill of adventure and discovery? It was a long time before Larry joined her. He came just before the food. Lisa had planned to be aloof but he never gave her the chance.

'That was Bob I was talking to. Haven't seen him in a year, not since his wife came looking for him one night down at Lyon's – that's our local. It's near here. I'd bring you but Samantha's bound to be there.

'Anyway, his wife comes in with a kettle of boiling water and an empty milk jug and a mug and she starts asking us all, all Bob's mates, for the price of a teabag and a drop of milk, because she's at home dying with the thirst and with no money. And just then Bob comes up behind her carrying three pints, two for himself and he hasn't seen her, so he puts a pint in front of me and says "I got the two for myself 'cause I'm dying with the thirst." You should have seen his face when he saw the wife and she saw him and all hell broke loose and they've both been barred since. She's a bit of a nutter, that wife of his is. Seriously, like, I'd feel sorry for him. She keeps too many cats and I've never seen her in shoes, always shuffling round in slippers.'

It was just as Lisa had hoped – a whole new world

with a man to mind her through it. She ate her cod and chips and listened and laughed and remembered her mum's story about her first date with Lisa's dad. It seemed almost fatally identical.

Lisa had kept her coat on to hide her uniform. And then she remembered her mum and she sprang up. 'I've to ring home. Is there a phone here?'

'Hold easy, there. You can use the one in the back if you leave the money. What's your problem? Have to check if Joe has remembered to take his bath?'

Lisa didn't answer. She was already almost an hour late home and she could think of no excuse. She wasn't used to lying to her mum but something about Larry wasn't conducive to honesty. She asked at the counter and they directed her to the phone. Her mum answered on the second ring and Lisa still didn't know what to say.

'Hi, Mum.'

'Lisa, where are you?'

'I'll be a little late home.'

'Where are you?' She didn't wait for an answer. Lisa understood that she didn't want to hear a lie. 'Joe's been on, worried sick about you. He said you rang him at work to say you were too tired to open your eyes and look at him. Well, it's just a good thing that May was coming. I suppose you forgot that we had arranged that Joe was coming over here tonight. I got a roast.'

'Sorry, I did forget.'

'You had better come home soon, Lisa.'

Lisa did try to. She knew that it would be better to face her mum sooner rather than later and it would be better to face her when May was there. Lisa did try to get away but Larry proved too big an obstacle to get around.

'Home? Now? No chance.'

'I have to.'

'You only have to do what you want.' He moved closer and his lips brushed her ear and his voice rumbled low, spilling into her. 'Do you want to go?'

'No.'

'Well, that's settled then. I'll finish these chips of yours and you owe me a pint.'

He brought her to a dark, smoky lounge bar that was half-filled with hard-faced men and hard-haired women. Larry greeted a few of them and directed Lisa up to the bar. She bought two pints and told herself that Larry was a feminist. Joe would never have expected her to go to the bar, but that was obviously a bad thing.

She brought the drinks over to a table and Larry joined her almost immediately. He had been talking himself through the pub. Lisa was proud of that. Larry seemed to know everyone and everyone seemed to respect him. He couldn't be as bad as he made out if he was so popular.

They sat in silence for a bit, side by side, drinking their beer, and then Lisa asked the inevitable.

'What's Samantha like?'

'Not as pretty as you, a lot fatter, no way as smart and crap in bed. But then I may be telling her the very same about you.'

And then, without warning, when Lisa's glass was midway between her mouth and the table, Larry swooped and fastened his lips tight over hers. She fumbled blindly for the table and splashed some beer over her hand and then she forgot about it and everything else.

He left her flushed and breathless and he grinned when he saw the effect he had had on her. She thought he was grinning at the joy of the kiss and she smiled back. She remembered her mum's story about her dad and the way they had kissed in public and how everyone had sighed. No one was looking at Lisa and Larry – Lisa glanced around to check – but she felt that she had experienced a kiss as full of magic as the one her mum remembered and that experience was worth any amount of explaining and even a little bit of betrayal.

It took them a long time to finish their drinks and when they had, Lisa stood up and insisted on leaving.

'All right then, Posh, if you really have to.'

'I do.'

'See ya, then.'

'Aren't you coming?'

'No, I think I'll have another.'

'But how do I get home?'

'Depends where home is.'

She finally pinned him down to specific directions, but she still had to leave alone. It was another example of his basic feminist nature and proof of his complete independence, she told herself as she marched through the dimly lit streets. She told herself that it was refreshing to be respected rather than mollycoddled and then she remembered his kisses and lost the need to convince herself any further.

It was only half eight when Lisa arrived home, but May was already gone. That was a serious sign. Her mum was waiting for her in the dim silence of the sitting room. There was no television on, no radio playing. That was a very bad sign. As soon as Lisa closed the hall door her mum called to her.

'I want to talk to you, love, come in to the fire.'

The kindness in the tone that should have been angry was an even more ominous sign. Lisa walked in and up close to the fire.

'Sit down, love.'

She sat.

'Have you eaten? Do you want anything?'

'I'm fine.'

'Well, take your coat off.'

Lisa did that, and then it started.

'Where were you? I have a fair idea, Lisa. So just tell me the truth.'

'There's no secret about it. I was out with Larry, one of the crew. I told you about him.'

'Yes, you did, and I don't like one thing I've heard about him.'

'Well, then, you don't have to meet him.' Lisa's tone hardened and she moved as if to stand and finish the conversation.

She felt bad about Joe, she felt guilty about the dinner and she felt stupid that her mum had caught her out. But it was none of it serious and it was very little of it anything to do with her mum. Lisa was a woman now, a working woman and, as such, was entitled to keep her own business to herself if she chose to. She was just forming that sentence – she thought it would be a good note to leave the room on – but her mum spoke before her.

'I'm not going to say much, but there are some things that have to be said.'

Lisa sat still and listened. The gravity of her mum's tone seemed to run deeper than a forgotten dinner.

'I know you are too young to settle down and I know

that you have plans that don't involve anyone special and I think you're right to keep things that way. You know that I'd rather if you stayed home next year and maybe I did think that Joe would keep you here but. . .'

'Joe, Mum! Did you think I was planning on marrying him?'

'No. I know you're too smart for that, but I thought that you might be too fond of him to leave. But that's not what I want to say. I just want to tell you that Joe is a good man and that maybe you should appreciate him a bit more.'

'That's none of your business. He's good, all right – good at being middle-aged.'

'Well, not Joe then, but not someone like Larry. You should know the difference between those types of men.'

'And what do you know about Larry?'

'What you told me and what May told me and I know enough of life to know his sort.'

'You sound just like Mrs Benson, do you know that? Oh, he's a bad lot, he's from a bad family, let's all just talk about him and not give him a chance.'

'Well, if I give him a chance I can't give you one. Why did you lie to Joe today? Scaring the poor boy out of his wits. It was all I could do to stop him calling around to check on you.'

'If it hurts you to lie so much you could have told him. I was going to anyway.'

'It's not just Joe. It's that I think you're looking for the wrong things in a man and I think that that might be my fault. I just want to put some things straight.'

'What things? All right then, tell me. What should I be looking for? Their wallets or their father potential?'

'No. Their standards and their morals.'

'Like you did?'

'Yes, like I did. Your dad was, is, a good, moral man.'

'And what about your morals then? What about Fran, all those years ago? What did you do when she came calling to you and you were out with her husband?'

They were both standing now. The force of their words had driven them to their feet. Lisa had never argued like this with her mum before. She was giddy with the excitement of it and the fear, and the frustration and the guilt of it. She could no longer control what she was saying. The words came out on their own and even as she spoke them she regretted them, and knew that they would be there for always and she would always regret them. Her mum shouted her answer. Her mum never shouted.

'I never did anything on Fran Burrows. And hasn't Fran taken enough already? She left me out of my home for years, she took my family, and I won't have her coming back from the grave to give you an excuse to throw yourself away on the likes of that Larry.'

'What do you mean, you never did anything? Didn't you take her husband?'

Lisa's mum didn't answer and her silence stretched between them. Lisa allowed it time to grow into a denial. The two women stood facing each other, shocked and scared, and then, in a voice as low as it could be, Lisa asked her question. 'Who was Jim Bowles?'

'Jim Bowles was your dad and he was a dad to be proud of.'

There was no more to be said, or there was no more that would be said. Lisa waited, but nothing else came from her silent mother.

'I think I'll go to bed, then,' she said. 'I'm tired.'

'Good night, love.'

But Lisa closed the door on her mother's endearment and for the first time she turned off her mother's bedside lamp and, curled up in the new darkness of her bed, she cried.

By morning, life had carried them beyond their row, but the words of the argument were still between them and everything they said to each other had to be layered with enough politeness to clear that wall.

CHAPTER 23

Lisa didn't see Larry again for a whole week, but she saw Joe the following evening and, though she had planned to break up with him, his concern for her well-being and his apologies for his treatment of her over the phone made it impossible for her to do so. Anyway, she wasn't even sure if she wanted to.

It was so comfortable to sit beside him in a cinema or a pub or a restaurant and relax into their easy flow of conversation. Or just to walk beside him and know that he saw it as his responsibility to guard her against the gathering cold. He would tuck her under his coat and wrap his scarf around her head. He made her feel more than beautiful – he made her feel perfect. And, raw from her fight with her mother, she needed someone to make her feel special.

As well as all that, his smile was sweetly crooked and his walk filled her with some kind of emotion, something softer than passion but something that made her feel worthy. All that seemed like too much to dispose of without a bigger reason than a couple of kisses.

So Lisa decided not to break up with Joe and she convinced herself that no harm had been done, that she didn't much care for Larry and that she would never see him again.

But she did, on the following Wednesday. He walked into the café towards the end of the breakfast rush, took a table and sat staring and grinning at Lisa. Mrs Moran saw him first.

'Well, hello, stranger,' she bellowed over to him, and then in a lower voice, but not low enough, she continued to Lisa. 'Well, there he is and I've no doubt it's a breakfast with you he's after. I've warned you to watch out for that one and I've done my duty. I can do no more. It's as much as I would do for my own daughter if I had one . . .'

Lisa knew the rest of the speech so she left Mrs Moran to continue it to herself and went to serve Larry. It was as difficult as she imagined that it would be.

'What would you like?' She tried to sound as official as she could.

'Now, there's an offer a man doesn't get every day. I'd like a lot of something that can't be served in public.'

'Well, what can I get you then?'

'Do you want me to spell it out?'

'If you're not eating you'll have to leave.'

'Now, is that any way to treat a kissing friend? Do you know that you didn't even say hello, let alone smile. What's the worry? Is lover-boy Joe on the prowl?'

He ducked his head and glanced around furtively with such a sudden and shocking look of complete terror that Lisa laughed. She stopped as soon as she realized that her laugh could be construed as being directed at Joe, but it was too late. Larry was smirking at her in that conspiratorial way of his.

'How are you fixed for tonight?' he asked, moving his face forward and up to hers as he spoke, running his hand up as far as her elbow.

She pulled away. 'I have to be home. My aunt and my cousin are calling over.'

But Larry just laughed. They both knew that Lisa wasn't going home, and she didn't. He was waiting for her outside the café at four o'clock. She walked straight into him and he closed his arms around her tight enough for her to convince herself that she didn't have a choice and she allowed herself to be walked into another illicit evening.

This time, when Lisa rang from the chip shop, her mum didn't expect any explanation.

Lisa said, 'I'll be a little late home.'

And her mum said, 'That's fine.'

Lisa hung up and imagined her mum and May and Elsie by the fire talking and laughing and hopefully missing her. And she imagined Joe spending the evening watching football in a loud pub filled with the warm camaraderie of his friends and she tried to imagine Samantha and wondered if she believed the lie Larry must have produced and she felt small and mean, but she still went back to Larry and her half-cold chips.

'I've eaten them, love. You weren't fast enough. You have to be fast around me. Like, last night, I was walking home and I got jumped on by three lads. They thought they had me, you see, with the element of surprise, but they got a shock – I was too quick for them. Look for yourself – not a scratch on me – but you should see them.'

'That's awful. Did you know who they were? Did you go to the police?'

He didn't even bother to answer.

The rest of the evening was much the same as the last one they had spent together, except that Lisa stayed a little later. There seemed no need to rush home to her new, polite mother.

Larry never explained why he just appeared on Wednesdays and Lisa never asked. She just built her week around him. Joe accepted without question that he wouldn't see her on Wednesdays and Lisa accepted that she wouldn't see May and Elsie and sometimes it was worth it. Lisa never saw enough of Larry for him to prove his potential, but then he hadn't sufficient opportunity to damn himself completely either, and sometimes Lisa felt that she was living the stories that she would tell when she was old. But only sometimes, and usually when they were kissing. It hadn't yet dawned on her that her stories were all the same. It was just the locations that varied.

Larry allowed her access to very little information about himself and he asked her no questions about herself. Initially Lisa had found this liberating. She had imagined a love unbounded by class or the clutter of past lives. But, as time wore on, she felt that maybe such separateness was, in itself, limiting.

It was the complete opposite with Joe. She had been invited and had accepted three invitations to tea in his house and by the third time felt completely at home there. Joe's mum had grey, curly hair and fat arms, plumped up from years of baking, and his dad called Joe's mum Mam and he smoked a pipe and was very fond of fishing. Joe told Lisa that they both loved her, but Lisa knew that though they were lovely to her, they hardly saw her, they were so dazzled by their pride in their only son.

And Joe had been invited and had accepted two

invitations to Sunday lunch in Station Road. Lisa was glad of his presence there. Somehow her family circle had grown too small for her. But even so, it was after his second lunch there, just before Christmas, that she was forced to break up with him.

She and her mum were perfectly pleasant to each other now. They never mentioned the row and her mum never mentioned Lisa's Wednesday nights, but Lisa could feel her mum's displeasure and maybe Lisa's mum could feel Lisa's distrust and her ever-present and never-spoken question. Whatever bonds had been fused or fluid between them were broken now and jagged with disappointment and dishonesty. They both pretended that everything was fine and they both took the time to politely avoid any form of confrontation.

And it wasn't only Lisa's mum who seemed distant. May was as well. Ever since she had arrived in Lisa's life, May had spent almost every Wednesday with Lisa and her mum.

Lisa used to love those Wednesdays. She still did and she missed them, but she assumed that they just went on without her. She never knew how her presence had alleviated the tension between the sisters. Baby Elsie was too young to cover over the past of eighteen years ago on her own, so the sisters were usually left facing it without being able to mention it, and in front of so much that was unsaid, the trivia of daily living dwindled into inconsequence and silence.

But Lisa never knew this and so she didn't understand May's new coldness towards her. She assumed it was because her mum had told May about Larry. And if May knew, then Bill knew, and sitting down to Sunday lunch,

Lisa would talk to her grandmother and baby Elsie and imagine disappointment behind every word the others directed at her. After the third Sunday, Lisa's grandmother noticed enough to comment.

'When I was young, we expected nothing from winter and so settled to enjoy it. Nowadays, with all this talk of Christmas, everyone is irritable waiting for it and irritable after it. A cross humour for a full quarter of a year is a high price to pay for a few presents.'

'No one's cross, Mother.'

'You are for one, Elsie, and you have that way when you're cross of making everyone around you irritable. You always have had.'

'That's just not true.' Automatically, May came to her sister's defence.

'And if it's not, what or who has got you in a pet? Or do you think it mannerly to snap at your elderly mother?'

For some reason, Bill laughed and they all had to wait for him to stop. 'Oh, don't mind me,' he said eventually. 'It's only what with "pet" and "snap", you'd think you were talking to a poodle. Reminds me, what's the difference between a dog that likes fires and one that hates them? One lights bogs and the other bites logs.'

The table of women sighed in exasperation. Even baby Elsie joined in, thinking it was a game of blowing.

It was the following Sunday that Lisa brought Joe along for the first time.

Lisa's grandmother treated the occasion with tremendous respect, overpowering Joe with the full force of her attentions. It was only after Lisa had introduced Joe that she realized that her grandmother obviously expected such a formal meeting to end with an announcement.

Mrs Gaskell had opened the door to Lisa, her mum and Joe, dressed in her usual sombre, Sunday frock but she had added a large glass butterfly brooch and a drooping chain of pearls that was weighed down with a heavy cameo.

'Good afternoon, everyone,' she said, extending her cheek to both Lisa and her mum. They kissed it obediently and didn't comment, even though this kind of welcome was usually limited to Christmas morning.

'And this must be Mr . . . ?'

'Joe.'

'Mr . . . ?'

This time Joe answered for himself. He stepped into the hall, extended his hand and said, 'Mr Greene, and thank you very much for the invitation to lunch. I hope you will call me Joe.'

'Very well, and you may call me Mrs Gaskell. Please make yourself at home. There are drinks laid out in the parlour if you want to help yourself.'

At this, Lisa and her mum caught each other's eye more in amusement than surprise. In an effort not to laugh, Lisa bundled Joe forward into the sitting room, and Lisa's mum went through to the kitchen and May.

Lisa was astonished to see that there were drinks laid out. Except at Christmas time she had never seen alcohol in her grandmother's house before. But on closer examination, she and Joe realized that the bottles were just for show. There was an empty sherry bottle, a bottle of ancient, sticky fruit schnapps and a congealed cream liqueur.

Joe and Lisa laughed silently and, out loud, for the

benefit of those in the kitchen Joe said, 'No thank you, it's far too early in the day for me to drink.'

As if poised on cue, the sound of a man's voice brought Bill into the room. 'So this is Joe, eh? The famous Joe.' He laughed.

Lisa groaned with embarrassment and left the two men together.

The lunch went very well. Joe's presence kept everyone interested and on their best behaviour. May was as charming as she could be and one or two of Bill's jokes were perfectly timed and very funny. Baby Elsie sat under the table throughout the whole meal, as usual, delighted by the extra pair of shoelaces to play with. Lisa's mum was a little territorial about the guest, but then Lisa reasoned that she deserved to be – she was the only one who had met him before.

It was Lisa's grandmother that was the problem. For once she didn't snap at Elsie or vaguely refer to her past mistakes or her lack of wealth. For Joe's benefit she seemed to be doing the opposite.

'A woman can never settle too young,' was her opening gambit, and although May tried to talk over her she was not to be distracted. 'Look at Lisa's mother, Joe. She had Lisa young and she started work young and she had all the time and the energy necessary to enjoy her child, her job and buy that lovely house. It's just the perfect size for two. It would be difficult to find another so suitable, don't you think? And in such a good neighbourhood.'

'Oh yes, it's a lovely house.'

'People call it small but I call it compact and practical. And I always think it's so important to have children early in life. I was almost thirty when I had mine and I know the toll it can take out of an older body. Are you from around here, Mr Greene?'

'Close, but my parents only moved here when they got married.'

'Well, that's a relief. I never hold with this sticking to your own. It's always the children who suffer. If you marry your neighbour your neighbour's children are likely to be as ugly as your own.'

This was going too far. Before Joe could collect himself to answer, the table erupted with diversions.

'How's Mrs Benson's hip, Mother?'

'Did you get to buy that dress?'

'Did you see the match yesterday, Joe, lad, or do you follow the game at all?'

'Has anyone thought about Christmas yet?'

'You weren't watching that documentary last night, were you?'

It worked for a while, but towards the end of the apple tart when every topic had been exhausted, Lisa's grandmother turned to Joe again. 'So now you have met us all, Mr Greene, all Lisa's family. Has she met yours yet?'

'I've met his parents.'

'And is that all there is to meet?'

'I have a sister working abroad.'

'Well, no doubt she will be home for Christmas. Perhaps then the two families might get together.'

Lisa didn't allow Joe time to answer. She thought that maybe he would like the idea.

'Goodness, Joe, look at the time. If we don't hurry we'll miss it.'

'Miss what?'

'The film.' She glared at him.

'Ah yes, the film. Well, thank you very much, Mrs Gaskell. It was a lovely lunch and I'm pleased to have met you all.'

He smiled around the table and then stood slowly, giving Lisa's grandmother all the time she needed to ask him for the following Sunday.

'I'm afraid I can't.'

'Well, the Sunday after.'

'That would be grand, thanks.'

Lisa groaned and Bill, sitting beside her, laughed at her reaction. She smiled down at him. He was right to laugh, the whole affair had been hilarious and a lot more enjoyable than the last few lunches at Station Road.

And so Joe came to lunch again and this time Lisa's grandmother kept the old bottles in her old cabinet and limited herself to wearing her pearls and cameo. It was a far more relaxed affair and Lisa and Joe stayed until the end.

Lisa was proud of Joe then and the way he fitted so well with everyone. May and her mum charmed him, Bill made him laugh and baby Elsie sat on his knee and he talked to her properly, telling her how exactly like Lisa she looked, and he chatted comfortably to everyone else.

Lisa was proud of him and his manners and his casual ease, but all of that scared her as well. Every joke her family shared with Joe, every bit of himself that he gave them seemed to bind him closer to Lisa and far too close to her future. It was too easy to let him laugh with Bill and eat her grandmother's food and eventually follow him into marriage and on and on and on with perfect ease.

Lisa wanted more. She wanted to present her family with something or someone of her own. Someone they would be forced to respect as hers, because they would have to admit that they couldn't understand them alone.

Someone whose presence could only be explained by a forceful emotion – not like Joe. She could almost see the reasons surrounding Joe: he was a fine-looking chap, he had a good job, he treated her so well, he was so easy to get on with.

And then she thought of Larry. Larry wouldn't fit into any of those reasons. Larry wouldn't fit in her grand-mother's house at all.

The previous Wednesday he had kissed her close to Station Road, by the park. She had been pressed up against the railings and above his head she could see a cold bare moon and two bright stars. Her face was warm with his breath and her hands were warm under his coat, but her legs were cold in her thin tights, her back was sore from his weight pressing her against the railings and her heart was heavy with guilt for Joe and for the Sunday coming.

She knew that she would have to break up with Joe and she knew that an extra Sunday lunch would make that all the harder to do and watching Joe beside the fire in the thick of her life, she knew that the task was almost beyond her. She decided to postpone any decision until after Christmas. But all that changed later on that evening, after she and Joe had left her grandmother's house and were walking aimlessly towards town and maybe a drink or maybe their separate buses.

'I liked your grandmother's idea about our families meeting for Christmas.' Joe was talking with complete confidence. 'You'll love my sister. She's really like you and my mum is bound to get on with yours. Maybe your lot could come around for a drink in the morning. They'll have to meet at some stage.'

'Not necessarily, Joe.'

But he wasn't listening.

'I think I know what I'm getting you for Christmas.' He reached for her hand and squeezed it and tucked it into his pocket. 'I saw it last week. I hope you'll like it. Do you want a hint? Some say it's a girl's best friend.'

It was too much. Lisa knew she couldn't take gifts from someone that she felt already detached from. Even if it wasn't a ring it was bad enough that Joe felt he could joke about such things. She realized now that a month would make all the difference. They had been walking automatically towards their favourite bar, but Lisa couldn't even wait until they were there. This had to be done immediately, out on the street in the cold depth of winter. She pulled her hand out of his and her nervousness, her guilt made her sound angry.

'No, Joe.'

'Don't sound so worried. Girls have other friends besides diamonds don't they?'

'No, Joe, this isn't going to work.'

He knew what she meant, but for a moment he tried to block the impact of her words.

'Do you not want a drink? Would you rather go straight home?'

'Yes, Joe, I'm going home and I don't think we should see each other again.'

She had stopped walking and he turned to face her. She didn't know what reaction she expected, but she knew that she hadn't expected this. He was perfectly calm, deadly in earnest and, though hurt hardened his voice, his eyes were still kind.

'Is there anything I can do about this or are you decided?'

'No. I think it's for the best.'

'Are you going to tell me why? Have I done something on you?'

'No. It's just, well, I am still going away and, well, it's just a bit too much, you know, families and all and. . .'

Her reasons trailed off. Even to her ears they sounded limp, but she couldn't mention Larry. She couldn't be honest and tell Joe that he was lacking in that crucial romantic spark. He waited to see if she had anything more to say and when it was obvious that she hadn't, he walked on towards the centre of town and their separate buses. She trotted by his side, embarrassing herself with clichés.

'It's just me, honestly. I'm still really fond of you. You deserve better. I would like to keep in touch still.'

Finally he spoke, and though his words were harsh, Lisa only discovered that later, when she remembered them. At the time he had just sounded sad.

'You're insulting me now, Lisa. You know you sound relieved. I always knew you were going and I would never have stopped you. I thought that you would have given me that much credit. I'm sorry if you thought that I was a bit much, but I never meant to frighten or insult you by being nice to your relatives, and I introduce all my friends to my parents, they expect it. I'll leave you to your bus-stop.'

They walked the rest of the way in silence. Lisa's bus was waiting there. She stepped on to it, turning to Joe as she did so. Standing up on the step, she was level with him. For a moment she faced him eye to eye. It was the only time she had ever felt cinematic in his presence.

'Goodbye, Joe. I'm very sorry.'

'Goodbye, Lisa. You can't apologize for your feelings.'

He walked away then. For the first time he didn't wait until the bus took off. Lisa watched him go and she ached for him or for herself – she didn't know which.

She arrived home tired and sad and wanting nothing more than to cry. She wanted the comfort of her mum, but without having to explain herself.

When Lisa came in, her mum was sitting reading, ready for conversation. 'Hello, love,' she called out.

'Hello.'

Lisa went straight into the kitchen.

'I'm in here.'

'I'm just making tea. Do you want a cup?'

But eventually Lisa had to go through to her mum.

'You're home early.'

'Yes.'

'Is everything all right?'

Lisa nodded.

'May really likes Joe. She was going on and on about him to me.'

Lisa nodded and turned on the television. Her mother took a couple of breaths and twice decided to leave her advice unsaid. Instead, she returned to her book and waited until later, until they were in bed and Lisa was breathing too quietly to really be asleep. She had noticed Lisa's face during lunch. She could almost see her daughter's thought patterns and it was right that she should – she was responsible for them. But her advice came out clumsily, as most advice does. She wasn't to know that she was too late.

'You seemed to have a nice time today, love, and Joe looked to be enjoying himself.'

'Yes, he did.'

'It's good he likes coming.'

'Well, I suppose if he didn't he wouldn't.'

'It's just that maybe if he didn't you wouldn't.'

'We're not joined at the hip, Mum. I go where I want.'

'Then it's good that you like going to your grandmother's. You know, May and Elsie miss you a lot on our Wednesdays.'

'I see them enough.'

'Not as much as you used to. I think May is a little hurt.'

Lisa knew her mum was right and was only trying to be tactful, not mentioning Larry, and if she was honest she would have to admit that she missed their Wednesdays too, but she felt that she just couldn't do without Larry's kisses. That excuse, however, did her no good. It was only a further reminder of her guilt, and so she sat up in her bed and snapped out her answer.

'If May misses me so much, there are another six days in the week. I go out one night a week and I'm treated like this.'

'You know that's unfair. It's not that you go. It's where you go and who you go with.'

'And when you were my age, you did as you were told all the time I suppose?'

'Please, Lisa, this isn't about me. It's about Joe.'

'And Joe is my business. Mum, I like him. I know he's every mother's dream but . . .'

'I know all the buts, love. Didn't I give them to you?'

And as was now part of their new norm, Lisa's mum turned off her light and they both tensely settled to sleep.

CHAPTER 24

Christmas came quicker than Lisa could have imagined. She had to work up until Christmas Eve, so for weeks her lunch-times and days off were spent shopping. Her nights were spent in school reunions, in a flutter of parties and absolutely necessary annual meetings and her Wednesdays, all except one, were spent wrapped around Larry.

One Wednesday he didn't turn up and Lisa disgusted herself by waiting for a full hour for him. He didn't ring the next day, or the next and she further disgusted herself by ringing him at work. She hung up before he got to the phone, but she had still rung him.

Lisa didn't really expect Larry the following week, but when he did turn up as nonchalant as ever, she disgusted herself fully by going out with him again and quizzing him on his absence.

'Where were you last week?'

'All sorts of places. What day and what time were you thinking of?'

'You know well.'

'Oh, do you mean Wednesday?'

'Of course.'

'Well, look who's turning into the right little wife. You'll not turn me into your next Joe, you know. By the way, I think you were a bit tough on our friend. A good man like that!'

'Leave him alone.'

'I will for a kiss.' And he kissed her. 'You know I'm glad you're finished with him. It's nice to think I'm the only one with access to these lips.'

'Don't fool yourself.' But she laughed. She liked to think that he was jealous of her.

What Lisa fancied as a new closeness between them was cemented when Larry produced a Christmas present for her. The next Wednesday was Christmas Day. They wouldn't see each other again until after the event. Lisa had known that, had agonized over it and had eventually decided that a present would not be in keeping with their relationship. She regretted her decision now, sitting in one of their dingy haunts, when he placed a small felt box in her hand.

'It's just something I got that I thought you might like,' he said, looking up at the television in the far corner. He obviously had no interest in the effect his gift would have. Lisa opened the box and gasped. Her reaction had more to do with the cost of the present than it's beauty. It was a thick gold link bracelet that was long enough to droop dangerously from Lisa's thin wrist. Larry heard the gasp and turned around with a satisfied grin.

'You like it, then?'

'Of course. It must be worth its weight in gold.'

But Larry didn't laugh. 'It's just something I got,' he said again and Lisa knew he was warning her not to ask questions.

With a thrill of excitement she slipped it on. 'I'll get it tightened. I don't want to lose it.'

'Okay, then.'

She had a perfect excuse to put it straight back in its box.

It was quite exciting to be given such a thing, but it was another thing to wear it. As soon as she got home that night, Lisa hid it under her mattress and left it there.

There was no real need to hide it, though. Her mum never came over to her side of the bedroom any more. She never sat on her bed to chat a little before getting changed for bed. She never dropped in a cup of tea or chocolate just in case Lisa wanted one. She would never have questioned a strange black box on her daughter's bedside table. She would have known that it was no longer any of her business and though this realization hurt them both, they neither of them knew what to do about it.

Christmas was coming. It came and nothing changed.

That Christmas started later than usual, but once it started it fell straight into ritual and so initially carried itself along quite smoothly.

Lisa and her mum woke early, but not as early as in previous years. Their bedroom was already bright with the day when they sat up and nodded across at each other, one, two, three and then shouted, 'Happy Christmas.'

Their Christmas hug was a little shorter than usual, but their stockings were filled with more expensive presents than ever before.

Ever since the year Lisa had discovered her mum's stocking stuffed with newspaper, she had insisted on filling it herself. This year was the first time she had any real money to spend though and it was also the first time she had ever felt the need to prove some emotion.

This year, she had filled her mum's stocking with perfumes and handmade chocolates and a beautiful finely spun scarf and those very expensive tights that her mum loved but seldom bought and then rarely wore for fear of laddering them.

Lisa watched her mum's embarrassed pleasure as she uncovered gift after gift and then she spilled the contents of her own stocking out on to her bed. The first thing she saw was a watch and she understood all too sadly that her mum was trying just as hard as she was to over-compensate.

They smiled over at each other and then Lisa climbed out of bed and shouted up the chimney, 'Thank you, Santa, but you've made a mistake. You've given too much to a girl who's not been very good.'

They both laughed and Lisa's mum shouted up a similar thank you and they went to their Christmas breakfast in their dressing gowns, arm in arm, warm in their unspoken truce.

It was like every other Christmas breakfast. They ate smoked salmon and cream cheese and they flicked through the comfort of an array of children's films. Afterwards they dressed in their chosen finery that was waiting, washed, ironed and aired, in their wardrobe, and then they walked across the park to Station Road.

Every year Lisa's mum filled in that walk with her story about her only Christmas with Lisa's dad, but this year she wouldn't be drawn and instead she asked about Joe.

'I haven't seen much of Joe recently.'

'No. Can we walk past the rose garden?'

'It's out of the way. Will you be seeing Joe today?'

'No, I don't think so. Tell me again about your rose bush.'

'He could call around later when we get home. You

still have to exchange presents don't you?'

'I know. We do have time to detour a bit.'

'It's not the time of year for the rose garden. Why don't you ring Joe from your grandmother's?'

'Because he's probably busy with his own Christmas.' Lisa finally snapped.

She didn't want to admit that she was missing Joe and this was definitely the wrong time to tell her mum that she had broken up with him.

Her mum humphed at the tone of her daughter's reply. They walked the rest of the way in silence and they walked all over their morning's truce.

Once they were in Station Road, though, everything was all right again. The house was loud with baby Elsie's excitement and May's and Bill's delight in her. Once Lisa and her mum arrived, the whole family gathered together in the parlour for a toast. Lisa's grandmother had covered the top of her sideboard with bottles of alcohol. The old bottles of schnapps were still there as well as a new bottle of sherry, one of whiskey, one of gin, one of vodka and at least six of beer.

'What would you like as a Christmas toast?' she asked, sweeping her arm proudly over her collection. Lisa and her mum gasped and May and Bill and baby Elsie laughed.

'Our mother has taken to the drink,' May explained.

'Which reminds me,' said Bill, 'what they used to tell us in school – the family that drinks together stays together, and them that prays together sinks together. Wasn't that it?'

Everyone laughed and he laughed that little bit longer, even longer than baby Elsie, who tried her best to outdo him, even though she didn't understand the joke. She saw it as just one more reason to be happy. She watched the adults get their drinks and ran between their legs while they toasted the day. After they had all clinked their glasses and sipped their first sip, Lisa's grandmother explained her quantity of alcohol.

'I've invited in a few of the neighbours for an afternoon drink. I've almost asked them so often that I think they've got together and put all their almosts into a pot and cooked themselves up a definite because I don't remember saying anything to anyone this year at all.'

Everyone laughed again, even though the threat of Mrs Benson was enough to ruin any meal. But it wasn't ruined – it was as tasty as ever. The dishes came and were passed around and emptied and then the presents came and were passed around and admired. Baby Elsie was alive with delight and pounced on each parcel taking as much interest in those that weren't hers as in those that were, often going as far as opening them. But no one minded. Her excitement kept them all occupied and talkative.

The neighbours were due to call at four. It was presumed that by that time the dishes would be cleared away and the dinner would be sufficiently digested and it was, but only barely. The neighbours were frighteningly punctual and by five past four the front parlour was filled with Mrs Benson, Mr and Mrs Elliot and Mrs Ryan. At ten past they were joined by Mr and Mrs Plunkett, even though Lisa's grandmother swore that she never ever even almost invited them.

The dining table had been folded up and squeezed back into the bay of the window and the side tables had been moved into the hall to make room for the extra chairs from the kitchen, but even so the room was very cramped. A subdued Elsie grabbed her new favourite doll and crouched with it under the table. Lisa soon gave up trying to tease her out and she concentrated on serving drink to her grandmother's guests.

'So this is Elsie's little one, eh? Not so little now.'

'Do you know that I knew your mum when she was only the size of baby Elsie there?'

'Any mistletoe here, or should I have brought my own? And any chance of a kiss without it?'

'Bob! Sorry about that. Now, that's your last drink for the day.'

Lisa smiled at them all and side-stepped the two old men and their wet mouths and pawing hands. They had lived too long, those men. They had lived past all they had associated with manhood, their jobs, their strength, their intellect and now they were forced into this women's world, a world bounded by a strict social etiquette and one that they didn't understand. Mr Elliot and Mr Plunkett both sat close by Bill laughing at everything he said and drinking everything he offered. His pity carried them along and, despite May's disapproving looks, his pity extended to matching his guests drink for drink.

May sat with her mother and her mother sat with the ladies of her circle. They each spoke at length about every member of their family and what they were all doing for Christmas. They sipped their drinks and nibbled at cakes and sandwiches and spoke loudly over the noise of the men. Lisa's mum hovered between the kitchen and the parlour. She tidied and fussed and offered too much food and too much drink to the wrong people.

Her mother tried to glare her back to her chair, but
Lisa's mum wouldn't settle. These gatherings and these
conversations still always ended in a sudden silence
around her – a silence that lasted just long enough to
remind everyone of what had happened, and Lisa knew
that that silence and that memory included her and so
she busied herself trying to tease Elsie out from under
the table and helping her mum to fill any empty glasses.

And then the silence came.

'It must be great for you to be home, May, especially
now with the baby?'

'Oh, it is.'

'But hardly a baby now at all, how time flies.'

'And it must be lovely for you, Mrs Gaskell, to have
your grandchild around you at Christmas.'

'I'm very lucky to have the two of them so close.'

'Oh, yes, because you were away as well, Elsie,
weren't you?'

'No, I was always just the other side of the park.'

'But we didn't see you for so many years, not since
. . . oh!'

And silly Mrs Plunkett slapped her first three fingers
to her mouth and then came the silence and out of it
everyone could hear the booming voice of Bob Elliot as
he clapped Bill on the back and shouted, 'Good one,
good one, but can you tell me the difference between a
broken hoover and a randy sailor? One is a sucker that
fails and the other is a fu—'

'Bob! We really must be going, Mrs Gaskell. It was a
lovely cake. You must give me the recipe. Bob!'

But Bob had a full glass that he wasn't leaving behind
and his wife had to sit with her coat on, prolonging her
goodbyes while he drank it. And when he had there was

nothing going to move him until he had sung his song. No amount of 'Bob!'-ing' from his wife could stop him, and so everyone was forced to sit back and listen to his tear-sodden rendition of *My Mother Far Away*. Five long verses later, he stumbled to a close:

> And though she lay there dying,
> Her heart it was still crying,
> For the son that left her door
> To return. . . never more.

Mr Elliot was on his feet before his friend's tear-filled eyes had time to empty themselves.

'What kind of a tune is that for the day that's in it? I have one now that'll start us all smiling again and if I was fifty years younger it would start me dancing.'

He winked at Lisa and his wife groaned.

'Ah, no, Paul, we don't have the time, we should be getting back.'

'It'll be a sad day when we don't have time for a song. Amn't I right?'

The assembled party politely nodded.

'Right so.'

He drew as much breath as he could into his puffed-out chest and rushed out the first two verses of *The Dance My Love Likes Most*. Then he stopped.

'Right now, everybody, the chorus.'

> 'Oh my love she likes the polka
> And she dances the waltz a treat
> But the steps she loves the most
> Are the ones that take her down my street.'

It worked. His generation knew the song well and remembered it too well. Their eyes glazed over and their wavering voices pulled them back to places and times that they usually found easier to forget. Their voices faded into a different kind of silence and this time their tears were allowed time to spill a little, and then May turned to Bill.

'Will you do a song now, Bill?'

'Ah, no, it's been too long.'

'Well, yes it has,' said Lisa's grandmother decisively. 'It has been far too long. I remember you had a lovely voice.'

'Had, before these years of whiskey and cigars.'

'Stand up there, lad.' Bob pushed and Paul patted. 'Give us an old rendition.'

'There's nothing I know the words of.'

'There must be, Bill, you used to know all the words. What was that one you used always to sing?'

May wanted him to sing now, quite seriously. She wanted them all to know that her husband had the best voice, and she didn't want to be so publicly denied a favour. 'For me, Bill?'

'Not tonight. I think I've even got a cold coming on.'

'We'll not push you, then.'

But Lisa's grandmother's tone was hard with anger. She felt her daughter's shame and she too had wanted to prove that she could provide a man capable of entertaining.

The silence that followed the polite family row was the last one of the party. Mrs Plunkett, still in her coat, stood and repeated a shorter version of her earlier goodbyes and the rest followed suit. Lisa's grandmother walked them all out to the hall and then, to show her displeasure, went straight into the kitchen. May, with an almost identical expression to her mother's, went and snatched baby Elsie out from under the table and in an overly sweet voice cooed to her, 'We're going to get you washed and brushed and in your nightie and wrapped in your quilt and in the car and home.'

Ignoring her husband and any views he might have on the matter, she left the room.

'I haven't sung in years. There's many a wife would be delighted by that. Bob's, for instance,' he said to Lisa.

She laughed because she was used to laughing at everything he said and went to help with baby Elsie. Bath time was always fun with May and Elsie, but when she went upstairs the door to the bathroom was locked. She turned the handle and May called out to her, 'I'm better on my own tonight, Lisa. Elsie is overtired and if you come in she'll just get herself all excited again. We'll see you downstairs.'

So Lisa ambled downstairs again, trailing her hand on the banisters, feeling more than a little lost. From the kitchen she heard the sound of her grandmother's final round of cleaning and through the half-open door into the sitting room she saw the backs of her mum and her Uncle Bill. They were sitting together on the sofa, facing the fire.

Lisa didn't mean to eavesdrop. She was only deciding where to go when she heard them speak and even then she wasn't eavesdropping, she was only overhearing.

'You should have sung, Bill. They would have been so proud of you and now you've upset them both.'

'I couldn't sing.'

There was a long silence that Lisa was going to walk

in on, and then her mum continued, 'There are more songs than that one.'

Something about the pathos in her mum's voice stopped her and something about her uncle's answer froze her. He was angry.

'It wasn't just a song I gave you, Elsie. It was my music. I was being honest when I said that I couldn't remember any songs. Afterwards, all the songs turned into *Moon River*.'

'You could have sung *Moon River*, Bill. Not all promises last for ever and that promise has lasted long enough.'

'My promises last longer than yours. I would have thought that you knew that.'

'You shouldn't be talking like that, Bill. You can't feel anything after all these years.'

'Of course I don't. You have some opinion of yourself, don't you? What do you take me for?'

And then, as if to himself, in something closer to the softness of his normal voice he continued, 'But that's why I have to keep that promise.'

Now Lisa really began to eavesdrop. She crept closer and curved her body towards the open door, straining her ears to pick up and her mind to keep every word her uncle spoke.

'Don't you see that the only thing that made what we did all right was our – or my – belief in it. I have to remember how I thought that it was so true and so lasting that it was worth sacrificing everyone for, and to think that I nearly did. For you! If my giving you *Moon River* means nothing, then everything we said means nothing and all it turns into was some nasty, lusty fumblings.'

'No!'

'I know it was only ever that to you, but I have to believe that it was something more, because I have to live with May and I have to live with my guilt, so I have to put some kind of weight behind it. Now, do you understand?'

His anger was almost gone. He just sounded drunk now, drunk and sneering.

'Not really. A bit, maybe.'

'Over the years, the promise grew. Maybe that's what all promises do. Maybe that's why they get so hard to keep, the older they get. Every song did turn into *Moon River*. I forgot all the others and so I don't sing any more and I loved it so much. But then, that's fair. It reminds me that I love May more.'

'I'm so glad to hear this, Bill. I thought today that . . . I was worried that . . .'

'Don't flatter yourself, Elsie, not on my account, not where May's concerned.'

He stood up and walked around the sofa. Lisa's mum's head followed him and Lisa caught a glimpse of her as she looked up at him. Her love far outmatched his disdain. The cruelty of his words barely touched her.

'I never would, Bill.'

He didn't answer. He fixed himself another drink and Lisa walked into the room and he laughed. 'Where's that little girl of mine? Is she clean enough to come home yet?' He laughed a little more. 'Tell me, Lisa, why can't a toddler ever get ahead in business? They take too many rusks.'

Lisa never had to react, never even had to laugh – May and baby Elsie arrived behind her and the room was almost immediately filled with goodbyes and baby

Elsie's last whimpers of delight. Lisa smiled and nodded and thanked everyone and stared hard at baby Elsie, snuggled in May's arms fighting against sleep. She had Lisa's square chin and far-set eyes and, behind her, Bill had the same. It was so horribly obvious that Lisa ducked her head, feeling suddenly naked.

They all said that it had been a lovely day and they all kissed each other and nobody noticed that Lisa avoided Bill and gave May an extra squeeze.

CHAPTER 25

Lisa didn't say anything on the walk home. In her grandmother's house she had been vocal and adamant about declining a lift, but once outside, alone with her mum, she couldn't talk. But her mum didn't notice and they walked on in silence, both dressed in their annual best, both weighed down with bags of presents and packages of food, both laden with all the trappings of festivity and both so silent.

They walked around the park. It was late now and the gates were closed. Lisa walked close to the railings and remembered all the stories – the rose bush, the dancing, the picnic – and into them all she placed her Uncle Bill, but he wouldn't fit. She stripped the years off him, she gave him hair and the fashions of the day, but she couldn't give him the necessary words or the charisma of her dad.

Her Uncle Bill never stood sideways to the mike clicking his fingers with a swing to the beat. He never painted words of love on to a daisy. He never swept her mum off and away in a dance that deserved applause. He never drove a scooter through the night to deliver a present to an old lady. He was never clucked at or pointed at for being undesirable, but he was her dad and God knew who the man Lisa loved was. God knew who Jim Bowles was.

They were almost halfway home when Lisa's mum spoke.

'I'm tired. The afternoon took it out of me. But if you want Joe around, that's fine. It's just that I might go to bed.'

'You'll have to stay up, Mum.'

Lisa was surprised at her own calm and her mum was obviously shocked by it.

'What on earth do you mean?'

'We'll have to do a lot of talking and I'm not prepared to start on the street.'

She strode ahead. Her mum called to her, but she wouldn't slow down. The rush of the night air helped, her mum's confusion helped and her growing tiredness finally blocked out all her thoughts. She arrived home about five minutes before her mum and took the time to try to settle her body and mind.

Her mum walked into the unknown and, as mothers do, tried to take the advantage. 'Have you gone mad, Lisa? What on earth is wrong with you? How dare you walk away from me like that!'

'I couldn't bear to walk beside you.'

Her mum dropped what she was carrying and sat heavily in her chair. Lisa had spoken as if she meant what she said. Lisa waited for a moment, wanting to form her words, but still they came out heavily and incoherently.

She had to draw them out of herself. She didn't want them in the room in their sweet little house where Santa was still respected. She didn't want the burden of them and the responsibility that came with them. She wanted her mum back, not this stranger who sat in front of her. She wanted her mum to hold her and tell her a story and rock her to sleep under the glow of her lamp and she wanted the memory of the dad she had loved. So the words came out heavily and they fell into the room.

'Who was my dad?'

'Jim Bowles.'

But Lisa's mum was only answering out of habit and Lisa wasn't listening. She had hardly given her time to reply.

'Who was Jim Bowles?'

'Your—'

'My Uncle Bill, wasn't he?'

'I don't . . .'

'Wasn't he?'

This time Lisa shouted and her mouth stretched and tears splashed out of her eyes. 'I heard you! I heard you! I heard everything he said to you and he hates you and it was Bill all along. Him! Him and his laughing! And he's my dad. And May! And you told me all the things you told me. You lied about everything and Fran! You let her believe. . . you let me believe some stupid, stupid story that I loved. I was so stupid, so thick, all those stories just to make you look good. I hate you and May will hate you and Bill already does and so did Fran and . . .'

'Stop, Lisa, stop.'

Her mum had been trying to talk, trying to stem the flow and now she just stood and shouted over it. Lisa stopped, not because she was told to but because she was breathless and she had run out of words. She slumped into silence and her mum, misreading the sudden curve of her daughter's shoulders reached out as if to hold her.

'Don't you touch me!'

'You don't know what you're saying, Lisa, love.'

'I do know and I'm not your love. God I even look like him. Does everyone know except me?'

'No one knows. Not even Bill.'

'So it is him?'

'Yes.'

'And all the stories, all everything?'

'I suppose I exaggerated them.'

'Exaggerated! They were lies, weren't they? And why? Why did you make me love some nonsense? It's no challenge to mess with a child you know. Did it make you feel big or something?'

'Will you let me talk?'

'Why? To hear more of your lies?'

But Lisa sat down and, after vocalizing her refusal to listen, she silently waited for some form of comfort.

'There's no room for lies in this. It's only a story of a few words. Bill was going around with May and we were all young. I never thought back then that actions or decisions could last for life or else I would have thought a little deeper about everything. I never thought that Bill and May would get married. She never seemed that keen on him, but I loved him, and we started seeing each other and I thought that it was going to be fine, that May would break up with him or he would break up with her and eventually I would be with him and no one would mind.' Lisa's mum was talking softly now. She was allowing herself to remember those golden days of potential, and seeing that glow about her thawed some of Lisa's anger. She began to listen with something deeper than her ears.

'Then the accident happened, down by the docks. You see, most of my stories were based on some truth. It was James Burrows and his friend that fell in. I think they were more or less pushed, just like I told you, by people they owed money to. But anyway, it was Bill who jumped in after them. It was dangerous enough, though Bill always did play down his part. I heard about it all when I was down town and by the time the story had got that far people were saying that someone had died. I was blinded with panic and I went racing home in a state and there was Bill, sitting facing me. I think I mentioned James Burrows because I had to give some reason for my hysteria and it was that that made the others put me and James together later.

'But what I remember most about that night was May. She warmed Bill and fed him and gave out to him for risking himself and sent him home with just a slight peck on the cheek, but once he was gone, she collapsed and I held her as she sobbed on and on. She kept moaning and saying, "I could have lost him, I could have lost him," over and over. I held her and I felt sick, because I wanted to cry for that same reason and more. I wanted to cry because I was beginning to understand that I would never be with Bill.

'I was pregnant with you then, but I didn't know it. I knew a couple of weeks later, when the crunch came. Bill got an offer of a job away and it was a job he always wanted. He planned for him and me to take it up. It's what we had always planned. The last time we had met, he was full of it, but I started off by asking all the wrong questions. I kept asking about May and how he was going to tell her and how much would he miss her and did he think he loved her and he tried but I could tell by his answers that he was confused.

'You see I wasn't even that good, Lisa. I loved him enough that I would have gone with him and left May if he had been sure about me. But I saw by him that he had real feelings for her, probably more realistic than the

ones he had for me, and between them and May's
feelings for him, I had no option but to step down, so I
did.

'I told him that I didn't fancy moving, that he was
asking too much, and that I didn't think it was fair of
him to ask me to go when I was expecting. His face lit
up, and then I did the hardest thing I ever did. I laughed
and laughed and told him that he wasn't the dad, that
I wasn't just his, that I had no intention of settling for
the likes of him. I went on and on. At first he couldn't
or wouldn't believe me, but finally, after as many
insults as I could think of, he left. A few weeks later, he
and May left for good and a few months later you were
born.

'I wouldn't tell anyone who your dad was and that's
where James Burrows stepped in. He hopped it without
a word just before I began to show – probably owed a
bit too much money – and, by not admitting to who
your dad was, I wasn't stopping the rumours, so they
took hold, and Fran came crying and screaming, and
your grandmother was disgusted by me, so I left.

'May wrote and wrote to me offering me all the
support I could want. She even wanted me to live with
her. But to take anything from her seemed like too big a
sin, so I cut her off.

'Bill wrote to me once. I suppose he must have heard
about the mess from May and he asked me again was I
sure about you. I said I was and so he assumed along
with the rest. As the years went on any doubts he had
faded completely. You see, it was his fault that they
couldn't have children up until now, up until modern
science caught up with them. You were a young man's
luck. If that hadn't been the case, he would have noticed

the likeness. I always have and I've always been scared that someone else would.'

She stopped there and looked up at Lisa, pleading for some sign, but Lisa had none.

'I knew you wouldn't be able to limit a story to a few words,' she said and got up and left the room.

Lisa's mum could see the red corner of the forgotten gift squashed down the side of the chair that Lisa had been sitting on. This year it was a cheque for far more than Lisa's mum could afford. It was supposed to have been the ultimate peace-offering.

CHAPTER 26

Lisa's mum gave Lisa time enough to get ready for bed and then she followed her into the dark bedroom. Lisa wasn't even pretending to sleep. She was just curled away from her mother, lying breathlessly silent. Lisa's mum sat opposite, on her own bed, and turned on her soft red light. Lisa didn't react. She heard her mum talking and she still didn't react and then her mum spoke on, knowing not to wait for a response.

'I never meant to hurt anyone. Not you, not May, not Bill, not Fran, not my mother, but I ended up hurting you all. You're right – not that they hate me, but none of them respect me. Not that I ever did anything to earn their respect, but I never did anything bad intentionally. I was never as bad as they all think I am. I never went with anyone's husband. I never turned my back on my family purely out of pride.

'I told the stories, Lisa, because I wanted you to love your dad and so I took the soul of Bill and imagined it into every girl's dream man. They were only meant to be bedtime stories, I never thought that they would grow so big.'

After every statement she paused and listened, but Lisa never moved. She became cramped and sore, curled into her tight ball, but she wouldn't give her mother the satisfaction of seeing her move. And so Lisa's mum talked on.

'I wanted you to love your dad, Lisa, and I'm not that subtle. I thought that I had to make up big stories so as to get that love across to you. I didn't think there would be any harm in it. I knew that I would never be able to tell you who your real dad was, but I didn't want you to hear the rumour about James Burrows. I didn't want you associated with the likes of him.'

'Then why did you give him to me?' Lisa didn't move. Her question was muffled by her pillow, but still her mum answered enthusiastically, grateful for any contact.

'What do you mean? I didn't give you James Burrows.'

'Jim Bowles, James Burrows. Sound different, don't they? I don't think.'

'Jim Bowles was a nursery rhyme. He had nothing to do with—'

'Are you going to tell me that he had nothing to do with a leather jacket, sideways looks, a sexy voice, a wild streak, a motorbike, with it all, all of it!'

Lisa was sitting up now, forced out of her tight curl by the passion behind her words.

'James Burrows was a—'

'Or maybe taking May's man wasn't enough. Maybe you had your eye on Fran's as well.'

'Lisa! Listen!'

And Lisa did, partly because she still automatically responded to her mother's orders, and partly because she dearly wanted to find something in her mum's excuses to believe in. She curled back tight under her blankets and pretended a sulky lack of interest while she listened.

'James Burrows was nothing like the man I described to you. Burrows was a thug. There was no beauty about him, no imagination. He was nothing. He wasn't even good-looking. But your father did have all I ever said he had. He had more than my words alone could ever describe, and so I made up stories for him. But even so, most of the stories were true in part. Your dad did save people from drowning and he did give me *Moon River* and he could sing and we did meet in the park a lot. He didn't do the things like the daisies and all but he did stand in front of the train once, for a joke, and we did plant a rose bush together for Christmas. The main thing, the only thing, was that he loved me and I loved him and we were happy together, so that was enough.'

Slowly the familiar drone of her mum's voice thawed Lisa out of her tightness, but she couldn't be thawed back into conversation. And so her mum talked on.

'He was all I had, Lisa. He was my only romance. No other man ever lived up to the way I felt about him. He might not be a prince, Lisa, but he is a very good man and a dad to be proud of. Maybe I should have remembered that myself, but I didn't. I made up those stories as much for myself as for you, if I'm honest. If you just say the facts, my one love affair does sound a bit sordid – a few meetings with my sister's boyfriend. Maybe I tried to make it too special. But I never thought of the stories as lies. I believed in them. I imagined Bill doing all those lovely things and somehow it seemed like it really happened.'

But Lisa wasn't listening any more, she was in her own world. For the first time she was confronting the reality of Larry.

Lisa stayed in bed late the next day, curled tight in her bed where she didn't have to face anything. It was the early afternoon when she finally got up, and then she just pulled on the clothes nearest her and walked straight out of the house. Her mum in the kitchen heard the front door slam and sank her head a little lower.

It was a cold day and Lisa was forced to walk quickly. She walked down the slant of her road and headed for the park. She was driven by an adolescent dramatic urge to twist the knife. She was going to sit cold in the park and remember every lie her mum had ever told her. But when she got there, she got no satisfaction from it. Knowing the truth, the stories all seemed pitiful, a lonely woman's fight for romance. Lisa walked on.

She found an open café and visited two school friends, but it wasn't a day for casual visiting, so she didn't stay long with either family. Towards evening she walked on to Joe's house and, after watching it for a while, she went home.

Her mother was there in the cold sitting room, waiting beside the empty grate.

'I was worried,' she said.

'There was no need to be.'

'You never got your forgotten present.'

Lisa opened the wrapped envelope that her mother held out to her.

'It's a traveller's cheque.'

'This is too much.'

'I can afford it.'

'So you want me out of the way this badly.'

'No! But I know you want to go that badly.'

'I do.'

'When you think about it, Lisa, I didn't do anything that bad and I have been punished long and hard by everyone. I couldn't bear it if you started on me too.

You're all I ever had, Lisa, love. You're my happy ending.'

'Goodnight.'

Lisa said it kindly, but it was all she could say. She had never seen her mum cry before and she was too confused to face those tears now. She left it until they were in bed, under the glow of her mum's lamp, before she said what had to be said.

'I'm going to go away as soon as I can, hopefully in the next couple of weeks.'

'So soon! Where will you go?'

'I don't know, but I don't have enough money to go too far or to stay too long.'

It was all she could give, but it was enough. Her mum accepted it as a promise to return and a promise of some future forgiveness.

Lisa was due at work the next morning. She walked to the café in a daze. It seemed like weeks rather than days since she had been there last. As usual she was greeted by Mrs Moran.

'Isn't this lovely, Christmas hardly here but it's gone, and all that fussing, wouldn't you wonder what it's for? How was yours? Did you have a lovely time? We tried our best, of course, me and Mr Moran, but it's a season for children, really, isn't it and as you know . . . well, we always have our health, eh?'

'I want to hand in my notice.'

'What?'

'I want to hand—'

'I heard you. Am I allowed to ask why? And how much notice do you mean to give us? We'll need at least a month.'

'I was thinking of a week. I'm paid by the week, so I think I need only give a week.'

'Need only! Need! What about what we want or what you owe us? Need, indeed! A week's notice, after all we've done for you. Taken you in as if you were our own. Like a daughter to me, I used to say to people when they asked why we didn't get someone with more experience. Trained you up in the catering trade for free and this is how you repay us. There's people your age that have to spend time and money in a classroom learning what we gave you for free with good money thrown in. Oh, I should have listened to Mr Moran. He always said that you could tell someone's moral fibre by their personal habits.'

'My personal habits are fine.'

'So you say but who are you to judge? Wait till I tell Mr Moran.'

It was a slow morning. The commuters who made up the bulk of the breakfast trade were not yet back at work. Mrs Moran had plenty of time to berate Lisa's decision and Lisa had nothing to do except stand and take it. And before the trickle of lunch-time shoppers swelled enough to take everyone's mind off the affair, Mr Moran arrived to have his say.

'I can have you up for breach of contract, you know.'

'We never had a contract.'

'A verbal one still stands in a court of law.'

'We never had even a verbal one.'

'You'll get no reference from me.'

'I don't want one.'

'I'll make sure you don't work in this business again.'

'I'm moving away. I won't be looking for a job here.'

'You can work your week, but expect no money at the

end of it. You'll have to work up enough to cover the cost of your uniform.'

'Well, if you make me buy it, I won't return it and you'll have to get another one for my replacement.'

'What are you standing here talking for? You've not left already. There are tables to be cleared.'

It was a horrible day at work and after the weekend it was going to be a horrible week, but Lisa knew she could face it.

It was that theory that drove her. Soon she would be away, soon she would be alone, soon it would be over and soon she could think.

Her weekend and the days that followed passed in a blur of activity. Her money had to be sorted, her clothes packed, a hasty farewell said to her friends; her mum had to be avoided and Mrs Moran tolerated.

'She's leaving us, you know,' Mrs Moran would shout over to every regular customer, 'without as much as the decency to wait till we're on our feet and like a daughter she was to me.'

At home Lisa's mum watched her daughter pack and sort her life, and she stopped trying to explain her past. Now she was only worried about grabbing a bit of their future.

'Where are you going?'

'I haven't decided yet.'

'When will you go?'

'As soon as possible. I may as well.'

'Are you still so angry?'

But Lisa couldn't answer. She didn't know if anger was at the root of her jumble of emotions. Did hurt stem from anger or did it turn into anger? When her mind settled would she hold her mother responsible for her confusion? Was a man that never existed worth grieving over? She didn't know. She only knew that she wanted to get away, and so she didn't answer, and her mum bowed under her silence and stopped asking questions.

On Wednesday Larry called early before Lisa was finished. He walked into the café and Mrs Moran's flat face lit up with the relief of a clichéd assumption, and for the first time since Lisa had broken the news, she smiled at her sympathetically and then nodded her into silence. A nod that obviously meant 'I'll take care of this one.'

'She's leaving us, you know,' she shouted over to Larry.

'Leaving? Better offer, eh, Posh?'

'But you'd know all about that, wouldn't you,' said Mrs Moran. 'Coming in here all innocent and taking advantage. Well, you took more than you bargained for with this girl, she's like a daughter to me and I'll not stand by. I warned you, Lisa, but I'm not one to say I told you so. I was young once and I know how hard it can be when you're up against a chap like this. You sit down there, girl, and take it easy and don't you worry about this nonsense of leaving and your story about going away. We'll not throw you out because of a little bump and you shouldn't give in to it and spend the next nine months sitting ashamed at home. No, we'll keep you on till the end.'

'But I'm not . . .'

Lisa was glowing with embarrassment. The half-full café was staring at her and Mrs Moran was keeping her pinned to a chair, holding her down by her shoulders. Larry was staring as well, but in horror.

'Well, don't look at me. I never even got the chance. I thought girls like her held out a bit longer. Does Joe-boy know, Posh, or is he in the same boat as me?'

'I'm not pregnant.'

'There's nothing to be ashamed of this day and age, love.'

'Oh, I'm off. Are you coming, Posh?'

'No.'

And he was gone, and that was the end of Larry. He was nothing now. Any echo Lisa had been searching for in him was an echo of nothing. She got her coat and walked home slowly. It was New Year's Day. Lisa and her mum had been asked to dinner in May's. Lisa had declined, but her mum was going.

Lisa was in bed when her mum came back, curled in her bed in the dark bedroom, ignoring any soft whisperings she heard. Only two more days to go.

On Friday morning she sat with her mother for breakfast. It was the first meal they had had together since Christmas.

'Today is my last day at work.'

'When do you think you'll go?'

'Early next week. No point in waiting.'

'Have you got a ticket?'

'I've myself sorted.'

'Are you going to see May? I told her about this, and your grandmother. I said that you'd see them before you go, that you'd explain to them.'

'That I'd do your dirty work.'

'No, no. I'll tell them if you want me to, but the decision is yours.'

'I can't see them. Don't you see that that's part of it?

Every time I see them now, everything I say to them is
going to be a lie or else some horrible truth that isn't
even my fault. Even baby Elsie – everything I say to her
is going to be a lie.'

'I know, Lisa, and that's what I've lived with. But they
love you. You can't go without saying goodbye.'

Lisa didn't answer, but she knew that she would go.
She went to May's that afternoon when she knew Bill
would still be at work. She had insisted on leaving the
café at three.

'I gave a week's notice, so now I'm working a day
extra and I worked New Year's Day. I deserve to get off
early.'

'Deserve! After the way you treated us, you deserve
nothing and us taking to you the way we did. If this is
what having children is like, then all I can say is I've only
missed out on heartache. Oh, I feel sorry for your
mother, you hard-hearted child.'

But there was nothing the Morans could do about
Lisa's going. She walked out at three leaving Mrs Moran
mid-sentence. The café door closed on her last familiar
speech.

'. . . and if it wasn't for my hips . . .'

May looked concerned when she opened the door, but
she smiled at Lisa and Elsie ran at her and Lisa smiled
back, but everything was horrible.

'Come in, come in and tell me everything. Elsie, if you
play by yourself for ten minutes, I'll make you chips for
tea and Lisa will stay and have them with us.'

'I don't know . . .'

'Yes, you do. We haven't seen you in an age and if
what Elsie is talking about is true we won't see you again
in a hurry.'

Lisa just laughed. 'Goodness, it's nothing that dramatic.'

She knew that she would never even hint at the truth.

Once she realized that much, she relaxed and the stories came easily. She was so fed up with work she said. She was so tired and she was beginning to see sense about college, so if she was going to go away she would have to do it soon. She'd saved much more money than she ever thought she would, so what was the point of hanging around? She had had a big row with the Morans before Christmas but she didn't want to tell anyone over the holiday so she would have been leaving there anyway and she might as well get her new job abroad. If she thought about it for any longer, she knew that she wouldn't do it. She could always come home. And finally she hung her head.

'But there's something else.'

'I thought there was.'

'I broke up with Joe.'

And the tears that came with the statement were real and, as far as Lisa could tell, they stemmed from that statement.

'Oh, Lisa, love, I'm so sorry.'

'Yeah, so it seemed like a good time to go.'

And there were no more stories needed. There was just a lovely tea and hours of games with Elsie, Lisa's sister. Even if it was always going to be a secret, it was still special. But Lisa left when Bill came home. He was still too much to cope with.

'What's this, a European wake?' He laughed.

'The end of a wake,' said Lisa and she got up from her game with Elsie. 'I have to be going.'

But he wasn't listening. He was smiling down at baby

Elsie and she was giggling up at him. 'Daddy, Daddy, why are owls so popular with the birds?'

'I don't know, why *are* owls so popular with the birds?'

'Because they have the wit to woo.'

She laughed longer than he did, but he waited for her to stop before he told his joke.

'I have one too. What's the difference between a feminist and a chicken breeder? One mates hens and the other . . .'

'Hates mens,' baby Elsie shouted and the two of them laughed all over again, although baby Elsie had no idea what the joke meant.

I knew him too late, Lisa thought to herself. *He's a child's man, and if I had grown up with him I would have loved him*, and she felt the loss of that much keener than the loss she had felt for her mum's dream man.

'So are you going away then, Lisa?' He straightened up from his laugh and was asking seriously.

'Yes.'

'Where?'

'I'm not too sure.'

'Next week, is it? Well, I'll give you a lift to the airport or wherever with your stuff.'

'Thank you, that would be great. I'll let you know the time.'

Lisa accepted without question. It seemed right and fitting that her father should see her off. Suddenly that was very important. It also softened her goodbyes to May and Elsie. She would see them again before she left.

CHAPTER 27

The next morning, Lisa went to Station Road. She was confident of herself now and her ability to gloss the truth. She had planned a more subdued version of the speech she had given to May, but she hadn't planned on her grandmother.

Mrs Gaskell opened the door to her granddaughter and immediately, without a word, turned on her heel and led the way into the parlour. She sat in her chair and waited until Lisa was settled opposite her before she spoke.

'So you've come to say goodbye.'

'Yes.'

'And about time. You're away then?'

'Yes.'

'Funny time to be going.'

Lisa took a deep breath, ready to start her excuses.

'I dare say you have your reasons. Funny Christmas we've had this year as well. Haven't seen much of you, not even on New Year's Day.'

'Well I . . .'

'I suppose you have your reasons. Christmas Day I think was a mistake. Bill is a very good man but he could never hold his drink and he needs very little encouragement to test his capabilities in that department.'

'Oh well, I didn't . . .'

'No, you wouldn't notice him as a drunk but he tends

to talk that bit too loudly and remember that bit too much.'

Lisa stared and her grandmother nodded.

'This wall behind me is no thicker than a paper partition, but I didn't hear anything I hadn't heard already. A mother knows her children and a woman knows what goes on in her own house. Sometimes we pretend not to, but what's the point in that? Don't be too hard on your mother, Lisa, love. She did one bad thing and spent many long years maybe doing worse things but always doing them for the best.'

'But I thought . . . why didn't you say anything. . . to Fran or anyone?'

'Best hurt a stranger than your own and I was never fond of that Fran anyway. Enough now, we'll have tea and talk about the future.'

But when Lisa's grandmother returned with her tea tray, she returned to the past. 'Young girls make stupid mistakes and old women aren't much better. If your mother had only upset Fran I'd have stayed by her no matter what, but I suppose for a while I sided with May and before I knew where I was, that while had lasted too long.'

'And May, does she know?'

'Maybe in her heart, but not in her head and Bill doesn't know at all and that's because men, even kind ones, don't have women's hearts.'

'So just no one says . . .'

'There's a lot in life that can't be said and that's why actions are so important. Can't you see how May treats you like her own child? And don't you ever forget how well your mother has always looked out for you. Because of her you are here today with all that life can

offer spread before you. What's gone never matters, only
the bits of it we choose to remember come with us and
who's to care what your mother chooses to remember
about your father or what you choose to remember
about what she told you?'

'But all I have to look back on is lies.'

'To some extent that's what we all have, that's what
keeps us sane. I truly believe that the summers of my
childhood were always sunny and the Christmases
always white, even though the met office can prove me
wrong. All I'm saying, child, is leave what's behind you
and what you can't change and do the best with what
comes your way and what you have to deal with now.'

Lisa nodded and listened on and left Station Road
with her past ironed a little smoother behind her. She
had planned to go into town, to a travel agency that she
had picked out, one with affordable fares to affordable
places that all seemed too foreign to her now. She
walked past it and on to the central rail station.
Eventually she might get a train to an airport but just in
case she didn't she bought a return ticket.

Afterwards she called to Joe's. She had stood for five
full minutes in a phone box, but in the end she had taken
the braver option. His mother opened the door to her.

'Well, hello.'

She made no movement to let Lisa in. The rudeness of
her stance and the sharpness in her voice made it evident
to Lisa that Joe had been noticeably upset. She hadn't
expected that. He had seemed so calm when they had
split up.

'Is Joe in?'

There was a long pause and then, with her eyes still
fixed on Lisa, she called out, 'Joe.'

He arrived almost immediately behind his mother and reached up for his coat hanging on a hook beside her. He squeezed around the other side of her and kissed her cheek in passing. 'See you later,' he said.

But she didn't move until Lisa and Joe were down the path and through the gate and so they didn't talk until they heard the soft thud of the door closing. Then they spoke together.

'Sorry about that.'

'Sorry for calling.'

They laughed.

'She's just protective.'

'I should have rung.'

They walked on, talking about Christmas and gossip, filling in the weeks they had been apart. They strolled aimlessly towards the park and, though it was cold, once they got there, they sat for over an hour. They didn't speak much but they said all there was to say.

Lisa told him that she was going away but that she would be back, that she wanted to go to college after all. She hadn't known that herself until the words were out. She said that she had missed him and that she would like if she could write to him.

He said that he would love to get letters from her.

'Did you miss me?' she asked.

'Of course.'

'Do you think that maybe when I come back . . . ?'

'I think things happen as they should if you always remember to respect your choices and recognize your options. If I'm not here when you get back, it will be because I've found someone I like better than you and if you don't come back to me it will be because you've found something or someone better than me. The best we can say is we'll see.'

The start of a story flashed through Lisa's head. *Once I knew a very kind, very wise boy . . .*

It was the first line of her first real romantic story and that was enough for one day. They got up and walked out of the park. At the main gate they pressed their bodies together and Lisa held her cheek against his for a long time. When they broke away they were both smiling.

Lisa was smiling most of the way home. For the first time she felt a happy excitement about her coming adventure.

In contrast to her new mood, her mum's waiting face was a shock. It was grey and tired with sadness. Lisa let herself in and an older version of what used to be her mum appeared at the kitchen door.

'Have you done everything you needed to do?' she asked apologetically. Even that much she felt was no longer any of her business.

'Yes.'

'You've bought your ticket?'

'I've bought my ticket and some nice new knickers.'

Lisa answered in a sing-song voice and she held her rail ticket out to her mum.

Her mum took a moment to smile and she swallowed hard before she took up the old chant. 'You've bought your ticket, some nice new knickers and gone to see your grandmother?'

'I've bought my ticket and some nice new knickers, I've gone to see my grandmother and I've gone to see Joe.'

'You've bought your ticket and some nice new

knickers, gone to see your grandmother, gone to see Joe and come home for your tea.'

They were both laughing now, laughing far beyond the joke. Lisa followed her mum into the kitchen, following the smell of her favourite dinner cooking.

'I've bought my ticket and some nice new knickers . . .'

It was going to be all right. Next week her mum, her dad, her cousin, her grandmother, her uncle, her aunt and her sister would wave her away from the station platform.

And they would all know their own truths.

And they would all be a part of each other's pasts.

And she would always call them home.